ALLAN STEIN

ALSO BY MATTHEW STADLER

Landscape: Memory

The Dissolution of Nicholas Dee

The Sex Offender

ALLAN STEIN

A Novel

Matthew Stadler

Grove Press
New York

Published simultaneously in Canada
Printed in the United States of America

FIRST PAPERBACK EDITION

Library of Congress Cataloging-in-Publication Data

Stadler, Matthew.
Allan Stein : a novel / Matthew Stadler.
p. cm.
ISBN 0-8021-3662-1 (pbk.)
I. Title.
PS3569.T149A45 1999
813'.54—dc21 98-24584
CIP

Design by Laura Hammond Hough

Grove Press
841 Broadway
New York, NY 10003

00 01 02 03 10 9 8 7 6 5 4 3 2 1

For Larry Rinder

Acknowledgments

Many people in many places have helped me. I'm grateful to them all. Among them are: Bernard Cache and Nicola Ehlermann; Jean-Baptiste Decavele and Kirsten Johnson; Gil, Françoise, and Blaise de Kermadec; Sylvia Calle; Miguel-Angel Molina; James Lord; Mme. Orsini at the École Alsacienne; Mme. Gallinetti in Agay; the library staff at the Musée Picasso; the staff of the Village Voice Bookstore; Vincent Giroud, Pat Willis, and Timothy Young at the Beinecke Library at Yale University; Ulla Dydo; Renate Stendhal; Calman Levin; Renny Pritikin; Jay Fisher and the library staff at the Baltimore Museum of Art; the staff at the Bancroft Collection in Berkeley; and Michael Stein. This project began thanks to the Guggenheim Foundation and was completed thanks to the Whiting Foundation, both of which granted me support when I needed it.

What is the use of being a boy

if you grow up to become a man,

what is the use?

—GERTRUDE STEIN

ALLAN STEIN

We arrived at noon and left our bags with a woman who said she worked for the hotel. There was no one else on the platform when the train pulled away, only this stout, very serious woman, some complacent mongrel edging along a ditch sniffing for scraps, plus me and the boy. She had a pushcart littered with dried flowers, and we put our bags on that. The hotel turned out to be more of a ruin, really, than a hotel, but she couldn't very well have said, Hello, let me take your bags, I work for the ruin. Off she went, with the flowers and the bags, down the one narrow road toward town.

I was light-headed from the air, which was breezy and, after two days of freakish winter snow without proper mittens or what-have-you, at last springlike and warm. Ocean and pine and dust mixed with heady currents of mimosa and the fresh iodine tang of seaweed left stranded on the rocks by an outgoing tide. The boy stared at the sea, probably exhausted by his fever and my having kept him up all night with the cool washcloth and the wine. It was unnaturally beautiful. Red, crenelated rock broke from the scruffy pine headlands, crumbling toward the sea, carpeted in patches with lavender, rosemary, and scrub brush. The sea was blue like metal. Where it touched the rock there was no blending, just the sharp brick-red rock against the cold metal sea. The strand of beach between the rigid headlands was white, the sand imported from some other shore so that it looked false, like a fancy ribbon or prize strung across the flushed bosom of a very determined young farm girl. (I remember her standing in a meadow of bluebells, this particular girl—not a farm girl at all, really, as it is my mother I am recalling, whose image was suggested by the falseness of the beach at Agay—sunshine raking the steep wooded hills that bordered "our meadow," and a goat she taunted to rage so she might show me how to vault over the animal as it charged, placing her two hands on the nubs of its horns, her legs in an elegant, inverted V sailing over the befuddled goat, whose violence turned to distraction when the target disappeared. The sea was visible there too, which is maybe why I thought of her.)

I will list the features of this final vista the boy and I shared: the disappearing train, a slinky metal worm, crawling along the edge of the rocks until it vanished beyond the third headland; small groves of plum trees in the broad, shadowed canyon carved by the river on its course from the hills to the sea; that woman with the flower cart, distant but still visible, pausing to shake dirt from her shoe, on her way through town to the hotel; signs, in French of course, pointing one way to AGAY, CANNES, NICE and the other to ST.-RAPHAËL, MARSEILLE; a calendar (notice how neatly these details triangulate our location) that was unreadable, obscured by distance and the warped glass of the stationmaster's office window; the boy's face (this my view), pale from sickness but utterly enchanting still, the wide gap between his rabbit teeth, small even nose, and brown eyes just slightly too close so that I kept focusing on the corners where they teared; a rounded chin and big mouth so soft he looked like he might still be suckling (he was fifteen); long, dirty, sand-colored hair, dull and stringy, pushed behind his wide blushing ears. The noon sun raised a painful glare off the platform and the boy put on dark glasses, which made him look like a pop star. The sky was squashed and bruised blue. To the south, beyond the sea's curving horizon (Africa down there), distance sucked all order from the sky and left it washed out and miasmic.

There is no hour of my life I do not see this vista obscured by signposts, around a corner, through trees, on a wrong turn past the ferry dock, or while scrambling to the edge of a sand cliff that is crumbling in the waves of another sea. I smell it in the scattering swirl of snow around an open-windowed car driving through mountains or on a crowded tram in some foreign city whose park has just opened its scrubbed, pale gardens of rosemary and gravel and lavender. It billows and collapses, this perpetual memory, continually verging on the real. The tram, my stop, and all the day's good intentions can be swallowed in the momentary rupture this constantly returning spectacle creates. In that breathless gap, marked by my reverie, space collapses into nothing and at the same time enlarges to monstrous, devouring proportions—rather like the panoramic view of a reader whose nose is buried in a book.

The boy went to the wall of the stationmaster's office and sat on a slatted bench in the shade. He was still feverish, and standing in the sun made him dizzy. I had his blue knapsack with the bottled water, and I offered it to him. The hum and clatter of the rails, transmitting the train's prolonged departure, diminished to nothing. Insects could be heard, together with the waves collapsing on the shore below us. The breeze made a huffing sort of dull whistle through the station's entrance, where there was no door to prevent it. The boy spoke English when it suited him but just now he understood nothing, neither the word "water" nor the obvious gesture I made with the bottle itself. He stared past me, looking puzzled.

Adults, so cruel, can be amused in the face of a child's suffering. Even while we comfort him, a part of us can be laughing at, for example, a hurt boy's exaggerated pout. This doesn't compromise our sympathy, it's just amusing in a way the boy can't possibly understand. It can't be explained to his satisfaction. When I cried my mother used to laugh out loud with pleasure and weep at the same time, while holding me. Her laughter was baffling and upsetting, and it made me cry all the more, which prolonged both the laughter and the embrace until in the end we were both just exhausted and sobbing, holding on to each other, having said nothing. I was never so cruel to the boy, but that was because I loved him and because my mother's cruelty had taught me not to be.

I have loved boys even when they despised me. This boy did not despise me, but that is perhaps because we had so little in common. In the garden he picked flowers and taught me to name them in French, but I quickly forgot all the names. I could only remember what his mouth looked like as he said them. What else do I recall? His bare hips, slightly turned as he lay in bed beside me. A glimmer of sweat limning the hollow of his back. Night, its gradual onset, and then our long slow recline. The boy (he was French, fifteen, as I've said, and he believed I could deliver him from a humdrum life and family that had begun to seem tedious and doomed) turned to me across the bunched pillows and let his soft chin rest on my shoulder. His nipples had softened and lay flat. His skin was warm from an increasing fever. I think it's okay for you to take pleasure in these things. He took my hand in his and drew it along his ribs to his belly and hip, and then he let my fingers touch the perfect lip of his shallow belly button, where I stopped for a moment to dwell.

His name is not important. I have called him, at one time or another, noodle boy, *le beau scout,* Blaise, Tony, your nipples are delicate as cherry blossoms, Miss Pants, my pal, *bougie,* Monsieur Steve, Mister Sister, *l'escalier, garçon vérité,* thrush or dove, Dogan, bastard, son of a bitch, kike, Jew boy, death-star-in-pants, my White House ultimate love, Aki, anodyne, Alex, Rex, and Allan, but his given name was Stéphane. I lived with his family in Paris for two weeks before the events that brought us to the seaside ruin, and I'm certain they would be horrified by my story. I loved Stéphane; I might have already mentioned that. Though my account will lapse into coarseness, flippancy, lies, and pure pornography, you must never forget that I truly and impossibly did love him. I lived with his family under a false pretense (which I will tell you about shortly), but we became friends and only the mother blames me for what happened to their son.

◆1◆

My story began properly in the perpetual darkness of last winter (almost spring, it was March) in the city where I used to live. Typically I woke up in the dark, 6 A.M. on most days, delivered from sleep by the icy stream of air spilling in my open window. The lighted clock of the railroad tower said six exactly. This round clock of black iron and creamy glass was the first thing I saw in the mornings. No one was ever on the way to work yet, nor had the lumbering buses and trucks started with their tentative, practice engine roars. (Later, in clouds suffused with the bright yellow and opium-poppy-orange of the risen sun, they would billow in every district of the city like grim flowers and release their belched gray emissions, which gave a pleasant taste to the winter air.) I am a teacher, or had been, which explains the early hour.

Opening the window from bed, only my head and one arm untucked, was my first habit of the morning. It was independent of me, like shifting the buried, cool pillows to the top in the deep middle of the night, neither conscious nor strictly unconscious—something between a dream and the address of a friend, which I had scribbled while dragging the phone as near to the table as it would go before absently tossing the newspaper on which I had written it into the garbage, along with the bones of a fish, so that it was lost both there and in my mind until, when the brisk air of morning rushed in the open window, the whole address, neatly printed, leapt to view, bright and clear as the pinpoint stars, noisy as a child, and my mind's eye, conscious, grasped it again, though only for a moment. Minutes later, in the chaos of morning, it was gone, but so was any memory of having lost it.

All my thoughts were thin and brittle when I woke. My expansive dreams, ideas that multiplied like the crystalline spread of urine released into space (which I have heard is a beautiful sight, witnessed only by astronauts, the discharge turning golden and immense in the black void), became whole great cities of geometrical fantasy, complex and beautiful as hoarfrost, before shattering suddenly into unreadable shards at the slightest touch of fact or feeling (a crease in the pillow bothering my cheek, for example, or the sour taste scraped from my teeth by a dull, swollen tongue). The scrim of night outside was fragile. Its thin black mask could not hide the sheer abundance of the day ahead, nor the fact that it was morning already elsewhere, evening again elsewhere still, and a bright summer afternoon somewhere so distant one passed through two accelerated days in the metal shell of a jet airplane just to get there. My mother, Louise, once asked me what separates one place from another. I was only a child, and of course I had no idea. Other places, I guessed, which begged the question.

The oatmeal I ate before bed and left too close to the coiled heater was covered by a film of dry skin, which burst under the slightest pressure, my thumb for example, if it strayed too deeply gripping the bowl. I always licked this thumb, after its plunge, and the cold sweet paste it unearthed from beneath the film was enjoyable. I could hear my friend Herbert, in the adjacent apartment, bellowing fragments of popular songs, which he only ever partly remembered. Herbert and I were always awake early, even while the rest of the city slept. He is the curator at the city's art museum, and they let him keep whatever hours he likes. I had no reason to be awake. The school where I taught resolved some misgivings that arose over Christmas by granting me a paid leave of absence.

I was accused of having sex with a tenth-grader in late December. This student, Dogan, was Turkish, lithe and very beautiful. I have a picture of him here on my wall. I tutored him on Saturdays at his apartment after his soccer practice, but I had never imagined molesting him until the principal suggested it by notifying me of the charges. Amidst the dust and gadgetry of the principal's meticulous office, his chair overburdened by the abundance he had squeezed onto its cupped seat, "had sex with the boy" floating in the well-lit air between us, my mind produced the following scenario (new to me):

On Saturday I arrive early. Dogan has showered after soccer, and water dapples the bare skin of his shoulders and chest. He's wearing shorts, drinking a soda when I get there, drying his wet hair with a towel. His lips and nipples enchant me. They have similar skin, rosy and supple, thinner and more tender than the olive skin around them. "Let's get started," I tell him. He takes the book and I stand behind his chair as he settles. "Read the first poem out loud." It is García Lorca. I put my hands on his shoulders as he reads.

"'No one understood the perfume of your belly's dark magnolia.'"

"Do you know that word, 'magnolia'?" Both my hands slip over his rounded shoulders, so that my fingers reach his nipples. He keeps still.

"Magnolia is like a tree or a bush, right?"

"Yes, and a flower. Keep going."

"'No one knew you tormenting love's hummingbird between your teeth. A thousand Persian ponies fell asleep in the moonlit plaza of your forehead.'" Here he stops and I'm worried he will get up, but he stays still. "Hmm, forehead." It's the imagery, not my seduction, that has him bothered. "'As four nights through I hugged your waist, snow's enemy.'" He slouches further into the chair as he reads, almost lying there, and I see his shorts tent and then relax. I move both hands over his ribs, then back up, pinching his nipples when he gets to the line about his waist. He is so slim I can feel his heart moving in the skin beneath my hand. If he didn't want it I wouldn't do it, I think I'm thinking.

"Those words should all be quite clear," I say. "Just continue."

"'Between plaster and jasmines your glance was a pale seed branch.'" He holds the book in one hand and pulls the waistband of his shorts down along his hip with the other. His thigh is pale where he has exposed it. I slide my hand over his belly and into his shorts, and he drops the book. His penis is very shapely, curving up onto his belly, and it's big enough to fill my hands. The glans of his penis has the same pink skin as his nipples and lips. I kneel between his legs and put it into my mouth. I pull it out and stroke the shaft and the head, pushing it around to inspect it. Dogan is tipped back in the chair with his hands entwined behind his head. His underarms are pale and damp.

I tell him, "Lorca's poem might appear to be unreal, but its dreamlike consistency can supplant waking reality by the force of a new coherence and logic, so that one becomes lost in it, like in fantasy or sleep, and the logical yardsticks of waking life that make its measure false are completely lost from view."

"Finish," he says, pouting. He bumps his thighs against my face, and I finish the blow job.

So you can imagine the difficulty I had denying the principal's charges. Why *hadn't* I molested the boy? For no good reason I could find, except maybe a failure of imagination. The fact I had done nothing seemed to be a mere accident of timing.

"I've never had sex with him," I said, in my defense.

"I believe you," our fidgety principal replied (and I believed he did believe). "I know you haven't done anything; the difficulty is proving it."

"What did the boy say happened?"

"Oh, he didn't say anything. His parents have accused you. They think he's covering it up because he likes it." He likes it? I was buoyed by this news, relieved to hear that my advances were welcome (never mind that there had been no advances, and no response and no victim, whose approval would still have been mere parental rumor).

"That's a relief."

"What is?"

"Nothing." Only minutes after hearing the accusation I was already planning a seduction. I cannot exaggerate how subtle and profound these chameleon confusions were. Placed at the scene of a multicar accident, I might become Florence Nightingale or a competent policeman directing worried traffic past the pools of blood and metal. At a boxing match, I have no doubt, I would've thirsted for the most horrifying results.

I pursued him. In the end I succeeded in committing the crime I had been falsely accused of. The parents never found out (no one did). As it turned out, sex was exactly what the boy wanted, and he became very much the happy, satisfied child they hoped he would be, where before, during the months that I was blind to him, he had been miserable and distracted (precisely the condition, noticed by his parents, that led to their accusation). In light of the boy's satisfaction, and the handsome salary I was then receiving for a great expanse of free time in which it became that much easier to meet him, clandestinely, for sex, I must admit that I sometimes looked on the whole horrifying affair as comical and ironic. After a while he grew bored or ashamed and stopped seeing me.

Herbert was the only friend I discussed this with. Others, especially my colleagues from school, were so moved by the weight of the "tragic accusations" that I could feel myself *becoming* tragic simply with the approach of their cloying, caring glances. Their eyes had the gleam and submerged instability of glaciers, vast sheets of luminous ice beneath which chasms creaked and yawned. One of them would appear uninvited before my table at a café, fat Mr. Stack the math teacher, for example, and shuffle toward me as if compelled by this hollowness behind his eyes, as slow and devouring as the ice that once crawled down the face of the continent. (My mother described a boyfriend of hers this way, one evening while she and I sat in a diner eating turkey sandwiches with gravy, a special treat she gave me far more often than I deserved. I was eleven years old. It wasn't five minutes before this very boyfriend appeared at the window with his face pressed to the glass, miming hello and making a fool of himself. She winked at me, then looked right past him, blowing smoke from her cigarette, saying nothing. Finally he went away.) I have none of my mother's cool reserve, so I avoided my colleagues when I could or, if forced by good manners to accept a repeated invitation to lunch, tried to speak cheerfully about my "new career" at Herbert's museum, a fiction I had devised, which, like most lies, eventually became true. I learned a great deal about art from Herbert during the few weeks that he helped me perpetrate this lie.

It first occurred to me one cold March afternoon while we sat at a café drinking. Herbert likes to drink and so do I. We are compatible in many ways, and being neighbors a great deal of our lives became shared; watering plants, checking the mail, and chitchat soon became socializing, shared travel, and a natural intimacy that has made me more comfortable with him than with anyone. This particular café (that cold March afternoon) was called Shackles, under which name it masqueraded as a pre-Victorian public house. Nothing in our city is pre-Victorian, except perhaps the famous lakes and the view out.

Dark wood, patterned velvet, newsprint advertisements for nineteenth-century ales (enlarged, scarred, and varnished for display), wall sconces fashioned from gas fixtures, and poor lighting made up Shackles's costume. Windows, curtained on brass rods at eye level, let us watch the street while easily hiding ourselves, if need be, by a simple crouch or slouch nearer the table. The unfortunate waiters were disguised as croupiers from Gold Rush–era Nevada (preposterous puffy sleeves, frilly red armbands frayed to the elastic, tidy vests with fake watch pockets and chains, plus anomalous cummerbunds), none of which kept the young students who took these jobs from supplementing the costume with beautiful earrings of silver or brass, chrome-pierced nostrils, ersatz-Maori cheek tattoos, braids and bangles twined about their elegant thin wrists or tied in colorful cloth cascading from their heads—the result being much more like science fiction than the vague nostalgia the owners must have been aiming for. One of the waiters was a lanky blond angel named Tristan, and Herbert adored him. Tristan was also a student at the university, and Herbert kept offering him an "internship" at the museum, to which the boy always replied, "It sounds completely fascinating," before shuffling off with our drink orders, and then nothing would come of it. We drank there whenever Tristan was working. When he wasn't working, Shackles became, to Herbert, "that hideous dive" and we went to a much nicer café near to our apartment house.

Our city is a virtual monument to indiscriminate nostalgia, sometimes (particularly when I look out my window at the nighttime buildings smartly lit by floods and spots) appearing like a grand, jumbled stage set for all the dramas of Western history. Muscular towers of concrete and glass, paid for by young stock wizards and software geniuses, offer a heady compote of modern forms and ornaments, collapsing three hundred years of the Enlightenment—vaulting skylights, vast glass cathedrals, forests of tall columns appended by apses (in which vendors sell coffee, magazines, and snacks), death-defying elevated wings of stone, granite monstrances balanced on steel pins, and sprawling webs of metal and tinted glass suffused with natural light (for the enjoyment of employees taking their sack lunch in the firm's "winter garden")—into singular monuments, so that one can review an entire history without straying out-of-doors. Lighted in the manner of Rome's Campidoglio, these generous knickknacks dominate the city at night.

Their grand theatricality is sadly compromised, for me, by the awkward, insistent fact that I grew up here. My childhood lurks behind these bright scrims and screens, unruly and constant, threatening to overturn the whole facade and reveal the actual place to me. Once, for example, about a year ago, on a date with a young friend named Herman, keeper of the computers at our school, the trashy glamour of the Downtown Fun House with its strung lights and carnival noise (a fabulous room of tilting pinball machines delivering their trilled ringing scores and piles of loose change which Herman, drunk, said was like Tivoli Gardens, which he described to me in German or Danish, making elegant gestures with his beer and singing God knows what song, so that for a moment I was far away in Denmark or Germany with my beer and this grandly sophisticated friend singing on the verge of some world war or depression) all dissolved when I spun (some would say reeled), and saw a dull canvas mural of two leering clowns painted in a hideous all too familiar greenish-pink. It had hung beside the Skee-Ball lanes covering a hole for the last thirty years, in a sad, dirty corner of this house of marvels, an eddy of quiet amidst the swirling noise. I had only ever seen it once before, when I was ten, and I had pissed there because my mother insisted it was all right to do so. You had better just do it, she said, and I unzipped my pants and did. A policeman came over, put his hand on my shoulder, and told me to stop. I could only stare at the clowns, which I've never really forgotten, and comply. Mama was kind enough to pretend it hadn't happened. "Look what some boy has done," she whispered, taking my hand and pulling me away from the corner.

Typically, the memory had ambushed me, replacing Denmark and the World War with my own messy life, and recasting my glamorous European date, Herman, as a loud, tasteless drunk. I knew all along it was there, waiting, but it sneaked up on me, rather like the smell of lavender, suppressed by the evening cold, that kept creeping out of the broad canyon of the Verdon River and stirring Stéphane from his sleep, rousing the boy enough to make me panic that he might get up and leave, might return to the world and abandon me in the shell of our last ruin, that he would walk out of his scripted fever into life, into a world we had shut out, at least for a few days. Isn't it strange how distant the boy is, was, and those last days near the edge of the sea in France where we left pages ago, ages ago, to meet Herbert, who's still waiting, too sober and impatient at Shackles, for our conversation to resume? And all the time the boy was *here,* hidden by a thought, behind a thin distraction, the noise of a conversation, in that gap between words when silence extends one beat too long.

I enjoy the noise of a good conversation, particularly with Herbert, who has opinions and a stylish way of talking, so that even when he is silent my mind is occupied by him, his nervous hands smoothing the table's edge, his fish-dart glances, and the way his face rearranges itself around the twin-ridged frenum of his upper lip when he wants something. Adrift in my chameleon instabilities—I could become as easily a society matron as a loud sports guy in the next second, should the right acquaintance walk through the door—I never knew from which blurry edge the next bright color would bleed; Herbert was a swath of singular hue (the dusty pink of

Travertine marble in the languid heat of Rome, late summer, late afternoon, for example, so antiquated and pleasing was his effect on me), a familiar resting place that imbued me with a clear, if slightly dated, identity.

"What exactly will Tristan be doing as your intern?" I asked.

Herbert stared at the retreating boy. "I think he's so talented, don't you?"

I turned and we watched him together. Tristan's rambling journey led first to a cluster of tables, where his drunk friends shared a cigarette and told him a joke, which Tristan didn't get, so there was a long period of explanation, including a great deal of scribbling on a napkin, arrows and words, until finally the boy burst out laughing while his friends sat calmly, passing their one cigarette like a last round of munitions. Tristan moved then to the bar, where he chatted with the newest "croupier" and told him the joke, pulling out the scribbled napkin, which he'd kept, all the while clutching our drink order and gesturing with it, even as the bartender cleaned the spindle of the slips that had been placed there.

"What talent? The way he deflects your interest without killing it?"

"His manner, and that cool reserve." If Herbert smoked he would have flicked ash at this point, but he didn't smoke. "I need someone with exactly his skills."

"I wonder what interests he has?" Herbert might not have heard me, or he didn't really care about the boy's interests. "What makes you think he knows anything about working at a museum?"

"What's there to know?"

"Well, social skills, at the very least."

"Exactly." Herbert brightened at the thought. "I can just see him, charming rich old homosexuals by the tableful." Herbert said "homosexuals" as if it were a Linnaen tag for some insect-devouring plant, with a lot of sibilance and spit. "No one would be safe. Entire prewar collections of sodomite erotica would flood the museum."

"I suppose he *could* worm his way into the confidence of some old widower."

"Mmm."

"Or the family of a rich industrialist."

"Mmm, fawning over the crayon scrawls of the twelve-year-old Scotch-tape heiress."

"The Infanta."

"Or her brother."

I said nothing, just stared at Herbert; maybe I lifted my eyebrow slightly.

Herbert took this silence as some kind of arch comment, an insight so enormous I could not deign to constrain it inside a few miserable words, so that while I was thinking nothing he believed I was thinking everything. He stared and bristled, then grinned at me and stammered, "No." Herbert often uttered this single word when he had stumbled across something he dearly hoped was true.

"Yes," was my obligatory reply. If I'd had my drink I would have sipped from it, but the drinks were still unmade.

"No." We searched the room for Tristan, but he was nowhere in sight.

"Probably." Someone kept tapping at the window with an umbrella, an older woman in Gore-Tex balaclava and rain parka, beckoning to her mukluked companion (parked at a table behind me) who responded in mime, Come in come in. Why should no one in the bar be allowed to hear the halfhearted invitation she was so obviously mouthing? Her friend shuffled to the doorway and brought half the afternoon's storm in with her, rain and leaves and lightning and such adhering to her billowing yards of weatherproof fabric. Herbert and I ducked down beneath curtain level and continued with our speculations. "Yes. He prefers boys, you can tell."

"No, I *can't* tell, which is what is so agonizing. He hasn't given me a clue one way or another."

"That is exactly what I mean. It's an obvious sign."

"You mean his failure to put me off?"

"No. He's put you off repeatedly. He puts you off every time we come in here."

"No."

"Yes. He just never does it by mentioning girlfriends or all that. If he was—you know—'normal,' he would have said so ages ago. He obviously likes boys."

"But he finds *me* repulsive?"

"An old, leering drunk."

"No."

"Yes."

"But he's always so chatty, serving the drinks and taking the tip and all."

"He's the waiter."

"Well, sometimes when I come in alone, I mean without *you*, in midafternoon when it's not very busy and poor Tristan isn't bombarded with all this work, he has gotten very, very flirty with me."

"Mmm." Suddenly he was at our table.

We looked up as this blessed angel lifted our drinks from his tray. (A small twinge here tells me it is demeaning and wrong to have condemned anyone, even one so incidental as our waiter, Tristan—though let me point out that he later, in fact, *became* Herbert's intern, excelled at courting collectors of all persuasions, was hired away by a famous art center in Minneapolis and then a museum in New York, where he has now become the golden boy of contemporary art curating, exactly as Herbert predicted and despite being just as stupid and poorly educated as I had suspected he was, a fitting poster child for America's fantastically undiscriminating upward mobility, where anyone with minimal beauty, a pleasing ignorance, and intitiative can rise to any height—to condemn him, that is to say, to the tired idealizations of romantics and colonialists [angels, sylphs, savages, and the like], such as have been routinely inflicted on women and other exotics, like children. Too bad. Herbert and I gave Tristan a *gift* when we elevated him to such heights, especially considering that the alternative was a life of dull, respectful sobriety and caution so boring we all might as well have been dead.)

"Scotch neat," our servile Eros mumbled as he set Herbert's drink in front of him.

"The usual," Herbert answered brightly, smiling at the boy.

"Uh-huh, whatever. And a gin and tonic here for your, uh, partner in crime." This absentminded aside sent a jolt of electricity through both of us, lifting Herbert's eyebrows as he stared at me across the drinks, silent, until the boy wandered off with his enormous tip (40 or 50 percent, whatever change was left on the tray).

"Partner in crime, did you hear that?" Herbert asked rhetorically, because of course I'd heard it. It was all either of us had heard. "He is such a tease."

"He probably thinks we're boyfriends."

"Don't be idiotic."

Tristan shuffled out of view—my view, in any case. Herbert kept his marksman's stare fixed just to the right of my face, beyond which the boy, to judge by the sound of what I could not see, was adjudicating a dispute between the two lady customers (one still unwrapping) and a wonderfully tall Nigerian "croupier" who, in the lilting British tones of a public-school boy, had ridiculed the ladies' objections to "an awful lot of indoor smoking." Shackles routinely allowed what state law evidently forbade. Tristan offered them a table near to ours (no smoke here), still behind me, and they took it. I could feel the weather arriving with the coats. I slouched a little closer to my drink so Herbert could see better.

"I wasn't being idiotic. We certainly *look* as though we're married."

"Mmm, that's a thought, not a pretty one." Herbert sipped his drink and continued his surveillence.

"*You're* handsome. Everyone says so." This drew a brief glance and a smile.

"Well, it's not true. I look like a doll whose head has been chewed on by a rat." In fact the description was a good one. "'Gnawed Doll's Head,' like some sort of Swedish porn star. You look that way too."

"Hmm, really?"

"Yes. Hank says we're practically identical. *We* would have handsome children, all sculpted and chewed upon."

"Would you have sex with our son?" I asked. "I mean, if we had one?" Herbert grimaced, as though his drink were bad. Tristan appeared beside us, and the grimace became a leering, amplified smile.

"We were just discussing you," Herbert announced, ignoring my question. "I mean the work you'll be doing for the museum."

"Hmm." Tristan might have been amused. At the very least he was cheerful.

"It looks fairly certain I can get you credit for that Stein project."

"Oh, right, the Stein project." Tristan squatted by our table and smiled. (I know for a fact Herbert was making this up. Tristan had been carrying a copy of Gertrude Stein's *Three Lives* one evening when we were drinking, and Herbert managed to turn this assigned text into Tristan's métier simply by prolonged badgering of the boy, plus Herbert's poor memory and fulsome imagination.)

"I mean in addition to the stipend. But you're going to have to start this—what is it you have here?—this term, or semester."

"Block." We both stared at the boy. "You know, seven blocks, five interims, plus the optional summer block?"

"Right. This block, which must be coming up soon, since there are so many of them. The work can go on however long you like, but we need to get started on it very soon." The boy's absent, cheerful face gave no clue what he was thinking. He might have been a genius or the victim of some experimental surgery. "You *did* tell me you were a big—what was it, fan—of Gertrude Stein, didn't you?"

"Oh, yeah." He perked up at her mention. "Big-time fan."

"Well, this is your chance to put that expertise to work—I mean, not *much* work, it's really very easy, but your enthusiasm for Stein will be an asset."

"Terrific."

"I have a sheaf of family letters, amazing stuff, mostly from her nephew and sister-in-law, which are just a joy to read."

"It sounds completely fascinating."

"Was he gay?" I interrupted, hoping to steer us, at last, toward the shoals of the Tristan question.

"'He'? Who 'he'?" Herbert's sour tone and grimace swatted at me, like hands chasing away some buzzing insect. "Gertrude Stein was gay, everyone knows that. You don't mean 'she,' do you?"

"He." I strained. "The nephew."

"Oh, I don't know. He was certainly miserable enough." Herbert turned his very broad and cold shoulder toward me. "Anyway, Tristan won't be concerned with all that. He'll be too busy going after these missing drawings. We'll probably have to send someone off to Paris to get them."

"Cool." It was me, interrupting before the boy could get this word in edgewise. In fact Tristan never used the word, nor was he about to use any word, because duty had called him away. "Super cool."

"Thank you very much for frightening the boy."

"What, with the word 'gay'?"

"With your rudeness. Why do you have to make a wreck of every conversation I have with anyone else?"

"I asked one question."

"You derailed the conversation."

"The question was in earnest. I didn't even know she had a nephew."

"'Was he gay?' What on earth does it matter?"

"I was just curious. Do you know him?"

"Do I know him? How could I know him, he's been dead for forty years. More."

"Was he cute?"

"Oh, God." Herbert left the table, and I fiddled with my glass. Outside the day had become grand and chaotic. Enormous sweeps of sun dragged down the boulevard, chasing sheets of rain (bright/dark/bright again) and transforming into glitter windblown accumulations of trash and prized trifles, after which schoolboys scattered in their slickers and boots. There was snow at a certain elevation (not high—it obscured the carnivorous pigeons in their third-story roosts), and large hail whomped down at one point as if released from some humiliating television game-show contraption, so that everyone looked up, and by the time they looked up it was sunny again.

Spring is always so marvelous here (our city sits smack dab at the northernmost reach of the American West Coast), and it stretches from February to July. The other season is fall, which begins at the end of spring and lasts through January. At some point, every year, shortly after spring has ended and before the first gray showers of fall have come, there appear, as suddenly as sleep, two weeks of honey-warm days stretching to near-Laplandian lengths, the noontime parkland trails burnished in gold, when our hilly metropolis is saturated with the big yellow sun—a fat baker's dozen of rich green days spent lolling on picnic blankets beside the child-strewn beach or drowsing with a book on one of the floating rafts. So sudden and delirious are these days, their memory is quickly buried under fall's gray return, alongside our more private night dreams, until the city is ambushed again the next year, when these days reemerge precisely where we had left them.

Regarding the weather of childhood, a harmless possum lived under the front porch of our fourth house—my favorite—which (belied by its trees, languor, and possum) was in a busy neighborhood near the city's downtown. It was our house for two years (ages ten to twelve), the house in which my mother and I were happiest. The trees, the languor, low-to-zero rent (the landlord died partway through our tenancy and no one noticed us for a year), plus my emergence into the age of reason and dinnertime conviviality, conspired to make of this place a brief heaven. The possum—I named him Larry—scratched at our door whenever it was going to rain. Louise called him our prognosticator. He wanted to come in, I think, because it got wet under the porch when it rained. We never let him (the only discord of these halcyon years) and I stopped arguing with Louise when she told me that possums love, more than anything, the spittle of sleep, and that Larry would find me at night and lick the saliva from my lips, from my tongue even, thrusting his ratty little mouth into mine, defenseless while I dreamt, to sip the sweet nectar of my boyhood mastications directly from its source, should we ever let him in the door. Later, when puberty began, this scenario became a fantasy of mine, the most horrible and forbidden of many imagined scenes and therefore (on a few intensely private occasions, of which I will spare you the details) the climactic one.

Why a fourth house? Why no father, siblings, or proper account of the scarring events of a troubled youth, etc., etc.? That is the part that bores me, all the psychiatrist's carefully hoarded trivia of "damage," gathered in his great pockets like loose change, grimy coins that he can then count out against the final bill, the great tabulation of failed dreams and dysfunctions he must balance against the purchases of a childhood. I can only tell what I remember, and what *I* remember is growing up. My father was gone, along with three half-siblings he enjoyed with another woman, and my mother didn't like him and neither did I. His absence was as meaningful to me as the fact that I lacked an elephant. There are times when a boy could benefit from the company of an elephant, and it's too bad if he doesn't have one. However, I was so involved with what I did have, the missing parts of the "normal" went unnoticed, until everyone started asking me about them—which was early, age six or seven, when a virtual forest of adult faces began pestering me with questions about Dad, etc. Had the world turned its immensely caring eyes toward me and asked, sotto voce, "But, little boy, where is your elephant?" I would have burst into tears more sincere than any I have shed about my father. There is so much in this world that does not love a child it never seemed terribly important to single him out.

Herbert returned. He settled in, casting a disappointed glance at the empty scotch glass. "Where is that boy?" We surveyed the room brusquely, but Tristan was nowhere in sight. "So, what happened while I was gone?"

"Nothing, really. Tell me more about this Stein nephew."

◆2◆

Allan Daniel Stein was born November 7, 1895, in San Francisco, the only child of Michael and Sarah Stein. Mike, the older brother of Leo and Gertrude, sold a streetcar business in 1903 and moved with Sarah and Allan to Paris. Gertrude and Leo had preceded them. Therese Jelencko, Allan's teenage nanny and piano teacher, went with them:

"Among my parents' most intimate friends at the turn of the century were Michael and Sally Stein. I was a so-called child prodigy but hadn't a good piano. So it was arranged that I practiced on their Steinway every morning. Their little son, Allan, four or five years of age, began to study with me. And a celebrated musician of the time, Oscar Weil, heard him play and was so enthusiastic that he begged to give him theory and harmony lessons and congratulated his parents on choosing 'such a marvelous teacher,' etc. I didn't realize then what a compliment it was, but the Steins made up their minds that when they went to Europe they couldn't dream of going without me. Of course I was then all of about fifteen years old, fifteen or sixteen.

"This was my first trip to Europe. Actually I never expected to be able to get to Europe, certainly not at that age, and there was great excitement. I left with Mike and Sally Stein and their little boy in December 1903, and arrived at Cherbourg and was met by

Mr. Stein's younger sister and brother, Leo and Gertrude Stein. No, Gertrude wasn't along; I'm mistaken there. It was just Leo. We actually arrived at Cherbourg about three o'clock in the morning, and I was thrilled and fascinated. I knew no French but was absolutely charmed. Leo took us to the old hotel; oh, dear, I've forgotten the name of it. The Hotel Fayot. It was the famous hotel in the Latin Quarter, facing the Luxembourg Gardens, where the Senators have their lunch; it was celebrated for its great restaurant. And that was an exciting night. I don't think anybody slept a wink.

"We finally found an apartment on the rue de Fleurus, 1 rue de Fleurus, which was the same street as Leo and Gertrude Stein, who lived at 27 rue de Fleurus. I remember ours was an apartment three flights up. There was no such thing as an elevator, and of course it had no bath. We had to go up the street to Gertrude's. They had a bath and were unique. I think in the whole street perhaps there was only one other bath. And the baths used to come around by cart. Pipes would be hoisted from the street into your apartment, the tin tub having been brought up ahead of time. And you 'bought' a bath, as it were. It was all very primitive and very exciting and very wonderful to me.

"The Michael Steins moved to the rue Madame, I think it was 58 rue Madame, and part of my duties as an assistant in the household was to take the little boy to school. I'm going back a couple of years. I'm going back a couple of years. He went to a private school a few blocks away. And each morning I would meet Degas, the painter, who lived a block away, and each morning he'd ask how my little boy was. Well, I was only ten years older than Allan, but just the same I never corrected him. I was very proud of him, this very handsome young boy. Degas was an interesting figure and must have been at the height of his painting career then. I was just stupid enough to be really only interested in music. Well, it's hard to follow in detail. There's so much detail."

The last days of March, all crazy with cold weather, swooped and shifted around me like the torn, blown pages of an old book. My forced holiday had brought new pleasures, but it had also robbed me of any enduring structure. I woke most mornings to nothing. For six years there had been some necessity to getting up. The stack of marked exams, toast in a paper napkin, plus my leather satchel stuffed with books and what-have-you (torn from their nooks as I rushed to the door), and my head full of plans and anticipation for the children and the day, I had to catch one of those monstrous buses that filled our streets by seven just to make it to school before the concierge, with his paw full of keys, locked the great iron door shut for the morning. Those were sweet, rapid mornings, full of flight and arrival. They loomed behind me like the shimmering, silvery peaks that frame our city's portrait, east and west: a magical, distant place—entirely unreachable. Now I was idle. I saw Dogan when he could arrange it. We had sex in the laundry room of his apartment building a few times. Twice we saw movies. I barely noticed the films, pinioned as I was to the minutest changes in his posture. I could never phone him. Lurking near the soccer field was out of the question, so I saw him less and less. The weather was terrible for a few weeks, and I stayed home and read. Herbert kept me supplied with books. It was an awful time, more destabilizing than I had then realized, and Herbert was my only reliable anchor.

On the last Friday of that disappointing March, Herbert called from work to invite me for dinner at the Hotel Grand. He'd made some great discovery about the Steins and wanted to share it over a meal with me and our friend Henry Richard. Henry always stayed at the Grand (a squat brick and glass monstrosity that rose from the edge of our "historic district" like a staging area for some kind of theme-park ride). Henry was in town just now, buying art.

Herbert, who really is extremely good at what he does, had discovered three "missing" drawings by Picasso—studies, he believed, for the 1906 painting called *Boy Leading a Horse*. (An utterly enchanting boy, standing nude beside a horse, which he seems to command without reins; the earth is tawny and burnished like the boy, while the sky is a festering storm of silver and gray, like the horse.) Herbert believed this boy might be Allan Stein. He'd uncovered a bill of lading sent by Allan to Miss Etta Cone of Baltimore in 1951, listing a portrait Picasso had painted of Allan, age eleven, during the same months that he painted *Boy Leading a Horse*—included with it were "three preliminary drawings." The portrait arrived in America, but the drawings did not. Herbert thought these drawings might have been for *Boy Leading a Horse*. If Allan had posed one afternoon, during his sittings at Picasso's studio, standing nude in the posture of the boy, he might, in some small way, *be* the *Boy Leading a Horse*. Finding the drawings could provide the link.

"Obviously nothing can be proven per se." Herbert rambled on as we sat waiting for Henry at the Grand. "Given Picasso's use of—well, virtually anything he could get his hands on to make his paintings, no one could *prove* Allan was the model in any conventional sense. But it's just so tantalizing to think of finding 'the boy,' I mean, a real boy stuck somewhere in that painting. It's a monumental piece." Herbert showed me a once-tipped-in color plate he'd cut from a book at the museum. The painting was very erotic. The contours of the boy's belly and chest were supple and inviting. "Any evidence linking it to Allan Stein would be, you know, more than delightful. No one ever mentions him in this regard." Henry arrived now, but that didn't keep Herbert from going on. "Everyone's so ga-ga about Cézanne's *Bathers*, Greek kouroi, or this weird grown-up Parisian delinquent who I'm sure was *very* important and blah-blah-blah, but why never a real boy?" I smiled hello to Henry, who looked very smart in his linen jacket. "Why *wouldn't* Picasso look at an actual boy?"

Henry Richard, first name English last name French (Herbert simply called him "the Day-Glo king" [Henry made a fortune with a 1961 patent on psychedelic poster paints {the patent was his even if the idea wasn't—his brilliant, druggy college roommate stumbled across it fooling around in chem lab, Henry saw the $$$ and offered the friend pot (to his credit a lot of pot) for the rights—and he licensed it out to manufacturers} without ever owning or running anything more than a postage meter at home] though Herbert only ever said this to me, not Henry), had spent the day with Herbert buying art. He liked to be called "Hank."

Hank bought art with Herbert's advice, while also buying Herbert's advice with art. The payoff for these friendly consultations was paintings, given to Herbert by the artists he pitched to the Day-Glo king (at that time building a fantastically high-profile collection)—a little thank-you for making their rent and maybe their careers. It all gets very complicated when Herbert later curates shows featuring these same artists, borrowing from the collections of the dozen industrialists he has advised in the past and writing lavish essays that create great reputations and markets for everyone involved: the artists, the collectors who own them, and not coincidentally Herbert, who just *happens* to have pieces by every last one of them, tossed his way free like a bone to a good dog who, in the last reel, turns out to have been the star of the movie all along.

Hank snagged the waiter, and we ordered more drinks. Herbert handed me a photograph of the Steins, winter 1905. It was enchanting. The family is standing in the courtyard of 27 rue de Fleurus. Allan is ten, the only child in a group of six. The adults form a dark wall and Allan stands in front of them, chest high to Gertrude, dressed in a white sailor shirt and knickers; he is wielding a stick. His eyes are dark flowers, barely opened. Gertrude has her hands on his shoulders, like the claws of a bird, though it's unclear if she means to protect or devour him. The Steins' faces are hard and flat, like the cut ends of tree stumps; they're all staring in different directions. Only Allan and Gertrude regard us directly, and this fact enchanted me—the directness of the boy's regard. Hank took the photocopied bill of lading from Herbert.

"Mmm, I see it right there. 'Three preliminary drawings.'" A good empiricist, Hank.

"I think Allan never sent them," Herbert went on. "He was never very good with details in the first place, plus being sick and all. The drawings probably stayed in Paris and ended up in the hands of his family when he died." The Grand management had scattered white narcissus willy-nilly throughout the dining room, so the air was pungent and cloying. Herbert performed a miracle with the encyclopedic wine list (thirty pages, possibly copied direct from the distributor's warehouse inventory), finding an Oregon pinot to complement the ubiquitous floral perfume. This acrobatic wine also had the virtue of going well with the lamb we ordered. We dined in a sea of odors: garlic, sage, rosemary, more garlic, someone else's cheese cut by my knife (an earlier dinner), lingering cleanser used to scrub grit from the tiles, plus the overpowering blooms.

"Do you know them?"

"Allan's family? I certainly know *of* them—"

I interrupted. "That's a very nice tie, Hank, very fine." Hank's tie interlocked salmon with clams in a kind-of Escheresque puzzle, a regional knickknack, I supposed, that he probably only wore on his trips north. It looked like a local bouillabaisse.

"Thanks very much." He tipped his fork to me, chewing. Herbert grimaced and poked at the pink lamb on his plate.

"It's a Jeffries," Herbert put in. "We bought it right off the artist's rack at his studio this morning. Hank is very lucky to have gotten the last one."

"Mmm, I thought it looked like a Jeffries," I improvised.

"Jeffries didn't *make* it, he simply owned it. Don't you read anything I clip for you? He's selling a bunch of his old clothes, you know, with all the grime left in, signing them and selling them. Each one is dated so you can tell when he owned it, kind of a record of his own evolving bad taste." Herbert cackled at this joke and then blushed when neither of us joined him. "This one's from very early, before he had any kind of name, you see, so it's especially sought after. Apparently it's got blood and cum stains, Jeffries says so, anyway."

Hank's tie, with its generous swirl of fish and bivalves, slipped neatly into a collar that was immaculate. Despite the pleasure of good company, the tasty lamb, the odors, the talk (a pungent, literate conversation)—all the epicurean delights, that is to say, of good company in a well-serviced cosmopolitan setting—I couldn't keep my mind from swimming into that beguiling collar, with its perfect single crease, which Hank kept lightly touching. The dry circumspection of this knife's-edge crease, tie snug as if folded within a thin and expert crepe, transported me to the moment of its creation—the firm hand of the laundress pressing her flat, hot iron to the cloth, the burst of steam, twined cotton fibers minutely loosened (breathing like Turks in a cave of heated rocks), then turned and pushed flat against the board into their traditional, more orderly arrangement. Handed to shirtless master in a flash, touching the fold (simple curtsy, a dry dollar pressed into her palm), the crease became a warm tunnel of delight for Hank's finger, which he slipped along the inner edge while flipping the collar up for the tie. And there was more in that fold, that neck-long fold of cotton—in the poorly lit, poorly designed, poor great dining room of the Grand—with its doing and undoing. My attentions slipped back and forth along the collar, following Hank's absent caress, his paired fingers mimicking the skis that rushed out from beneath me down the steep snowy ridge of Hurricane Hill, high above "our meadow," where my mother and I watched the trails of jets tracing their course across the bright ice-blue sky to Tokyo, LA, Bogotá, Miami, Corsica for goodness' sake, because there is so much in this world to see (she said, laughing and pushing off to race me down the hill), so much; and with the guilelessness of a twelve-year-old I felt the great wobbling globe spin forward beneath us toward a future of fantastic communications and swift, glamorous transport across promising skies. It disturbs me to realize this is *not* an interruption; this blossoming, this rupture, is what is permanent, and the hollow wooden box of conversation, our simple evening meal at the Grand, the way Herbert glances at me when he drinks his wine, the timely, clever remark, are the disturbances, interruptions that distract us from the more permanent ether in which our lives swim. Herbert, who never knew my mother, tells me this is crazy. But how could anyone call such transports insanity when they dwell in something as plain and sober as the crease of a well-starched collar? Hank's fold, at dinner, was a portal into life's pleasing enormity.

"You know, Herbert, I still can't find the cum stains," Hank pointed out. "I checked the whole tie front and back before dinner." He lifted it toward the inadequate candle. We scrutinized the tie.

"Up by the top." I pointed, helpful. "You see, next to the clam's neck, or whatever they call that thing. It kind of disappears into the knot." Herbert and I leaned closer, but Hank couldn't see because it was too high.

"Did Jeffries say it was *his* cum, or just cum generally?"

"Oh, definitely *his* cum," Herbert assured Hank. "Commodification of the artist, the artist's 'body-of-work,' and blah-blah-blah. I know the ideas are getting pretty stale, but he *is* limiting the number of items, and with his signature on it there's no doubt of the value. We could ask him to stain it again if you like, I mean, if there really is no discernible mark. I'm sure he'd be happy to do that for you, Hank."

Hank paid no attention to Herbert's offer. He smoothed the tie proudly against his chest. "I'm giving it to my son," he pointed out. "For his bar mitzvah."

"Oh, hell yes," I let out. "He'll love it. Kids love goofy ties."

An arcade ran around the periphery of this broad high-ceilinged room, with tiny shops full of gewgaws and magazines, sewing kits, tooth care and soaps, all the miscellanea of travel. The shops opened up both toward us—articulating glass walls drawn back like the flaps of a surgical wound—and outward to the surrounding streets (mere doors there) to encourage "flow-through." Dogan, my very erotic and beloved ex-student, flowed through, his two parents in tow. Then they flowed right back out again. A miracle of architecture!

"Look, the important thing about the family, Allan's family, is that they are *very* sharp, and if they catch wind of any *reason* why I should be pursuing these particular drawings, if they even suspect I want them at all, for God's sake, the price is going to go right through the ceiling."

"They're not priceless already?"

"No, I don't think so. Picasso drawings aren't all that rare. He must have scribbled on every surface in Europe, like Napoleon sleeping. These are probably undated, maybe even unsigned. In any case, I've got to let the family believe there's no special value in them, that just by selling me the drawings they're taking advantage of me."

"Maybe they sold them already—I mean, decades ago."

"They might have. But the family is the only starting point, unless the Baltimore Museum turns up something."

Hank held the photograph of Allan next to the color plate of *Boy Leading a Horse*. There was no similarity, per se. The face in the painting looked more like a mask than a face, a reduced emblem that seemed to hang in space before the body, not a rendering of something you might touch in real life. The genitals were a mess, so that he looked uncircumcised but you couldn't be sure. It might have been a poor reproduction. His slim chest and belly were achingly beautiful, warm and rounded enough to feel with your hand. I kept catching glimpses of Dogan in the shopping arcade (with Mom and Dad, apparently returned). His loose-limbed grace and elegant head would flash at me like a snapshot from the shifting crowd.

"I wonder if Allan's classmates cared that he knew Picasso?" (Dogan's association with me, even when it was mere parental rumor, had lent him a glamour and worldliness that dazzled the mock sophisticates of Urban Country Day's upper school. The girls flocked around him—martyred sexual decadent, grown-up seducer of men—and began to pursue this slim little boy who just weeks before had been nothing more than a charming but infantile halfback on the soccer team. Dogan had sex with many of these girls, seduced by the rumors of his homosexuality, and I could only swallow the bitter reports of my jealous heart.)

"You know, Herbert, if you're not going to finish that lamb—"

Herbert slid the tepid plate to Hank, who smiled and asked me, "How *is* that school of yours?" deflecting attention from the flap of meat he then slipped into his mouth. Hank took a great interest in my school but thankfully had no information except what I gave him. He'd even met Dogan once, when I took the boy to the local sports palace to join Hank and his teenage son in an opulent sky box, replete with swiveling chairs, nifty curtains, sniveling help hauling beer and snacks, plus a huge TV, which was a big hit all around.

"*My* school?" It was doubtful Hank knew anything. "Actually, I've quit teaching." Herbert glanced at me, then, pointedly, away. "I'm working with Herbert now, helping him out at the museum." I could have caused two deaths with this single utterance, as it caught Herbert in mid-swallow of a glass of water, on which he began to choke, and Hank in the depths of chewing a tongue-sized lamb chunk, through which undercooked sinew he tried exclaiming, "Why, that's just terrific!" A long draught of wine dislodged the meat and kept us from the ugly exertions of the Heimlich maneuver (invented by Dr. Henry J. Heimlich of Cincinnati, whose charming twin daughters I have met and enjoyed).

"That's just terrific," Hank repeated, after the wine. "Working together like a team. There's nothing better." Herbert didn't seem to think so. "Herb kept mum about it the whole day."

"Yes," Herbert said. "I didn't want to spoil the surprise."

"What are you now, an assistant or a consultant of some sort?"

I was silent.

"He's my assistant," Herbert said, drinking my wine because his was empty. "I let him fiddle with all the machines, the faxes, the mimeographs, and all that."

"Herbert's no good with machines," I explained.

"That's right. It's really very helpful having an assistant around to take care of them."

"Sometimes I make the coffee." I added. Hank laughed because this was obviously a joke. "Actually, I'll be doing a lot of the footwork on these Stein drawings."

"That's right." Herbert smiled at me. "Which is why I was so glad, Hank, that you were interested in seeing both of us for dinner tonight, because that is precisely the project we need your help on."

"I'm always interested in helping," Hank allowed. "Particularly if it's going to be some kind of fun."

"It *will* be fun, Hank. I want you to buy the drawings and donate them to the museum."

Hank looked a little unhappy. "Just buy them?"

"Uh-huh, and donate them to the museum."

"It sounds pretty dull to me."

Poor Herbert. He looked completely undone by this small defeat. "Actually"—I rallied for my new boss—"the way, uh, Herbert has it all worked out"—here I smiled broadly at brooding Herbert—"we need you to *go* to Paris, Hank, for the whole . . . arrangement to work, am I right, Herbert?" Herbert nodded glumly. I went on. "Well." I rattled the empty wine bottle, then sipped my water, while thinking. "*We're* going first, or Herbert is"—I tipped my fork to him—"to poke around and see if these drawings are even what we think they are, and then, *if* they are, Herbert will insist on their worthlessness and make his pitiful little offer."

"Which of course they'll reject." The curator spoke.

"Right, which of course they'll reject . . . which is when you show up, Hank, and buy the pieces right out from under us. You see, this will give the family the pleasure of thinking they've taken *you* to the cleaners, because Herbert will have established that the drawings are nearly worthless except as wallpaper for some children's hospital, and then you sweep in, the big rich bumbling American who doesn't know his ass from his elbow—that's the masquerade anyway, the part you'll be playing—and the family sells to you at twice what we offered, thinking they've hit the jackpot. And voilà! you've got the drawings!" Herbert rolled his eyes.

"Voilà!" Hank echoed, smiling. "That sounds like fun."

"Oh." Herbert sighed. "I'm sure it would be."

"I can do that," Hank announced. "I mean, why not? April in Paris." Herbert looked strangely disappointed. "Say, isn't that one of your students?" Hank pointed his bent fork tine toward the crowded windows of the Hair Health and Vanity store, and there was Dogan, Mother beside him clutching a fresh wig bag, with Daddy evidently gone. "Donald, wasn't it, or Doogie, that kid you brought to the football game?"

"Hank, have you seen the Grand Marble Bar yet?" I asked. "It's really the highlight of the whole hotel."

"Noah certainly did have a good time with him." Hank strained to follow the swiftly moving boy but was distracted by his bladder.

I turned toward Herbert. "Herbert? The Grand Marble Bar? We seem to be out of wine in any case, and I'm sure Hank is sick of this dreary emporium."

"I'll join you two in a sec," Hank offered, rising. "Gotta go to the pisser." We waved a feathery good-bye, and Herbert glared at me.

"Are you mad about something?" I asked. Dogan, fragmented, drifting, afflicted my periphery.

"Where do you come up with these fantasies?"

"With what?"

"You certainly improvised well. I just can't believe Hank swallowed all that garbage, flights to Paris to hobnob with the rich."

"Come on, you'll have a great time."

"Look, Miss Double-oh-seven, the sort of espionage you described has nothing to do with art acquisition. One buys drawings at galleries. You know, like at a store?"

"You made these sound like the Dead Sea Scrolls."

"Did I? Well they might be worth a small fortune, but I'm afraid the chances of their being at all important are remote to none. I was just fishing around to see how far Hank was willing to go with that checkbook of his."

"Do you always rely on swindling the rich?"

"I wouldn't say 'rely.' I'd say I 'delight' in it."

"Well, Hank's willing to go to Paris."

"Going to Paris on this kind of wild goose chase—with Hank, no less—would be sheer torture."

"It looks like you're either going or backing out."

"I can back out easily enough. Hank won't mind. I would just appreciate it, Madame Assistant, if you would leave the whole affair alone for a while, the rest of the evening at least, and let things settle."

In the bar, the Grand Marble Bar (massive countertop hauled from Firenze, installed on broad cedar stumps with a rough fir trim, brass fixtures from Berlin—spoils of the last World War—all this from the napkin supplied with my drink), we found Hank, and voilà! Dogan, without his mom or dad. The pair was installed at a small round side table with two beers, Dogan's in a tall pewter stein (Hank's largesse, no doubt, plus a nimble bribe of the waiter). The boy watched me.

"Look what the cat dragged in," Hank announced. "Doogie's here." I smiled at "Doogie" and Herbert shook his hand, introducing himself as my new colleague. Sweet Herbert.

Dogan sipped from the beer, leaving a mustache where no mustache could be. "I saw you eating."

"Yes, that was me. Hello, by the way."

"Hi. My mom and dad left."

"I saw you shopping."

"Yeah, Mom got her wig and they both had headaches."

"Well, long time."

"I guess so; I mean, a month."

"A month's a long time, though you must be busy with studying and sports and all, so it wouldn't seem so long to you."

"Doogie tells me the soccer squad has made it to the playoffs this year," Hank put in, hoisting his beer. Herbert, utterly bored by the soccer squad, ordered himself an expensive scotch (Day-Glo money) and a Bombay for me.

"Oh?" I was surprised. "That's terrific. It's hard for me to keep track, you know with all my work at the museum." Meaningful glance at Dogan, met, puzzled, returned. "I'll probably be seeing them on TV before long." The round table was minuscule, built for crowding onto the tiny sidewalk of a Parisian back street, and we were rather large. Getting anywhere near the drinks meant navigating an intimate slalom of knees and chair legs; I paid no mind to the press of Dogan (left thigh and calf) and Herbert (right knee).

"There was a picture in the newspaper," Dogan announced, grimacing at the beer stein as he sniffed it and took a sip. "But I wasn't in it."

"Hardly worth clipping."

"Are you gonna be in the yearbook?" my little waif asked.

"You know"—Hank leaned in, disturbing almost everything—"I don't know if you're on the yearbook squad or anything, Doogie, but I recall in fifty-three, my senior year, when Professor Schmatza—you're a senior, right?"

"Sophomore."

"That's right. Well, when Professor Schmatza left our school midyear to join the Lucy expedition, the kids got together and dedicated the yearbook to him, just as a kind of tribute." Herbert accepted his scotch from the waiter and handed me my gin. "I'm sure someone's already suggested it in this case, I mean, it's probably a fait acompli." Hank smiled at me.

"I'm not on the yearbook staff," Dogan said, but Hank wasn't really listening to him.

"My goodness, Professor Schmatza was surprised—and pleased, of course. It was a terrific surprise for everyone."

"As it would be for me," I added. I clinked my glass to Herbert's, Hank's, and, with some prompting, Dogan's nearly full beer stein.

"They're putting extra pages in for soccer, if we make it to finals." Dogan spoke only of what he knew, a habit that always charmed me.

"The *I Love Lucy* expedition?" Herbert asked. Like Hank, he didn't seem to notice that the boy ever actually spoke. "Or was it *The Lucy Show* already?" He and Hank laughed at the joke.

"What are you drinking?" Dogan asked me.

"Gin. You wouldn't like it."

"I don't like this beer. It's warm." I looked into the tall stein and saw a dark well of stout, rimmed with scummy foam.

"What is it?"

"It's called Guinness. Your friend said since I'm a soccer player I'd like it." How cosmopolitan the Grand Marble Bar was, serving Irish stout in a German stein to an underage Turk.

"You don't have to drink it. Hank was just being friendly. He likes to buy things for his friends."

"I remembered him from the football game. He's really nice."

"Did he see you shopping?"

"No. I saw him so I said hi."

"That's very nice of you, and nice of Hank to invite you along to the bar."

"He didn't invite me."

"That's not just Guinness, you know," Hank pointed out, thinking I cared about the beer, "that's a Guinness triple-X. This bar's terrific. I haven't seen triple-X since Hattie and I took Noah to Dublin for the horse races."

"He didn't invite you?"

"I told him I was supposed to meet you, and he said you were in the bar."

"You don't mind, do you?" Hank asked rhetorically, taking the boy's beer and lifting it up to my face. "Just look at that foam, thick enough to raise kids on. You could build a house with that foam."

"It's remarkable, Hank." Turning to the boy: "Is that what you told your parents?"

"Oh, no way." Dogan dismissed this lunacy. "They didn't see you. I told them I ran into a friend from soccer camp who was staying at the hotel. They think I'm staying overnight with him. They don't care."

"You don't mind if Herbert tries it, do you? Go ahead, Herbie, after a sip of the scotch it's a real high-class boilermaker." Herbert sniffed the stein suspiciously and then tried it. I was surprised he seemed to like it.

"Tastes kind of like oatmeal, Hank. I mean with dirt and alcohol in it. That's very nice, a very fine beer."

"Well, that was kind of dumb," I whispered to Dogan. "Now you can't go home, plus there's no 'friend' here to stay with."

The boy rolled his eyes, then just looked at me.

So that now, to the delight of many of you and the horror of some, Dogan and I are going to spend the whole night together in the same bed (my bed, by the ill-paned window at home) for the last time, and in some detail. We'll have unskilled, enthusiastic sex, minimal but valued conversation, and a snack at what was probably three in the morning. Those of you who can't stomach any more of this sort of thing can skip ahead to page 47, where the narrative resumes.

We shared a taxi home, Herbert, Dogan, and I. The boy insisted I make a ruse to Herbert about some book I was lending him, which I did, halfheartedly, and which sweet Herbert led the boy to believe he believed and also found unremarkable ("Oh, he mentioned that book to me just yesterday, didn't you now, and how it must be lent soon; how convenient for everyone; I hope I don't miss the eleven o'clock news"). Since the narrative hounds have all skipped forward anyway, I'll just dispense with the clumsy linkages and survey some of the highlights of that night.

The slight weight of Dogan's hand on my shoulder when we leaned in the doorway, worrying the lock open. The fact that he let the same hand drift along my back when the lock slid shut and we walked in. The ease with which he stood and peed and talked to me while peeing, and that I heard him through a bathroom door he hadn't bothered to close. The vista in the dark. Him still fiddling with the buttons of his fly when he came out. Dogan—I don't think I mentioned he was 5 feet 8 inches or so (two or three inches shorter than I), with a lanky floppiness that wobbled between puppy dog and deer, that his messy hair was fine and dark brown, that his eyes were large and deep beneath a single brow, or that he habitually kept his lips slightly parted as if about to speak—looking out the window at the city's nighttime profile, then flopping back on the bed as if he lived in it. The elegance of his prone posture, like a poorly drawn swastika or a spinning ninja weapon that had tired and fallen in the midst of its long trajectory. These words: "Use both your hands." Because we'd only ever had sex before in a nervous hurry, how he lay on the bed talking to me not undressing or rushing himself at all. I didn't know what he thought, but *I* thought there were ruses ahead, long conversations or fidgeting, feints toward the couch or a sleeping bag, when in fact he lay down on the bed because he was there to sleep with me. I sat down so my hip touched his, and I let my hand drift onto his leg. "Use both your hands," was his final instruction.

The spring of his puckered fly, when both my hands got there after traveling the length of the inseamed thighs. That he watched and smiled. His long arms fiddling against the window glass behind his head while he reclined. The crushed and folded paperback (Rousseau's *Émile*) stuck underneath him, produced only after five or ten minutes when the arching of his back to push a tremulous and exposed organ deeper into my mouth made it convenient, I suppose, to grab the book and toss it to the floor. At this point he was just a long baggy bundle of soft clothes with an engorged penis protruding from the middle; I had my shirt partly undone—hardly the picture of romance. There was traffic outside, honks and the late-night blatting of taxis, periodic bus roars, and the drunken chatter of partygoers returning home. The railroad tower became especially interesting for a protracted minute or two that is difficult to account for. I simply lost my focus on the great slobbery organ for a stretch. It had slipped from my mouth again and, poking haphazardly, had found my eye socket and brow so that I pulled it aside in one hand, still enjoying its remarkable heat in my fist, and stared across Dogan's pulled up shirt and long arms (drawn back behind his head) at the beautiful lighted masquerade of the window-framed city. The railroad tower, as I said, looked especially homely and real amidst the delicious fakery. It appeared, just then, to have an actual history and function. I wobbled the boy's organ like a joystick, absentmindedly, then saw him in the dark, staring out from the hutch of his baggy shirt like a rabbit in the nighttime forest. I kissed the head of his cock, then pushed it down flat against his belly, where I smushed it for a while. He groaned some, thrusting like an infant trying to reach the taut nipple, only not leading with his face: thrust, groan, thrust-thrust, groan, which was endearing, so I petted him like a dog. He turned on his side, and this petulance aggravated me. Rolling him over I pulled at his clothes without explanation, dragging the unbuttoned jeans and boxers sharply down to his shapely ankles and slipping the baggy shirt over his head so that he was all just flesh and startled as I rolled my hairy head all over him and began kneading his body with both great grabbing hands like a panicked shopper unleashed in the midst of a monetary collapse. This was quite unlike our usual furtive blow jobs. He took to it like a boy to wrestling, tore my shirt, and tugged my trousers down, all the while smushing himself in acrobatic variations on and against me and whatever else got drawn into the maelstrom: pillows, sheets, clothing, and the like. His breathing became furious and uncontrolled, his brow and back wet with sweat, until, flopping me down against the twisted bedding and straddling my hips to drive his soccer-drenched open-air thighs and slobbery organ over my tummy, he let out a great fart. We both stopped, and then he laughed. I really shouldn't include this with the highlights at all, but it provides such a nice contrast to the idealized Dogan I've tried to preserve. Other contrasts: his chaste pucker when I whispered, "Can we kiss?" I don't know if he had never kissed with an open mouth, or if mine offended him, but his closed eyes and pert, expectant lips endeared him to me. I pecked his cheek and whispered "there." My alarm when, while rolling in our romp, I found myself on top of him, impressing the enormity of my body on the true prematurity of his; Dogan wasn't merely lithe or gangly or slim, he was a little boy, a nervous, pulsing envelope of flesh and growing bones whose sexual development had rushed in advance of the rest of him so that this great, potent organ was appended to the birdlike frame of a tall twelve-year-old (by the calendar he was fifteen). I had to hold myself slightly off the mattress with a well-placed elbow or two to avoid crushing him.

Our conversation, after our last shared orgasm, lying now in the manner of spoons, Dogan in front, me behind, the boy dressed in hastily found boxers and T-shirt, me in nothing, while outside the window the city was mostly silent and dark:

"Are you really working at a museum?"

"Yes." (Would I ever stop lying to him?)

"Do you have to? I mean, I thought the school gave you pay even though you had to leave and everything."

"I prefer it. The work interests me."

"What do you do there?"

"I'm a curator." It felt oddly pleasant to be Herbert for a moment. "Do you know what a curator does?"

"Not exactly."

"I help decide what paintings the museum buys and displays. I organize shows for them—not just paintings, actually, but drawings and photographs too."

"Wow."

"I'm going to Paris in a few weeks, to buy some Picasso drawings for a show."

"Pablo Picasso?"

"Yes. You know Picasso?"

"Oh, sure." Here the boy began singing—melodizing, I guess—in a soft whisper. "'He was only five-foot-two, but girls could not resist his stare. Pablo Picasso was never called an asshole, not like you. . . ."

"I don't think that's the same Picasso."

"Sure it is. 'He would drive down the street in his El Dorado, and the girls would turn the color of an avocado; oh, he was only five-foot-two . . .'"

"Did you make that up?"

"No, it's the Modern Lovers, 'Pablo Picasso.' He was an artist, right?"

"Yes."

"Come on." He shook his body a little, like wiggling an eyebrow, only in the dark. "Everyone knows Picasso. My mom took us to the Musée Picasso all the time when we lived in Paris."

"Of course. I'd forgotten." I let my hand turn the corner over his hip. "How long did you live there?"

"We moved there when I was six, and I had my bar mitzvah there, so seven years." He stopped, everything stopped, while the boy evaluated the trajectory of my hand. "A little more than seven." Now he stretched his leg out slightly, enough to let the hip turn open and encourage my hand.

"I need to hire a translator for the Paris trip."

"You don't speak French?" Where my hand brushed his boxers, a rounded fold of cotton pushed up, one pulse and then another.

"Not very well."

"I speak it better than my English." We both laughed a little. I had been hired to change that fact, but neither of us ever cared or worked hard enough to change it. I drew my other hand up along the backs of his thighs, along the crease where his legs met.

"I wonder if you could go with me, be my translator. You'd get paid very well."

"Uhn." He turned his hip a little more, pulling his free arm over his head, so my hand slipped onto the tented middle of his boxers, and I let it lie there, just cupping the drifting organ that moved and struggled under its weight. "I'm at school every day." He kind of sighed. "I mean, and soccer."

"Maybe during your break. You'd be an excellent translator." Now I lifted my hand so the cotton lifted beneath it, then moved my fingers up and down its length.

"Yeah." He simply breathed, pushing his hips out toward my wandering hand. I had turned too, to lay my other arm along his parting legs, brushing both thighs along the inside and up into his shorts, and now he tugged the waistband down and his erection flopped out onto his tummy, where I licked it, pressing my tongue along the underside onto its head, and he groaned, then lifted my head from him and whispered, "Can I, you know, in you?" And he slipped over onto me, pushing my legs up with his body, and we did.

Oh, yes, our snack, at 3 or 4 A.M.: a bland cheese (jack) and crackers, plus gulps of orange juice from a cardboard container in the fridge, first tasted leaning in the cool white light of that marvelous icebox, then seated on the bed, silent, puzzled, exhausted, looking out at the utterly dark and sleeping city.

◆3◆

Allan Stein was the spoiled only child of progressive Jewish parents. A cultured, upper-middle-class boy in a prosperous city, he was the happy recipient of endless lessons: piano, tennis, boxing, language, crafts, horseback riding. He liked streetcars and went with his father to the "car house to watch his dearest cars being shampooed." At his mother's behest, he "played man, to show what he will look like when he is a man." A raft of cousins from Sarah's side kept him company in Berkeley, while back in San Francisco, at 707 Washington Street, Allan played with his bearded, bearish father, Mikey.

His mother posed him for photographs, once a week, and then every month of the first four years of his life, costumed for outlandish scenarios, which she mounted and labeled in great albums to be shared with friends: A Young Don Quixote, Paderovsky Up to Date, No More Dresses For Me No Sir, Champion of the Brawl. After nearly dying from loss of blood and an infection caused by the difficult birth of this ten-pound baby, Sally wrote to her sister-in-law, Gertrude:

"He has Mike's forehead and horrifies me by moving the entire top of his head just as Mike does. Above an exquisite upper lip he has a nondescript nose whose nostrils he inflates in an alarming fashion. On the whole he is considered a very intelligent-looking but not a beautiful child."

And later, "There certainly is nothing in the line of happiness to compare with that which a mother derives from the contemplation of her firstborn, and even the agony which she endures from the moment of its birth does not seem to mar it, therefore my dear and beloved sister-in-law go and get married, for there is nothing in the whole wide world like babies."

Sarah was devoted to him. "I doubt if a happier, more attractive youngster can be found," she wrote. When Allan was two, Sarah reported the boy's "cute little sayings" to Auntie Gertrude—

"'Poor mamma has wind in her odder leg, its a hoyyible fing to have wind, dear me!' The little fellow will not play with children his own age and he regards younger children with disgust, but he dotes on boys and girls from eight to fourteen."

In Paris, Allan was the only child of the four Stein adults, great big children themselves, who, with the sour exception of dour Uncle Leo, adored and doted on him. He went to the private École Alsacienne, an innovative school in their Montparnasse neighborhood. I imagine him on a cold day in the late winter, the rue Madame smelling of ice and coal. I have been studying the maps. M. Vernot, in blue coveralls, throws grit on the stone sidewalk to make it safe. Allan watches his breath in clouds and crosses the street to walk where there is no grit. The sky is slate gray and empty. On every street there are children rushing to school. Allan hurries down the rue de Fleurus and crosses the rue Guynemer to the iron gate of the Luxembourg Garden. He pulls his mittens off and fixes the satchel, then runs with it against the fence, making a dull accelerating noise. At the rue d'Assas, where bombs would fall during the Great War, Allan slows and walks. Boys from his class call greetings or hit his head with their mittens. His friend Giselin bumps his shoulder and they shake hands. Older boys stand by the wall at the Lycée Montaigne, blowing smoke and staring past them. Allan and Giselin say nothing. The courtyard echoes with shouting and the smack of hard shoes on gravel. Allan's cap is grabbed and pulled down over his eyes, and he pushes it back up again. Cold mist hangs among the shouting boys, muting light from rooms where teachers write lessons on blackboards in chalk. The hard ball comes flying, unseen, toward Allan, and he feels the sting and then a sharp burn of pain on his bare calf when it hits him.

"*If* you went to Paris, Herbert." We were at Shackles again. The day was sunny and warm, and Shackles had their articulating windows thrown open to the spring breeze. I was trying a rosé Tristan said was typical of Provence. Herbert had scotch. "I mean, to find those drawings: Wouldn't the museum tack your vacation on *after* the work was done? I mean, a week or two of business, then 'Herbert's vacation'?"

"Naturally I could do that. I'm the one who accounts for my hours. It's not like a factory time clock. What are you getting at?"

"I think you need a vacation."

"Of course I need a vacation, just not in Paris. Are you fixing to send me away for a *long* time so you can take over? Madame Assistant leads the revolution?"

"No, I've got a much better idea." I left an obnoxious silence, which Herbert didn't bother filling. He just stared, sipping his scotch. "I should go to Paris in your place." This made him laugh, which I preferred to the silence.

"You're delusional. You *don't* work for the museum. That is a fiction, a lie we told Hank, just for—for I don't know what reason."

"I know that. I'm not proposing that *I* go to Paris, per se."

"Well then, how *will* you go, if not per se?"

"I'll go as you. As Herbert Widener. I'll get the drawings, have a fine time doing it, and take however long you want me to, and you can just disappear into whatever vacation your heart desires—paid, I might add, while everyone thinks you're off in Paris working." This put him into a much more involved silence. I fiddled with the decanter, holding it up to the sun as if this could tell me something about the wine. Herbert thought and thought and thought some more.

"You'll go as me."

"Mmm."

"What if you run into someone who knows me?"

"Why would I?"

"I don't see why you would."

"The Steins don't know you."

"No, they don't."

"Does anyone in Paris know you? I mean by sight."

"Well, a few friends of course, but no one you'd have any reason to deal with." A long pause. "You *can't* stay at the Mahler."

"At the what?"

"The Hotel Mahler. All my friends *know* I stay there. They're probably checking the register every day, just waiting for me to show up."

"I won't even stay in the neighborhood. What neighborhood is it?"

"The Fourth—"

"Send me to the Fifth."

"No, farther. We've got to put you somewhere out of the way. It is, I would say, an intriguing plan, as long as no one who knows me sees you."

"So I'm going?"

"It's unthinkable." A sip of scotch. "Let me think about it."

My first passport was shared with my mother and our dog, Max. In the picture she is seated, holding Max, and I'm standing at her side. I was twelve. Louise wanted to take me to North Africa.

Louise kept a shrine on a small credenza in her bedroom. Among photographs and candles, postcards, and especially memorable traffic citations, Louise always had propped her folded and dirty, lipstick-kissed, grad school transcript. She had studied anthropology—in fact, was studying to become an anthropologist—when the pursuit was interrupted by her pregnancy. Louise took a leave. After I was born, the plan went, she would return, Dad splitting the day care, but that never happened. She had two years of grad school, the last devoted to a professor named Margaret Chang-Sagerty (*her* red lips on the transcript), whose specialty was something about Morocco. We were going to North Africa to spend a month among the "Mohammedans" Louise had studied at school.

We planned to travel in winter, stretching my two-week Christmas break into four and deflecting the objections of my teachers with the promise of hard study and a special report when I returned. Louise insisted I take the report seriously, and I did, and she did too. Our report was astonishing, but I'll get to that. Louise liked to smoke, and she smoked more when she was happy. The weeks leading up to our trip were shrouded in a bluish haze, saturated with lists, borrowed luggage, special hats and phrase books, and punctuated by lessons in Spanish and French from friends of Louise who came to our house with bottles of wine and talked.

It was hard to concentrate at school. At lunch I pretended there was no water. I thought Fez was in the desert. Doug Hedges was my best friend, and I told him Louise and I were going to ride to Fez on camels.

"Fez isn't in the desert," he said.

"I know that," I told him. "We could still ride on camels."

"Why?"

Louise made maps and "itineraries" after dinner on beautiful, translucent onion paper that she'd lifted from work. We used different colored pens for the different days. She hated her job (insurance receptionist—"deflectionist," she called it) and asked her friend Constance Pruitt to phone in sick for her the first two weeks, then call and get a "medical leave." Constance sounded like Louise on the phone. She hated "assless bosses" as much as Louise did, and this subterfuge appealed to her.

We thought of everything except the passport. On the day before our departure, Louise went to pick up the airplane tickets and they asked for our passport. We didn't have one which is how Max ended up in the picture. Three bulky suitcases and a knapsack ("only what can be carried"), one frantic boy, and a calm mother, all stuffed into Constance's car with Constance and the dog, we went in the morning downtown to Immigration on our way to an afternoon departure for Madrid. Louise held Max on her lap in the photo booth and I stood, and then we waited several hours for the paperwork to be completed. The dog was well behaved. Constance kept me happy playing cards. On the way to the airport we left Max with Jean-Baptiste (of the drunken French lessons) and arrived with about an hour to spare before our flight.

My private life at that time (every child has one) had become exceedingly complicated, mostly because of puberty. I stared in the mirror constantly and was embarrassed to be caught at it. I began forming elaborate ideas about myself and my mother—who we were in the world and who we ought to be. On the airplane I insisted on wearing a tie. It was ridiculous. We had to buy a clip-on at the drugstore because neither of us knew how to make the knot. Somewhere I'd gotten the idea that I was the kind of child who should travel in a tie. This evolving scenario included Louise, who needed to become a kind of Auntie Mame in order for the tie to really resonate properly. It wasn't a huge stretch—she had so much life and spine and humor—but no woman is Auntie Mame, and Louise had no interest in becoming her. On the airplane to Chicago, the first of three links to Madrid, she ordered a club soda and I was disappointed. I gestured to the champagne and said she should have some.

"Why?" she asked, wrinkling her brow.

"You love champagne," I said.

"Not on airplanes. It gives me a headache on airplanes."

"Well, I'd like to try a little." This from a boy who had always complained that wine stank like vomit, beer was urine, and liquor poison.

Louise laughed and turned back to her magazine. "What a ridiculous boy." Her rebuke surprised me but did nothing to diminish the elegant vision I had conjured. The story in my head was not a lie but a kind of reality-in-progress. I had all the guileless relativism of a child. Louise's rebuke didn't mean I was mistaken; rather, reality had not yet caught up to my imagination. (And of course at this point, in the guise of memory, my childhood has become exactly this kind of mutable, irrefutable thing.)

We made it to Spain but never Morocco. Morocco required a visa we didn't have, and now it was too late. Louise wrote most of my report in a wonderful cheap hotel in Barcelona where we stayed for four weeks, a long, elaborate fiction about our adventures in the market culture of Fez. The report was encyclopedic and stunning, with photos taken from a reference book and drawings, by me, of a Fez based largely on Barcelona's old quarter. Afternoons were spent in cafés on the Ramblas drinking colorful sodas and playing solitaire (or rummy with Louise, when she wasn't busy scripting seventh grade paragraphs). The nights went on and on into hours I thought even adults could not inhabit, and I was a great hit in my clip-on tie, dancing with Louise at a club called El Sol, where the waiters gave me free snacks and admired my cards.

I was pleased that my second passport would not include Max. When Herbert finally agreed to my plan (against his better judgment, he said), it was a Friday and I had three days to get ready for my trip to Paris. Among the felicities that finally swayed him was the availability of a place to stay deep, deep in the Thirteenth arrondissement with a family that had nothing to do with art or museums. The Dupaignes offered a "suite of rooms" on the ground floor of their house to foreign scholars visiting the Cité Universitaire, just a few blocks away. Herbert had a friend in the university's history department (another fruit) arrange everything on his behalf, and the rooms were secured for two weeks. Herbert Widener was expected in Paris April fifteenth.

Outside, the afternoons had become legendary and warm. I rescued my tired and neglected leather datebook from its place on the dusty window ledge. Traversing its many barren pages, its vast white field of empty days and weeks, I penned in this single appointment, *Arrive Paris April 15,* punctuated with a swift underline.

"I'm only doing this to rescue you from the scandal you're courting here in town."

"Courting? I'm not courting anyone."

"You can't go inviting twelve-year-old ex-students to sleep with you and expect nothing to come of it."

"Oh, everything came of it. He's fifteen, by the way."

"Exactly my point. You could be arrested."

"I've already been punished for it by the school. It's the least I can do, you know, to make the charges valid."

"That's certainly selfless—and stupid."

"I wish Dogan could go with me."

"It's out of the question. I'm the one who's going to Paris."

"I'm sure I'll keep to myself."

"Maybe you'll get this Turk out of your system, or at least develop the good sense not to sleep with him anymore."

"Hmm."

The bright blue days became crowded. I hadn't packed bags like this since my second trip with Louise (France at age sixteen), and it was relaxing to lift them in two hands and feel anchored by their weight. The neglected datebook got filled with errands and addresses, lists, phone numbers, and the pleasing finality of sharp check marks stabbed beside those tasks I managed to complete. Herbert was disappearing to a vast ranch near Petaluma to take pharmaceuticals, drink chilled fumé blanc, and lie in the sun with an architect friend of ours who had everything one could ever want in life except company. The "rest cure," Herbert called it.

"Jimmy asked if you were free too."

"What did you tell him?"

"That you were in jail."

"No."

"I told him you were taking some school group on a trip. I didn't say where. I doubt he'll press me for details."

"Maybe I'll join you. I mean, after Paris."

"Mmm, you should. I don't see any reason *not* to stay on at Jimmy's."

"I could bring you the drawings."

"Yes, you could; that's very good. I'll tell them I'm flying back via San Francisco. A week in Paris and then a week in San Francisco. I've got to get back by the twenty-ninth."

"The museum won't collapse in your absence?"

"Not so anyone would notice."

The prospect of vacation at Jimmy's was already giving Herbert a blush of health and vigor I hadn't seen on him in several months. He still looked gaunt and drunk, but his mouth was more relaxed and his eyes sparkled. The arrangement promised to be as good for him as it was for me, and this equanimity was pleasing. It assuaged the guilt I felt for the one truly wrong and completely unconscionable thing I did to my dearest friend before going to Paris. I don't know why it was important to me. I can't say how the compulsion became so irresistible and the act so plausible, but I took his passport. I stole it from his apartment while he was at work, rifling through the desk to find it, together with his birth certificate—and then I mutilated the passport, so it would have to be replaced. I wanted a new one with my picture and his name, to make the masquerade of my Paris trip complete.

Our last drink was at Shackles. An air of melancholy settled with the balding assistant manager's news that Tristan was gone for two weeks. "The kids are all off for spring break," he told us. "How glum," Herbert said, and indeed the whole place was glum. The assistant didn't bother to wear the croupier's disguise. He wiped our clean table with a filthy cloth and stood waiting for an order. We split a bottle of heavy Bordeaux and then a Napa Valley red zinfandel that was like drinking a brick wall. A little bon voyage.

"Is that a new watch? You never wore a watch before." I'd bought a watch and Herbert was right, I had never had one before.

"I know. I thought I might need one." I fiddled with the mechanism and ran my fingers along the soft leather band. I had been doing that all evening.

"What time is your flight?"

"Afternoon. One o'clock, I think." The bar was crowded but it seemed empty, the drinkers subdued by the fact it was Monday evening, stunned by the recent weekend's end and the terrible recurring surprise of work again.

"It takes forever."

"Eleven hours. I change planes in Copenhagen."

"Oh, SAS?"

"Mmm." I'd bought the ticket with Herbert's credit card, as per instructions; I also had it issued in his name, with his passport, but he didn't know that.

"I love SAS. All those little sandwiches, and you know they'll give you aquavit, chilled to absolute zero."

"Delicious." We drank wine without speaking for some time.

"Thank God I'm leaving for California. I couldn't stand another evening like this, here without Tristan."

"Thank you very much. I'll miss you too."

"I mean without Tristan or you, obviously. That kind of thing goes without saying."

"Tristan's probably waiting for you at Jimmy's."

"Don't tease me. I would die to spend a few weeks with him at Jimmy's."

"He looks Californian, maybe he's back home for break, just over the ridge at the next ranch. Jimmy probably hires him every spring to, you know, mow the range. The neighbor boy, out mowing the range, all shirtless and sweaty." I smiled weakly, happy to give my friend at least this small token.

"Maybe he *does* live down there. I wonder if he'd visit, I mean if I invited him?"

"He'd have to stay overnight. Can't drive drunk."

"The bursar would certainly have his family's address."

"A scented note in the letter box."

"I should probably just phone. Though maybe a note *is* best, so he doesn't feel pressured in any way."

"A simple note: Jimmy's phone number and a condom."

"You're so crude."

"What's so crude about a condom? It's a very normal thing. You're so anachronistic."

"It isn't normal to send one in the mail as a dinner invitation."

"Mmm, just dinner?"

"Obviously just dinner." Herbert tried the zinfandel and made a face. "Or maybe a day trip, a hike in the hills and lunch somewhere, like that fabulous place near Point Reyes. Jimmy could get us reservations, I mean if anyone could."

"Just send the condom."

"Oh, shut up."

I would miss Herbert, but that went without saying. My well-kept secret lent the evening some of the poignancy and glamour of the Last Supper, but only for me. Herbert was a Christ without a clue, unaware he'd been betrayed by his most ardent friend. The betrayal was minor (certainly by comparison), but its resonance was deep. The torpor of our stalled conversation felt profound to me. There was nothing left to exchange. I had already taken the last token of his identity from him.

4

The airport was torn up and confusing. I had my two bags and knapsack (only what can be carried), plus the passport, clutched in one hand with my ticket. I hadn't slept well despite all the wine—excitement, I told myself, though approaching the airfield (the only passenger that hour in the ExPorter Express Van) it was clear that leaving also frightened me. This trip was a precipice and I was going over. Herbert, who is always nervous about airplanes, had given me some pills to take.

It was difficult to find my terminal. Men with hydraulic tools blasted paint from the concrete floors. Flapping gray tarpaulins covered steel frames where the glass walls were missing. I asked directions, but noise from the tools drowned my voice out. Normally the gates are coded by color, but there was no color left. A woman touched my wrist. She looked at my ticket and motioned for me to follow her. Because of the noise we said nothing. This woman was kind but her face was hard and expressionless, like the floor. She set a brisk pace and only looked back to see that I kept up. Wooden barriers and strung tape channeled us past the torn-open places. The sun through the tarps was dull and even. We found my gate and it was crowded, so I had to stand. The woman nodded at it, then left me.

Everything about my flight had been changed. The airplane would leave late and fly to Paris directly because of heavy snow in the north. Danes argued reasonably at the ticket desk. I was in business class, which meant I could board early. In my knapsack (all I had after the gatekeeper snatched my suitcases away) were *Émile*, *Walks in Gertrude Stein's Paris*, some Henry James, *A Very Pretty Girl from the Country*, *Paris As It Is*, old guidebooks from Herbert—Ward-Lock & Co.'s *Paris* (1911), C. B. Black's *Riviera* (1905; how very intriguing to see what has changed, he said)—and *Zigzagging in France*, all unearthed from the bulky suitcase when it was taken from me, panicky and convinced I would read at least six books on the flight over (I read none of them).

Because I boarded first, the magazines were still available. I picked out a half dozen and stuffed them in the netting of the seat in front of me. Cool air blew through a nozzle and over my face. I sank into the cushions and watched men outside groom the metal wings. Luggage dragged on belts dropped into the plane's belly, then bumped and settled in the hold like ice into a glass. There were engines humming, small engines that soothed my nerves. It might have been the pills.

I rode the airplane as if into sleep, motionless, transported. The ground fell away, and the air inside became thick and busy. The city, my home, rushed away, beyond my reach. Through the scarred plastic window unreal tableaux lurched and turned, then disappeared into clouds. I drank a lot of alcohol and could not stay awake. The flight was very long. It felt like days with meals that came suddenly and too soon. Dinner arrived during a prolonged morning that seemed to be moving backward into night. We had a snack and breakfast in the middle of a dream, then a second morning. The night between was caricatured and flat, an emblem of night that fell and withdrew as suddenly as the backdrop of an opera. The sun appeared, a dull metal disk on an empty curved horizon that was stained yellow and blue by the sun's arrival. A woman across from me said good morning. She took her breakfast from the steward and thanked him. There is an easy camaraderie in business class. In coach I would not speak to anyone.

"Hello," I said. "Herbert Widener."

"Margaret Carlson." She had work to do and set up a small computer on the tray beside her breakfast. I took my meal from the steward but fell asleep again.

On photocopied pages in my knapsack were these details: Allan Stein's journey with his parents, San Francisco to Paris, 1903 (age eight)—eating biscuits at a table on the train, crumbs on white linen; the pleasure of Allan's window at night, the soft rumbling of the engine, his head pressed to a pillow; the city of Baltimore, kissed by aunts and cousins; boarding the ocean liner in New York; torn bread thrown to diving gulls in the harbor, cold salt air billowing Allan's coat; bright sun; playing shuffleboard on deck with Mikey; a basket of pastry, coffee in a silver pot beside the bed; the sighting of a whale through binoculars, near to dawn, the coast of France; Allan, curled in a deck chair, wrapped in a blanket, watching land; the smell of manure, earth, and coal dust; crates hoisted by cranes onto docks; the weakness of Allan's legs, arriving; passport stamps and shouting; baggage carts, a vendor of pastries, then tea; trains like giant worms asleep in a cavernous station of iron and glass; steam and metal, fog, rain on the rattling window; Allan asleep until Paris.

The airplane shook, descending, and I woke up with my head pressed to a pillow by the small plastic window. My body felt awful, sick from the alcohol, and cramped. I had slept with the arm of the chair pushed against my ribs. What time was it? It was morning. There was land, bright and green, then patched white with snow or ice, spotted by clouds and crisscrossed by roads where I could see traffic. Buildings cast shadows to the north and west. There were towns with churches surrounded by checkerboard farmland. The shadows of clouds made patterns like swells in the ocean where they moved over hills below us. Paris could not be seen. I arranged my seat and strained to look forward through the scratched and cloudy window. I saw nothing but dull light. The airplane turned, descending, and I saw farms, again, and a busy highway. It all came rushing toward us, and then the airplane touched down and we had landed. A car waiting at the terminal had been provided by the Cité Universitaire. M. WIDENER, the hand-held placard said. Herbert was treated very well.

"Paris is like a fruit divided into two halves by the gleaming steel of the river," [this from one of my books] "and over each half on either side rises a height which augments the impression of immensity. On the left bank it is the mountain of Sainte-Genevieve crowned by the Pantheon, with its belt of columns on which rests its enormous dome. On the right is the white church of the Sacre Coeur, gleaming on the hill of Mont Martre like some celestial vision. It is at its threshold, rather than from the Eiffel Tower or anywhere else, that you get the most poignant impressions of Paris as a whole. It lies spread out before you, with its setting of distant hills, its swarming expanse of houses dominated here and there by palaces, and broken by the green of gardens; and from that distance the sounds of the city come to you only as one great suppressed murmur, a murmur palpitating with this great heart of the old world."

We drove along a raised highway. The driver was African and did not speak to me. Boxy modern flats sprawled below the road, half occupied and in disrepair. I watched the buildings grow closer and more busy. It began to sleet; then the sleet turned to rain and I closed my eyes, wanting more sleep.

While I try to be gracious I am in fact made uncomfortable by strangers. Paris was a stranger, and I was in it. That fact, plus the airplane ride, had so drained me that when we pulled up to the forlorn garden wall of the Dupaignes' house—a quaint cottagelike building wedged between towering apartment blocks in a rather ugly district—I asked the driver to find a hotel where I could rest. He stared at me, saying nothing, then drove on. Out the car's back window I saw a boy watching from an upper story of the house, leaning on a window casement, his oversized sweater falling from one shoulder. This was Stéphane.

The hotel lobby was cold and empty, like a drained aquarium, and I took my bags upstairs and collapsed onto the bed. I dreamt of nothing, flopping on the covers like a stunned fish, kept from my dreams, from anything beyond sensory impressions, by some kind of synaptical failure I blamed on the long trip. I felt cut in pieces, diced, like a man pressed through a sieve, as if a web of knowingness, a coherence, had been dragged out of me when the plane took off. Sleep helped. Waking up, several hours later, I looked at my watch and it told me the time back home. Herbert was alone in the city now, without me, not due to leave for Jimmy's until the next morning. For an instant, as a kind of reflex, I considered inviting him out for a drink, but of course I couldn't do that. I showered and got dressed and asked the concierge for a map. It was half past five and my appetite and humor had returned. I thought a drink would be nice, and maybe some fresh oysters, after which I'd take on the Dupaignes.

The biting cold and sleet of my arrival had disappeared and a deep blue sky, evening to the east, tapered away between buildings. The breeze smelled of flowers and rain and car exhaust. It was pleasant where it touched my face and neck. I undid the heavy coat I'd brought on the plane and looked around the nearest corner, wondering if the morning's storm might be lodged there, hiding in the shadow of some courtyard, but there was nothing. The concierge had made a map on which he marked a garden, the Jardin du Luxembourg, and I could see it, grand chestnut trees all billowing and wet behind a forbiddingly spiked black fence, just a few blocks away. I walked there first, in no great hurry.

The garden was crowded with boys, some of them playing basketball at a hoop among the chestnut trees. I sat on a metal chair and watched them. A small fist of cloud shifted, blocking the last sun, and it became dusky where I sat. These boys did not move well. Their bodies were new to the game, and they lurched and stopped like apprentice drivers maneuvering trucks. They had no idea how poorly they played. Each success thrilled them, so they would strut and slap if a simple layup went in. I smiled at their successes, as I did at school when my students discussed philosophy.

Smaller children sailed boats in a pond and their mothers sat on benches with nannies, smoking cigarettes and talking. I read that Allan Stein played in this garden when Gertrude took him on walks. How odd to be sitting in it. (Once Allan played with an American girl, Edith Rosenshine, and Edith was horrified when he asked her to go to the toilet with him. Gertrude assured her it was the French custom, and she went.) Evening came and policemen cleared us from the park. The boys unlocked their bicycles from the fences where they'd chained them, and mothers and children drifted away through traffic.

I walked alongside the park, enjoying the smell of trees, to the rue Vavin, where a perfectly fine café was open. It was simple and fairly crowded, and that appealed to me. I wouldn't bother with oysters, not at so plain a place, but wine must be decent everywhere. The evening's chill was coming on, so the outside tables were empty and I took one. Two young women watched through the glass front of the café, their table only a few feet from mine. They talked easily and laughed. I caught the eye of one, a fat girl, and I smiled. The waiter came and I ordered a *pichet* of Côtes-du-Rhône with a baguette and Gruyère. My accent sounded fairly good, casual and dismissive like the French of my mother's drunk friends at home.

A gate of the park was visible across the street, and it emptied for another ten minutes before the gate was finally shut.

The park was empty, closed now. Gravel paths led from the gate into trees that were heavy and shook water on the grass when the wind came up. Traffic and birds made a noise like wildfire. The sky was dead or hollow like a painting, and it made me lonely sitting at the café on a slatted chair. I looked around for something, a boy, to admire and found a group of them with worn leather satchels strapped to their backs. A taller black-haired one, in particular, seemed as delightful as the wine I drank. Twisting to swat the shoulder of a pal or grab an arm he caught my eye, right across a long pause in the traffic, and I returned it with a broad smile, amplified by the wine, so that he noticed me. It was nice, this familiar boy, like a kind of universal welcome home, and I felt drawn to him. He grabbed the shoulders of two friends and this trio stopped. The boy was a type: baggy, low-belted American jeans, oversized white T-shirt, and a jacket with logos from basketball or soccer all blossoming on a frame as thin and gangly as Dogan's. He had the arrogance of the spoiled kids I'd enjoyed at my school. His posture and the sudden dash he made, two friends in tow, showed it. They crossed the busy street and came abruptly to my table, so I could see there was nothing that made him bashful. He bellied up to the table so close I could have touched him. He must have been thirteen or fourteen.

"Toi entre suc mais?" or something like that; it was hard to make out. He smiled at me, then at his friends, who just looked on in amazement. I had no idea what he meant, but I smiled back to show I appreciated his company.

"Bonsoir," I tried, in a poor accent. All three laughed at this.

"Toi entre suc mais?" or whatever it was, repeated. He enunciated it strangely. "Yes or no?" This part I understood. The women at the table through the glass noticed him too, and I'm sure we be-

came a topic of their conversation. The boy's face was smooth with a blush of red high in the cheeks matched by his full lips. Soft fuzz feathered the nape of his neck and where his sideburns would someday be. Dark eyes and thick black lashes made him look like an Arabian girl; he might have been Algerian. I could see the waiter hovering inside, busy with a tray of drinks and bread.

"Mmm, yes," I guessed, still smiling. Maybe the boy wanted some of my wine. I hoped his two friends would leave, and they did, racing back through the traffic as the boy bumped his crotch against my table so it moved slightly.

"Too bad," he said, in his poor English, "fucking *pédé*," and now he ran away after them and I was left at my table. I didn't recognize his curse exactly, but I could guess its meaning from the tone he gave it. A few people stared, walking past my table, but it wasn't worth taking time to explain. The waiter arrived and wiped up the wine where it had spilled. *"Je m'excuse,"* he whispered. I think he was embarrassed by the boy's bad behavior. Obviously the boy knew nothing about me. This was just his cruelty, a misunderstanding, less than nothing, and I didn't let it spoil my mood in the cool, promising evening.

The wine became satisfying, plain and clean like the café. It tasted like a good paint job sometimes looks, even and unremarkable. It left a lot of room for the Gruyère and the bread. Water shook from the trees and startled me, and I put the boy out of mind. The door to the café opened and the noise became bright and leering. Rising laughter and conversation swarmed out with the brisk waiter when he brought more water and bread. The women through the glass were angry now, and one pushed the arm of her friend so sharply the coffee she drank spilled and her friend slapped her and there were tears. The air was heavy with electricity, or I was, and the birds suddenly seemed much louder. Fatigue, of course, so I closed my eyes. The night smelled marvelous now, full of bus exhaust, but it was getting late. I found a taxi, picked my bags up at the hotel, and went, finally, to the Dupaignes'.

The taxi should have simply been a final compartment, the antechamber concluding my long corridor of travel. I had departed through the work-ravaged portal of my city and was about to be delivered back into the bosom of humanity. The airport, the plane, the car, my hotel room, even the pleasant café, were in between. Now I was on the verge of arriving. So that it's hard to explain why, sitting comfortably in the upholstered back seat of the taxi, coursing the crazy circuit of Paris boulevards, I had a little breakdown. It began when we merged onto the Boulevard Montparnasse and, looking to my right, down the broad nighttime avenue, through the streaming red taillights and stripped trees, west, I saw the last glimmer of evening getting sucked into the edge of the earth and I knew that that same light shone brightly on my home back home. Somewhere beyond the curving edge of France, beyond the cold Atlantic and the next crowded continent, that same light reached my apartment. Sitting nine thousand miles away in the comfortable taxi, straining my neck to look back through traffic, I could see it. I turned away to face front and felt my throat tighten. I wasn't homesick, just impressed with the enormity of my transport. Paris jumbled around us, spread out like an old idea. My eyes broadened so I could see it too, feel the whole city like a host for this taxi-borne virus that capsuled across its middle, and this awareness, my isolation, started the tears. Everything became dispersed and unlocatable. I cried, loosening something from the broad middle below my heart, while gasping for enough air to fill that space back up again. The driver held a tissue box on his open palm, elegant as a butler serving canapés, but otherwise he ignored me. By the time we got to the Dupaignes' I was fine. I suppose it was simply the sort of thing that happens when one travels, this rupture, when something new or old is emerging. The same way a disappeared pair of socks or underwear is sometimes found when we unpack our luggage at the end of a long day's travel, settling for the night in some foreign place.

This time I got out of the car and rang the bell. The small house was bright with lights. Two stereos played, some sort of jazz and Nirvana. This second, the louder, diminished when I rang again, and that was promising. Maybe the boy I'd seen in the window would greet me. I felt sorry I had cried so hard. An inner door opened and closed, shoes shuffled, and the door in the garden wall opened.

"Hello." It was a skinny old man with long wet hair and a vast beard like frozen weeds, an arctic Neptune freshly risen, bare-chested and wet there too, with ratty torn shorts to cover his middle. He grasped my hand and pumped it vigorously.

"*Bonsoir, Monsieur Dupaigne.*" I recited what I had practiced. "*Je m'appelle* Herbert Widener, *et j'ai rendez-vous avec vous monsieur.*"

"I'm afraid my French isn't very good," he said. "But neither is yours, so it's better we try English." He took a bag and led me through the tiny garden. Its plot was triangular and crowded with three fruit trees plus long turned beds running beside high brick walls. A short path led to the porch.

"You don't speak French?"

"Well, I'm Danish, and I'm not Serge, I'm Per." Per moved like an eel, all sinewy and lithe.

"I'm sorry, I've never met the Dupaignes. I was supposed to fly here via Copenhagen, by the way, so that's odd. You're with the City University?"

"No." At the porch Per slipped his wooden sandals off, then bent down to undo my shoes, and we left them by the door. His bright black eyes and smile broadcast a kind of bovine contentment that seemed to attach to nothing. "Serge," he yelled up the winding stairs, "Herbert Widener *arrive pour 'un rendez-vous avec vous monseiur.'*"

The narrow stair twisted up into darkness and down toward flickering candlelight from the *cave*. The jazz came from there. Per gave my hand a hearty last squeeze. "You will excuse me. I am in the middle of an important lesson." He bounded up the stairs, and Nirvana was turned on again at a tremendous volume. The jazz increased in reply and the stairway light shut off so that darkness swallowed the vestibule.

It was pleasant in the dark. The house smelled of heating gas and sweet dust. The dust was books. Cold air clung to my coat and smelled of the day's rain. I saw ghosts emerge from the dark, coats on pegs in a line and two bicycles, plus the white frame of a doorway that I could only see if I looked sideways past it. Garlic and mushrooms fried in butter somewhere. The jazz got switched off and the basement candles snuffed so now I could see nothing, only hear the rush of sock-padded feet ascend the stairs, fly past me (did everyone *bound* upward in this household?), and bang through the door on the next landing. The stairway light came on.

"Herbert," a man yelled over the noise, pronouncing the name "air-bair," with a kind of soft growl at the end, which was a charming way to say it, "I will come down the stairway in a moment, but your room is right in front of you."

"*Merci,*" I called back cheerfully.

"You're very welcome, and I'm sorry for this moment's delay but it is unavoidable. You see the doorway?"

"Yes, I do."

"The light is made with little switches. You will see them in the dark." A tiny switch glowed and I pressed it.

My suite was several rooms strung together like a many-chambered cave. Its few windows were covered by metal shutters, which put me in mind of the world wars. Crazy uneven shelves of books, blandly colored—white, tan, or yellowed—so that I thought they must be statistical records (they were French literature), covered the walls. A toilet with no bath, just a thin closet really, featured posters of trees, a small head-high window with a view of the garden, and, by some accident of poor remodeling, a letter slot through which the day's mail came. I scooped the mail from the floor and took it to the bed (wedged into an alcove), then lay down. Despite the chill the room felt heavy with sleep and I enjoyed the gravity of it. I would simply need to find the heater.

Nirvana was dimmed by a thick ceiling and walls, so that now it murmured like a soft, persistent heart. The walls must have been made of stone. A desk opposite the bed was supplied with paper and pens, plus delicate blue airmail envelopes. I arranged the lights so the room was dark except where two small lamps pooled buttery light on the bed and the dresser, and then I took my time unpacking shirts and laying them neatly in the deep wooden drawers. Herbert would have complained about the noise, but I liked hearing a little music. It reminded me of my childhood, when Louise would play Ella Fitzgerald records in one room while I went to sleep in the next, sometimes on Sunday nights (that supremely melancholy bruise at the tail of a weekend). I was always sad on Sundays. My best friend, Tony, would have stayed overnight and we'd sleep in and spend the long gray day together, sprawled on the bedroom floor with my cards and crushed foam weapons. The hours would drift out of reach and drain all initiative from our bodies, so that we could only lie there through the dusk, not speaking, just toying with the cards, until my mother finally finished her book and announced, passing by my door on the way to check the laundry, that Tony ought to be going home now it was dinnertime and Sunday and what did I have for homework tonight? After dinner, after the wine, she'd put me to bed, drop the Ellas on the spindle, and I'd fall asleep listening. Walking through neighborhoods now that I am a man alone on these same empty days that don't begin or end so much as they go on all day ending, when I hear a knot of children in an unfenced yard, drained by their weekend of play walking dutifully through familiar games to fill the last hours, I feel a strange sadness, as painful and pressing as a heartbeat, rush through my body, so that tears form and I can hardly keep from sighing.

Someone knocked at my door, a woman, a beautiful blond woman my age, square-jawed and ruddy, with her hair pulled back into a barrette, and she came in carrying a bottle and two tiny glasses.

"*Bonsoir,*" I tried, not knowing which language was correct.

"Hello." She sat down on the bed, easy as an old friend, and handed me a small ice-cold glass. "A 'welcome' drink." We clinked and swallowed, and the chilled liquor warmed me all the way to my stomach.

"I found your mail by the toilet."

She flipped through the bundle and then put it in the trash. "So much of it is junk."

"Are you Danish?" I asked, happy with the drink and her good English.

"No." (Someone yelled from the top of the stairs— "Miriam," her name, I guessed—but she didn't answer.) "You look exhausted."

"Thank you. Your English is very good."

"I'm Dutch, French by my marriage. It's always worse flying east, I don't know why."

"I'm Herbert, by the way."

"Yes. Miriam." We shook hands, and Miriam settled back onto the bed. "You've met Per. Serge is upstairs." The bedroom door was pushed open. "And here is my boy."

Miriam's boy, the boy from the window. This long day had at last delivered me. "Stéphane," Miriam said, "I'd like you to meet Herbert." A little wet from a shower, long hair in his eyes, and with damp, chaste arms folded across his chest, Stéphane watched me, smiling. I smiled back and said nothing, still unclear about the language.

This moment made a tear in the fabric of my day. The boy's wrists, his silence and proximity, held my full attention. I stood in the warmth of his regard. As I said, I said nothing. I felt only the hollowness of my throat, robbed of its pleasantries, and an uncertain drop when I shifted my posture at the hips. How flighty dear reader must think me, birdied back and forth by the day, undone by strangers and taxi cabs alike, driven to revery by the merest profile, a delicate wrist, the nape of a neck. It helped that this particular boy's head was full of a language I could not understand. Paris was the correct frame. Herbert tells me that fate is made by our own choosing, that character is etched into the surface of the days, when in fact fate billows like a combustible cloud of gas, a cataclysmic crystal of arrangements, delicate and temporary. I would like to understand myself—choice by choice as Herbert would have it—and arrive at some peace or resolution, but how is it that everything can be erased and remade all at once? In that slim instant I saw the vast territory of my own disappearance open up. You must understand, it was simply the boy—the boy was sufficient. This moment was nothing more than the boy's feet, aristocratic and long, his high arch, the gentle laxness in his joints, his ankle, bared for scratching, delicate and pronounced, with soft golden hair ceasing abruptly along a stirrup-shaped border just above the knob, the french curve of his calves leading to simple knees whose greatest features were the hollows behind them—soft, deep as eggs, warm and bordered by the firm stretch of twin tendons from above—the great haunches of meat he stored in his long thighs (soccer, I supposed, so that his butt, too, was firm and rounded and kept the baggy blue jeans perched at a tilt), his loosely belted pants, over-sized enough to fit two hands snugly down the front, resting and carressing, riding the back upper-mid butt serenely, bordered all around by a brilliant billow of flannel boxers, his fly, with its battered, dented buttons half-loosened from their nooks, puckering where his languorous organ pushed and nudged so that I could fairly see it, breathing and sighing behind the folds of distressed fabric, and the pleasure I could feel in my flattened palm (if pressed against the fly, which press would be returned from within, amplified). Am I only to the waist? Surely everyone has seen the boy shirtless, and in the grand array of life's exertions: half stripped and sweating at work in the shop stacking boxes; speeding down the left wing in his wind-torn shorts chasing World Cup dreams; emerging from the pool all arms and gangly legs, dewdropped and shivering; or asleep in the shade of a summer tree, shorts askew, drooling on the pried-open pages of his required reading; the dizzying vertigo, running your eyes along his tattered waistband, riding so low and loose off twin-ridged hips it seemed whole religions could be founded in the space between that drifting lip of cotton and the boy's trim, shallow belly button. I'd stroll along the rim there, tasting the rounded flat of belly, stretching out from its spiral origin, driving hands across the broad flat plain, dusky horizons distant on either side, then up along his slim torso (alarming how thin he is where the hips gave in, so small I imagine wrapping two hands around him, twin thumbs pressed into his belly button, fingertips touching on the other side) over the knobby-ridged ribs, moving visibly as he breathes. The boy ran his mindless hands over his ribs, up to fold the soft nipple, then back down to his hips, as he stood shirtless, regarding me. His shoulder blades were delicate and pronounced. They moved like angel's wings when he moved. Face front, where his ribs converged, a singular divet, pulsing with the exertions of his heart, invited my tongue to rest. He smelled like sweet milk and dust where my hard stare then pressed, flat against the plate of bone his taut skin hid. Shifting my eyes to either side, the slightest rise of muscle defined all horizons and led to nipples that put me in mind, for a sad millisecond, of Dogan (supple and thin as rose petals when warm, and taut if pulled on, cold, or agitated, I think it was). Above the shadowed hollows of his collarbones, his shoulders, as slim as they were rounded took drops of water from the boy's long, wet hair. A delicate necklace of flat, linked gold lay along his throat like sleep. I could easily wrap my hands around his little throat and squeeze. The veins and striations, everything vital, was pressed to the surface there. His arms dangled, angular and elegant, when he fiddled with his belt loops. A filthy braided twine was tied loosely around one wrist, which it never left. No one can capture the weak beauty of his wrists. I imagine them crushed in the jaws of an industrial menace, or motionless amongst the ferns of a brook in the springtime woods where the boy has drowned. In either case the wrists beg to be touched, their knobs caressed as the last pulse of blood plunges through the soft underside where the veins are. I read in the newspaper about a man who murdered boys, and on the eve of his execution he said "everyone thinks this is the end, that it's all over now. But where do you think *I* came from?" And all of this blossomed in that instant, that glance, so that you can imagine how it formed a pivot and the days, my life, everything, now turned, as flimsy and compelling as a dream. That is what I thought, in any case. Who knows what the boy thought?

Stéphane showed me the house in his poor English, pointing at things, oblivious to my clumsy attention. He tried out all the doors and switches and ignored my questions about showers and soap. Dinner was much too late, a midnight snack really, and I was too tired to join them for it. I went to bed and passed that first night at the Dupaignes' without eating.

In my room (two duvets, pillows from the nineteenth century, thick-walled silence of this nether district of Paris, plus the metal-shuttered darkness) I drifted toward sleep, and space collapsed so that home, everything, drew near again: Herbert's voice soft and clear, telling me to pick up my newspapers from the hall; the view of the city from my window; Louise, located like pins in a map, still, in every house we ever had there; my school, the one where I had taught; and the sense, always with me, that the mountains hid our city and beyond them the earth curved over oceans until finally it turned in on itself, moved past the mountains again, and entered back into the city.

• 5 •

The next morning I had no plans and no urgency. The house was empty when I got up, and a set of keys—plus a bicycle—had been left for me. There was no sense being idle on my first real day. Herbert had made it clear he really didn't care about the drawings (and in any case I had no money with which to buy them), but I thought it would be a great triumph and a terrific gift for poor wronged Herbert if I at least came back with the news of their location. If finding that out involved little more than a leisurely pursuit of the Stein family and some archival research (for background), then I was ready for the task.

The air was cold and fresh as a pail of water when I set out after a pleasant breakfast, which I ate alone in the Dupaignes' kitchen. Bread and marmalade were on the counter, and the heat of the stove where someone had baked eggs a little earlier kept the chill away. Miriam had left hot chocolate on a tin warming plate with a candle burning beneath it. Outside, the day was bright and blue and the metal of the bike was cold to the touch. I took my map of Paris and rode to the Musée Picasso. The bike was simple to maneuver, so I was at ease even when I got lost. Paris felt otherworldly still, a sequence of pretty pictures, but I was beginning to enjoy the effect. While the city's grid of boulevards kept ribbons of cars coursing across it, the streets where I rode were a lost country beneath the grid. Traffic bled onto them but slowed or disappeared before reaching me.

Everything was interesting, even the trash on the street was exotic to me. It took two hours to get to the museum. An unusual hill where the rue Jeanne d'Arc dropped from the Boulevard de l'Hôpital gave me a jolt at the bottom. I drifted into one-way traffic past an old slaughterhouse, now a historical site of interest (interesting because they slaughtered horses here for longer than my city has existed), which smelled like almond pastry, and then cigars and diesel fumes. Overgrown trees spilled up the stone wall of the Jardin des Plantes, cluttering the sky, and the wind shook them. I waited for a light and watched the trees. The wall stretched uphill, away from me, and the sun got blocked by a flat gathering haze so that it became a bruise of light above the feathering trees, like an eye bearing down. It was warm in the saddle of this shallow valley where I relaxed on my bike seat. A silvery bus discharged tourists, pasty and dazed, white-haired, and they shuffled through the gates into the garden. The light turned and I went on through this picture book.

The museum took up a whole château, and the library was hidden in the eaves. My poor French was a problem. Kind Madame Gogny smiled and asked me to write out my request. I wanted pictures of Allan, anything of Allan, and details about the *Boy Leading a Horse*. She brought books to my table, which made me feel childish. The other scholars had files filled with original papers, letters in a tight concealing hand, yellowed bills of lading, the postcards friends sent to Picasso. I had three fat textbooks. But there was Allan, featured on several pages of the American volume. The boy was stubborn. His impatience with the photographer had been frozen so that, staring at me now, he was still impatient, still waiting, and would be until the photo was put away. His face pleased me, and I took my book to the copy machine and enlarged his picture.

He resembled me, his firm mouth and soft chin, and I packed him in my satchel and returned to the Dupaignes'.

The clock had been shattered by my travel so the afternoon felt like midnight to me, the hazy, glorious day lost behind my shuttered windows in this shadowed canyon of unlikely high-rise apartments. Herbert was awake now—6 A.M., 7 A.M.?—bellowing his fragmented songs, washing in a tub of ankle-deep cold water—a ritual I discovered when we were made to share a hotel room in Philadelphia on some little junket of his. Neither of us was very comfortable with the arrangement, and Herbert dealt with it by simply pretending I wasn't there. We lay side by side in the gargantuan beds, reading, and then he turned the light off and began to snore. I lay half asleep, pleased with the clean cotton sheets (Paris now), until the boy knocked on my door and called me to dinner.

Dinner was served in an alcove which hung from the third-floor kitchen like an oversized flower box, seeming to hover in the air above the small courtyard. Beneath this alcove's sloped roof, built-in benches surrounded a low table. Windows on all three sides let the light in, and candles made multiple reflections in the uneven glass. Cushions lined the benches and we slid into our places. "Like dining in the prow of a ship," Per said.

"I sit by the house," the boy pointed out. He slipped onto the near bench, hair toweled and combed behind his big ears, in a fresh white T-shirt and khaki shorts. I sat down beside him. Serge—compact and handsome in a white cotton shirt tucked neatly into belted wool slacks with leather loafers and no socks (and with a great shock of white hair)—looked well beyond sixty. The family mathematics did not add up, but I put the equation out of mind for the time being, smiling at the pleasure of their company.

"English is our *lingua franca* whenever there are guests," Miriam announced. "Even when there are no guests Per doesn't really like French at all, and naturally Serge doesn't know a word of Danish."

"If you prefer French we can speak it," Per allowed. "Some guests of the university are disappointed to find the meals aren't in French." In fact it was a relief. I dismissed his offer with a generous shrug.

"No, the English is excellent, everyone's English."

Together with two musty bottles of brackish red wine from Normandy and a winter stew, Serge served a basket of warm baguettes and yogurt in a cool earthen crock. Stéphane, who seemed to have warmed up to me, now that we were at the dinner table, leaned close and unfurled his napkin.

"I am the devil," the boy offered, apropos of nothing.

Miriam apologized. "Sometimes the level of conversation here is very low."

"It is a lyric from Metallica," Stéphane explained, flush from the effort. With a delicate gesture he pointed at its source. "Per played it for me."

The boy's shoulder brushed mine. The stew and its fine perfume, the great piggish grunt of a wine, plus the good company, blurred a little beside the demanding clarity of this point of contact. I shifted against the boy as we maneuvered through dinner. Pleasantries fluttered from my lips like butterflies, alighting here on Serge, there on Miriam, while my mind retreated into exile, camped out in the monastery of my upper thigh where his hip now touched me. Pinioned to him throughout the conversation, I missed a great deal of what was said.

"Were you also in Paris during the manifestations?" I asked Per, trying to keep up. Stéphane reached for the stew and Miriam swatted his hand from it, then pushed the crock of yogurt toward him.

"I was at sea."

"For many years," Serge put in. "Per was a pilot of a masted ship the Danish navy used to train its sailors." The boy squished yogurt through his teeth, making a sound, then stopped, mocking boredom with a great yawn. "*Fils*, if you are bored by us you can leave and do your work in your room," Serge reminded him. "Such impertinence." He showed off this unusual word.

"Eat more yogurt, *mon petit*, or you know what the night is going to be like." Stéphane stuck his tongue out at Miriam's suggestion.

"*Merde,* Stéphane. That's too much, go now to your work."

The boy withdrew from the table like a fever that, at last, breaks.

"Here we've talked so long about ourselves and asked nothing about your work," Miriam observed.

"Oh, it's nothing." Really, it was. What could they know of Herbert? "I'm researching the American writer Gertrude Stein." Serge smiled benignly while Miriam and Per took some dishes from the table. "And a nephew of hers, though you've probably never heard of him."

"Didn't you know Stein?" Per asked Serge, shouting above the clatter of his chores. "She gave you a tinned ham, didn't she, Serge, after the war?" I'm sure my jaw dropped. In any case, I stopped chewing. A sort of immaculate, disembodied double, a dybbuk of Serge, floated before me, a perfect, unreachable Serge, bleeding irretrievably into the gray photos of Gertrude and family in Herbert's STEIN folder. A kind of tug-of-war was set off in my head, with the silent, flat Stein dragging Serge into the sealed vault of history, while my host dragged Gertrude back into life.

"No," Serge corrected. "No, I never knew Stein."

"Oh." Per sighed, disappointed. "I thought your father fixed her car."

"Your father fixed Gertrude Stein's car?" I asked, a little slow to keep up.

"No. No, he never did."

Serge lit another cigarette and offered more wine, which I took. His smoke drifted out the open window.

"You realize," Per interrupted over the noise of coffee, "that a mechanic was a real artist then, especially a car mechanic."

"Like a great chef," Serge said.

"Yes, like a chef. Monsieur Dupaigne was a famous car mechanic. He worked on the car of my parents when we traveled into France. That is how I met Serge."

"Was the bicycle all right?" Miriam put in. I supposed she had heard this story often enough. "The car reminded me."

"Herbert has my bicycle," Serge pointed out. "Of course it's all right."

"You'd heard of him in Denmark?"

"No, it was coincidence. Our car broke down near the Jardin du Luxembourg. That was before the war."

"The Second War," Miriam added.

"Yes, of course, the Second War."

Miriam smiled at me. Her face was like a fresh-drawn bath, or a bed I could sleep very well in.

"I'm sorry if this is impertinent, Per"—I used Serge's word—"but when were you born?"

"Nineteen-twenty, as was Serge." Now the mathematics tumbled through my head and I couldn't keep from staring at Miriam, who was certainly no older than forty, mother of a fifteen-year-old boy who was almost a decade closer to her, in age, than her husband. The boy was downstairs just then, pinned by duty to his desk and chair, his head full of Metallica (good for concentration), while he struggled with algebra.

"Mmm."

"The year of diamonds, isn't it?" Miriam remarked.

"In May, and it will be grand."

"Who is the nephew?" Serge asked, leaning to get sugar from Per.

"Allan Stein; he was born in 1895."

"He lived in Paris?"

"For most of his life. His family moved here when he was eight. I think he died in Neuilly, in the American Hospital, in 1951."

"A nephew is . . . ?" Serge.

"*Neveu.*" Miriam.

"Was he an artist?"

I glanced at my watch intently, as if it and not Serge had spoken to me. "No, no. Allan was painted by Picasso, when he was a boy. He is the boy in the *Boy Leading a Horse*, I don't know its French title."

"*Meneur de Chevaux Nu*," Miriam said, leaning forward. "It's a very important piece." Another cigarette took shape in her hand. "The end of the *période rose*, just before *Les Demoiselles d'Avignon*."

"That's right." News to me. "Picasso also painted a smaller, less important portrait of Allan, at the same time." I sipped a little wine onto my tongue and simply breathed it, letting the aroma billow in my throat. "I'm interested in his adolescence, from the Picasso paintings to the First War."

"Did he fight in the war?"

"He was here in Paris, as an army supply manager. The family lived on the rue Madame in a great loft above a church, where his parents had their collection of Matisse paintings. They were the first great patrons of Matisse." I rambled through my dossier of facts. "In the summers they went to Agay, on the Côte d'Azur."

"Why this part of his life?"

"Mmm?"

"Why his adolescence?"

"Oh, it's my specialty." The truth at last. "I used to be a schoolteacher, and—well, the boy makes the man, and all of that."

"But was he an important man?" Serge wondered. "I don't understand what makes this man's boyhood interesting."

I was silent and fiddled with my glass. I wasn't stumped so much as baffled. What did it matter if Allan was or wasn't important?

"All boys are important." Miriam. "But so few men are." Sainted Miriam.

"Yes, exactly."

"This is one of the features of the Picasso Herbert speaks of, the most erotic and moving aspect of it—that it is a boy. He has a tremendous power because he is nothing yet, no one, and so he has the power in him to be a god, like all children do, you see? If Picasso had painted a man leading the horse, just imagine it. This man would be someone, some man who will never be a god at all, just a man, without the limitless power this boy has." Oh, God bless her. A mother knows so much most men will never know. It didn't matter if Allan was or wasn't important, he was a boy, and that was sufficient. Per and Serge looked at each other and laughed, not maliciously, not really *at* what Miriam had said but around it, with it; their laughter was easy and meaningless, the way children hold hands. This pair intrigued me, and so did Miriam, who drifted in and out of their orbit. Serge poured more coffee from the scorched chrome pot. I had drained my wine and he offered to get more.

It was 2:30 P.M., according to my warm new watch, when I went down the stairs to bed. Two-thirty at home, that is, and eleven-thirty in Paris. I'd gone past exhaustion into a second day, and now that too seemed to be ending. The stairway was dark, and descending rickrack shelves of books spiraled along the wall. Off the second-floor landing Stéphane's door was open, and it led into a nest of rooms, with a small bathroom where the door was open. I knocked timidly and peeked in. No boy. Full bathtub, plastic morphing men afloat face down in the water, a mirror obscured by steam, interesting toiletries, muppet shampoo, deodorant stick, floating boats and ducks, plus a superfluous razor and shaving cream. The room stank of sneakers. Garish strings of beads filled a second doorway, clattering. Thin music drifted from the speakers, and I pushed through the beads. "Stéphane?" Still no answer. A worse smell, mixed with futile incense, which I saw now, still burning on the homework desk. A body bumped me, slipping through the beads.

"Miriam. You startled me."

"God, it smells in here. I told him to eat more yogurt." She stared past my shoulder, to a dim alcove. And there where *maman* gazed, on a bunched pile of duvets, with a toasty heater glowing red near the bed, the boy slept. He was still dressed, his flushed face pressed into a book on which he drooled. Miriam unplugged the heater and tugged his socks and shirt off, as if this meant nothing. She threw a duvet over him and squelched the lights as we left. "Charming, isn't he?"

"Mmm."

Allan Stein, who had just turned ten, woke up in the cold bedroom above the church at 58 rue Madame and listened for his parents. There was nothing. Birds, a very few, sang in the small garden beneath the tall window. The sky was still black. A broom could be heard, straw raking over stone, very near. Madame Vernot kept the steps so clean. Who could tell at what hour she would begin? Allan shivered in his bed and saw that his fire was out. He reached toward the coal. If he stretched far enough, and kept one ankle pried beneath the brass rail for leverage, he could fill the stove and restart it without leaving his bed. He had asked Sally, his mother, if the bed could be moved closer, but she said it might catch fire and must be kept where it was.

Today is November 28, 1905, a very special day for Allan. He will meet his Aunt Gertrude at nine o'clock and travel across Paris to Montmartre. The painter Picasso will paint his portrait. It is a gift for his birthday, from his mother and father, who like paintings very much. Really it is a gift for themselves, like so much of what they give to Allan.

Allan got the fire started, then curled into his blankets and listened to the birds. They made a weak, diminished sound, a very sad bird sound. Allan felt the room grow warmer. He had not eaten much at dinner, wanting to be slim for Picasso. He might pose without clothes, Auntie Gertrude told him, and that would be an honor. Sometimes, when he ate very much, his stomach stuck out like those of the cherubs in paintings he had seen. He wanted to look like a boxer, not a cherub. Allan felt the muscles of his chest and then his ribs. He ran his hands over them, stopping to push his finger into the shallow depression of his belly button. He flexed his stomach and enjoyed the pressure against his fingertip. He raked his fingers through his hair and left them there, warm.

There was dim light in the sky. Today he would miss school. Paintings were not made in a moment, Sally had told him; some took a lifetime. Gertrude said Picasso did not need to see Allan to paint him. The sitting was a formality, a chance for conversation. She insisted on going with him. Picasso would be bored by a child. Under his tent of blankets, Allan pushed his closed fist hard against his stomach. Surely he and Picasso could discuss boxing.

The weak fire did not warm the room. Sadie Vernot knocked and said breakfast was ready. Sally and Mike were still in bed. Allan sat with Sadie in the kitchen, where the stove kept the room very hot, and Sadie served butter with bread and hot chocolate. Allan made an argument to get marmalade and Sadie gave it to him. Sadie talked but Allan didn't listen, and soon it was time to go.

Allan meets Gertrude at nine on the rue de Fleurus. She gives him a sack of coal to carry to Picasso's and fifteen centimes for the omnibus at the Place Saint-Michel. Gertrude dislikes the underground, especially on fine days. They walk through the Luxembourg Garden. The air is bright and cold. Mist hangs above the pond and Allan asks if they can see the Bouguereaus, but Gertrude says no, the galleries are closed. Allan hugs the sack of coal to his chest, watching a man sweep leaves. The boulevard is crowded and exciting. They cross without stopping and are almost hit by an automobile!

The omnibus is waiting. They sit outside on top. It is, Gertrude says, as poorly horsed as it is driven. The Seine is high and makes eggs from the arches of the Pont des Arts and their reflection. "Look," Allan points out. "Eggs." But Gertrude does not see it and looks past the bridge to the Louvre. A man beside them speaks English. He is a tourist and comes from Tenby, the Naples of Wales. He smells like cheese and alcohol, and Allan looks away. Gertrude says, "The Louvre, Allan. Observe its mass and carelessness."

It is 11:18 A.M. exactly. The sky is ice blue, the stones of the buildings gray. The Opéra looks like a great mint hat on a box. The Grand Hotel has automobiles waiting in line by the entrance, "pretty swifty." The Welshman gets off. Picasso lives in Montmartre, Gertrude explains, because it is higher up so he can see more. Everyone else lives in Montparnasse because everyone else lives in Montparnasse. The Boulevard Haussmann is very dull, but they aren't on it for long. A commotion. The pealing bells crash as the *pompiers* are released from their scrubbed building to fly down the boulevard behind the combed and lathering horses.

"Is there a fire?" Gertrude asks. Yes, I see it there beyond the Gare Saint-Lazare, a column of smoke, a trace in the air above the gray roofs, snaking away from the street of its origin, above flung windows and hung laundry, spiraling from the narrow streets on the butte of Montmartre. It is thin and twists upward before disappearing like a sound in the crisp blue air. Can you see it, Gertrude? But she cannot, or she does not find it interesting. The *pompiers* were interesting, weren't they, Allan? With their black uniforms and rigid postures, flying into the mouth of hell? They are gone now. "Yes, now they are gone." The fire has been put out.

They walk from the Gare Saint-Lazare, and Gertrude carries the coal for a while. The rue Lepic is very steep. At 59 rue Lepic, Allan draws in chalk on the sidewalk:

The chalk is given to him by another boy. The view down rue Tholozé is very beautiful. Allan has tired feet, but Gertrude does not like tired feet so he doesn't tell her. They stop to look at a menu.

The door is closed at number 13, and no one answers when they call. Allan can call very loudly. Perhaps they are early, perhaps they are late. Gertrude suggests they have a hot chocolate and wait. They go to Le Ressuscité, leaving a note for Picasso. Allan has not eaten last night or today, wanting to be slim for Picasso. Today his stomach is flat and very fetching. He asks for a glass of gas water and Auntie Gertrude has *épinards* with cheese and a *porc grillé*, which she says is very good. Madame Rossi is kind to Allan and brings a creme caramel when Gertrude is in the toilet, but he tells her the doctor will not let him eat. She takes it away.

It is 2 P.M. and Picasso is home now. He kisses Allan and Gertrude and holds her hand when they walk to his studio. It is very cold. Gertrude and Picasso are laughing. He thanks her for the coal. Allan's pants feel loose on his waist, and this pleases him. The studio is full of junk. Gertrude sits in a large stuffed chair, and the boy goes to stand near the stove. There are boxes set on a cloth. Picasso points there and tells Allan to undress. Gertrude asks for some tea. Allan pulls his undershirt off and becomes entangled, so that Picasso must help him. He says that Allan's belly is perfect. Allan is glad he hasn't eaten. He is undressed now. He stands near the stove and leans against a tall box for a while with his arms relaxed at his sides. Picasso touches Allan when he wants him to move or not move. His eyes are very strong, always looking. He talks to Gertrude while he works. Allan's *zizi* is standing, very much, but they don't notice. His feet are tired. After some silence, and the fire collapsing a little in the stove, Picasso asks him, "Allan, what is it that you love?" And Allan tells him, "I love horses."

•6•

Miriam phoned the Musée Picasso the next morning and badgered their research librarian on my behalf—to no avail. Her friend Denis had suggested trying, and Miriam made the call because my French is poor. Denis knew someone or had worked there. In any case, I would meet this Denis soon at dinner. Serge and Miriam had planned a garden party in honor of Herbert and spring and the flower beds and fine weather. Miriam hung up on the stubborn librarian, left for work, and the house was empty.

Anything at all could fill the hours, but a small insecurity kept me from relaxing. My hosts seemed to know a great deal more about the Steins than anyone really should. It wouldn't do to be caught in my lie, so I went to their bedroom to snoop for a few clues. In Serge's desk drawer (oak, Danish), I found a letter from the Cité Universitaire announcing Herbert's date of arrival, appended to a fax from the fag friend in history. *Vraiment génial,* he assured them. (I felt I'd been living up to it.) *Les Américains d'Amérique* by Gertrude Stein had been dragged out by Serge and lay splayed open on the bedside table. Bingo. *Titre Original: The Making of Americans.* Surely I could find an American bookstore and catch up on my required reading. In the drawers I found money (some U.S., $5 and change); a dozen letters in loopy, girlish script (Serge's), stacked beside addressed, unstamped envelopes (blue, it would be nice to lick them, the paste was so even and glossy); oils, pale yellow, amber, and almost nut-brown, in glass amphorae with stoppers and not much scent; incense cones and a blackened metal Buddha to hold them (a cone of ash in his lap now). I climbed into the bed to push my bare feet around, and the sheets were smooth and clean—Egyptian cotton—and I was impressed that the guest room sheets were as good.

The living room wasn't interesting except for the hard black piano tucked up to the wall, and I settled onto its sturdy bench. What a pleasant and peculiar light the surrounding buildings allowed into the garden, diffuse and luminous all at once. I propped open a window, and the air was fresh.

When I was ten, just before we moved to the house with the possum, Louise and I lived in an apartment with an upright piano in the den. The den was our only room, except for the kitchen and bedroom, and since we did everything in it Louise gave it that exotic name. I loved our den. It had everything: a television, the piano, and a certain stuffy, overheated serenity. The heat was on continually, I think because we didn't have to pay for it. This was our only place ever with a piano, and Louise gave me lessons during the winter we lived there.

The piano was in bad shape. A dozen or so keys produced no music at all, just a dull percussive thump, while others made aggravating dissonances or simply the wrong note. I found ways to play a simple minuet by Purcell, plus some two- or three-finger chords of my own invention, and I played these over and over again until Louise made me stop. Louise played whatever she wanted (I think she was very talented but no one else ever said so), while I became fairly proficient and signed up for the third-grade "talent" show. I would play Purcell. The piece was easy and "Minuet" was such a dauntingly sophisticated title I thought I was a shoo-in to win everyone's admiration. There were no other prizes.

Louise came to the show. Some girls danced (boring), and another made her dog hold a living bird in its mouth, a parakeet, and she was a great hit. Two boys played the piano, four-handed chopsticks, which always sounds flashy but everyone knows it's easy. I'd look like Horowitz to their Liberace. I was nervous walking up to the stage, and Louise's loud applause didn't help. When I sat, though, the only thing in view was the tall brown piano and its keys and I was able to relax.

Then I began to play. Although every key I hit was exactly the right one, the sounds they produced were hideous, full of crazy chords and booming round wrong notes. Dead keys I normally rolled my wrist across, reaching for the high notes, gave out a wobbling glissando, and by the time I stopped I was completely humiliated. Polite applause, an arm around my shoulder from Louise, and then Peter Narver juggled coffee cans. That night at home, Louise laughed and apologized for not having "forethought" this hazard.

Has every childhood tale I've told been a litany of humiliation? In fact I was very happy with these disasters, as if the richness of my melancholy brought a compensatory relief—if I was sad, Louise was obliged to be happy. In the psychic economy of the family, my agony required her good cheer, or at least solicitousness. If I've always been drawn to melancholy, maybe it was to keep Louise from it. She was always kind when I was sad and went to great lengths to console me through my daily reports of disaster. And I *was* miserable and it was important that she think so, as it guaranteed me the delight of long tearful evenings full of attention and sympathy over dinner in the stuffy, steam-heated den—a rich and exquisite pleasure.

At three I showered and shaved for the boy's scheduled return from school. Surely he could direct me to a bookstore. Herbert would be dragging himself from Jimmy's guest bed (futon on a cedar frame) in another few hours, a jet stream away, and then only to fetch a fruit smoothy and arrange his pale body by the pool, where he could sleep with a book on his lap until lunchtime. Was there really an ocean between us? And another continent? Broad grass hills, burned golden and dusty, rolled on to the next blue sea, still under a mist, doubtless, cradling Herbert and Jimmy (who didn't bother waking up until lunch) in a vivid expanse of land, pretty as a travel film that I had running continuously in some tiny back screening room of my brain. It played there even while I was busy with Paris, 3:50 P.M., and the puzzle of French dish liquid (which one was it?) for my filthy bowl and cup, plus last night's still-soaking pans. The school back home, "my school," would just now be blossoming into life. Barret cleared garbage from the door and harassed any students who had the poor judgment to arrive before seven. "Teachers only," he slurred, and spat at the kids, so it sounded like "T-shirts only," which is what they said back in mockery, walking past him through the door. So much was going on all at once. Miriam worked, but what at? Serge and Per were gone, and I supposed that meant Stéphane and I would be home alone. Life as Herbert so far was good.

The garden door opened, *click-clack,* and I bellied up to the sink and the pile of half-done dishes, preparing myself for the boy. Sleeves rolled up, top shirt button undone, relaxed shimmy of the back and hips for tone (whistling? no), humming an unplaceable tune. I could hear the boy bounding up the stairs. Top door, *click-clack*! Best to be casual. I clattered some dishes into the rack (still dirty, who had the time to clean them?), hoping he would sidle up and pinion me to that hip again.

"Hey, handsome, 'you know I'm a sex machine.'" It was Per.

"Oh, hello, Per." He wore bright striped bell-bottoms, one leg smeared with house paint, cinched above his hips so the cuffs wouldn't drag, plus a slinky rayon top, bright red. The sheen of the top matched his machine-tooled boots.

"James Brown. 'Sex Machine.'" He seemed as nimble as the boy. How could a seventy-two-year-old bound up the stairs so effortlessly, and in boots?

"I was just doing the dishes."

Per glanced at the crusty pots and pans skeptically. "A little."

"This is the prewash."

"Mmm." He took the metal scouring tool that I'd left hanging and cleaned the ugly pans while I rinsed and dried. "Have you been out yet to see the pretty sunshine?"

"No, just work this morning." I gestured vaguely at the table, while Per beamed into the dirty dishwater. "I have a lot of reading to do."

"*L'adolescence de Monsieur Stein?*"

"Yes." Three bowls, nested and wet, defied my prying and I left them upside down in the rack. "I know the name of his school, but I'm not at all sure of how to approach them."

"What is the school?"

"The École Alsacienne."

"It's a nice little school. You could visit this afternoon." Distant banging of the garden door, louder bang from the front, and then steps bounding up to the boy's floor. "We could walk there together."

"Mmm."

"It's a remarkable day. We'll pick up that sausage for Miriam." Stereo blast (floor-rattling volume, turned down to plain old loud) plus leaping and pounding alarmed me, but Per took no notice of it. "And that American book for Serge."

"Is that Stéphane?"

"No, Serge; he needs the crime mysteries of Ann Rule. I think they're only available in English."

"I meant downstairs." We paused. The stereo stopped, door banged, downward bounding, *click-click-click-click*, bicycle wheeled to the door, then clatter, slam out to the garden, and bang again, away down the street.

"I think he goes to basketball now."

"Hmm." Too bad. "There is a bookstore with American books?"

"Oh, yes, one with quite a few of them. We'll go there and then walk home, past the sausage man and the École Alsacienne."

The late afternoon was mild and warm, with a breeze like a shimmering fabric and the only clouds elegant and puffed as light pastries, scattered in a broad field of blue. The last night's rain must have been partly responsible, scrubbing the air and brightening the blossoms that made such a pretty scent. Per tossed one of Miriam's old wraps over his blood-red chemise as we hurried out the door.

We walked uphill toward the Parc Montsouris, along bordered paths, to the sand-blasted brick entrance of the metro. They were still blasting. Spasmed hoses squirmed and wriggled beneath our feet. Per slipped two tickets through the mechanized gate and we went to the platform, which was dusty and littered with interesting trash: flyers, foreign candy wrappers, newspaper pages in French (interesting to me). A saxophone player, that is, a man who owned one, stood idle, reading the scraps of newsprint at his feet. The golden glowing horn hung from his neck on a string.

Per narrated the fleeting journey with views through the gaps between buildings, until the saxophonist reached our car and his bellow drowned everyone out. The train plummeted into darkness for two stations and we got off.

The great trees and black iron gates of the Luxembourg Garden were visible across a boulevard at the lip of the station. "I went to the gardens my first day," I said. "Before coming to your house." Car exhaust filled the air and the paths of the garden were packed with people, sprawled on pale-green chairs or strolling coatless. Per took my hand and led me directly through traffic, seven lanes of it, if this disorderly sprawl could be measured in lanes, on an unhurried and divinely blind straight-line stroll to the street corner. We walked along, opposite the park, for awhile. Per never released my hand, but squeezed it lightly. People passing noticed but Per did not, and I marveled at how dry and soft his palm felt. Probably they thought he was my father (my father, the bearded Danish Sly Stone in furs).

The bookstore was small and crowded with books. A charming Frenchwoman bustled toward the door, cooing. She kissed Per, maneuvering delicately past the fur trim, then fetched tea from a back broom closet into which computers, a desk, and two employees had been stuffed. I was given tea too, plus an introductory handshake and terrific respect when I asked Madame if they carried Gertrude Stein's *The Making of Americans*. Actually, she beamed her frank admiration directly at Per. He'd brought in a good dog. My refined tastes were evidence, first and foremost, of his.

Herbert is a great book snob, making a fuss over bindings and years and keeping most of his books from me because of their rarity. I just like to read, often in the tub, and this kind of thing horrifies him. He offered hundreds of dollars to keep me from reading my copy of Doughty's *Arabia Deserta* that way, which was embarrassing since it only cost $50 and I simply wanted to read it. In the end I just gave it to him in exchange for a newer, more compact copy. Now the original sits in a glass case in his apartment, unread. Admittedly, his books are beautiful. I can think of no more relaxing and pleasant decoration than walls and walls of books. They provide a barrier while also functioning as portals into other worlds. A wall of books is like a mass, a crowd, with its thousands of faces blending into one field of color. Each speck is so rich and individual, once you peer in closely enough, but it's just as easy, and pleasant, to draw away and admire their anonymity.

"Oh, Gertrude Stein, but of course we carry everything we can of her, she is a giant, an absolute giant, how could we not? But *The Making of Americans,* this is very difficult, very hard to get." Everyone was sad for a moment, and I sipped my tea. "Of course you want the unabridged edition."

"Yes, naturally." Had it been abridged? "However, the abridged would be fine." (In fact *Cliff Notes* would have been better.) I tried offering my flexibility as a second coin to buy her affection. "Why, the abridged edition wouldn't bother me in the least." Madame's smile disappeared with this crass admission and she shuddered (again at Per), turning to the shelves to find the filthy little abridged edition that tried to pass itself off as literature. My stock was plummeting like a stone to earth. "I mean, if that's all your shop is able to carry." Madame perked a little, looking back at me. "There must be other shops, but Per told me this was the best." I sipped the tea with distaste.

Madame rallied. "Well, you can't imagine how hard this book is to find. If it is available at all, we are the shop that would have it, Monsieur Per is absolutely correct about that, if you'll just wait a moment for me." Per tossed his eyebrows and smiled nervously as Madame disappeared into the closet.

"It's good you didn't settle for the abridged," he whispered. "She likes a challenge." There was shouting. A mewling, defensive man tried getting words in edgewise while Madame riddled him with stray fire. French sentences machine-gunned, with a few pauses for reloading. At one point she peeked out the door, smiled sweetly at us, then pulled it shut and had at him again. Per and I browsed new American editions near the empty front desk, cupping our warm tea mugs, enjoying their steam beside stacks of gargantuan best-sellers in their shiny brash jackets spiraling up from a low table, topped by propped cards extolling their virtues. A narrow stairway led to a balcony with more books and a man, who could be seen sleeping, in a chair with a coat on his lap. I strolled to the window and couldn't make out the weather, the street was so deeply shadowed. Madame emerged from the back, smug, triumphant, holding a book.

"Voilà, monsieur, the Stein you were looking for." She handed it to me and smiled tightly at Per. "Now surely Monsieur Per has something more interesting he is looking for, something of rare value?" Per recited his list of Ann Rule titles, and I held the fat Stein like a fetish, feeling its broad edges and heft. I didn't dare ask the price. Beyond the book's rarity, it seemed clear I would be made to pay for the struggle Madame had just enjoyed. Cold air rolled in with two noisy kids, waist high, and then the door slammed shut. Their coats smelled of snow, despite the clear air outside. I stepped to the window, craned my head sideways, and made out a narrow strip of blue sky. Still spring, I gathered, somewhere. Stéphane, maybe, just then, shot baskets at the Jardin, beneath the great green chestnut trees, lurching and leaping with the rude boys. Bikes parked outside, cool hand slaps, tennis *pop-pop-pup* across the gravel path. The air must be marvelous and warm there, soft on billowed T-shirts and skin. I missed my dear dear Dogan terribly, even as I painstakingly erased him.

Per finished and we left. Evidently my rancor had been a hit with Madame. We walked down the lane and turned the tight cold corner into a great burst of sun. It shone from the west (my house visible again beyond the earth's curve), the sun so broad and low the whole happy street turned Aztec, cobbled in gold. Nervous scurriers relaxed, became droll strollers. I recall the same sun glimmering off Louise, astride the low diving board at Desolation Lake car-campground, after the glamour of an "atom burger" at Tiny's nearby snack stand made us halt and stay there rather than pushing on to the trailhead for a hike and two days of dreaded backcountry tenting. God bless you, Tiny.

"Isn't the sunshine pretty?" Per.

"Marvelous."

"The rue du Four is where our car broke down." Solid well-kept buildings curved toward the lowering sun. I looked behind us, as if through a door, at the bleak winter along the shop's narrow alley, then turned forward again.

"When you met Serge?"

"Yes. I was thirteen. It was our first car vacation, which for me was a very glamorous thing."

"Where did you go?" Dog shit, old and new, littered the pavement, brown blossoms, and I stepped in some.

"Only Paris, it turned out. We were going to drive to Colmars, where I had an uncle, but the car was difficult to fix." I scraped my foot behind me like a lame man, leaving trails of the shit along the walk. "Serge's family took a great liking to us, and we stayed for more than a month, then drove back to Copenhagen."

"You stayed with Serge?"

"I did. My family took rooms in a cheap hotel—you'll see it up here in a minute—but I stayed with Serge at his house. Do you know Colmars?"

"Is it German?"

"No. Colmars is a fortified hill town in the Basses-Alpes, near Digne. Are you all right?"

"What?"

"You're dragging your leg."

"It's just a cramp, go on." Per halted, concerned. We'd come upon a great boulevard, and the sidewalk was thick with pedestrians.

"I could massage the muscle, or, if you don't mind it, I will show you a pressure point to make it relax."

"No, thank you. It feels a lot better actually. Actually, it's fine."

"We'll stop. I'm a little hungry." Per pointed to a café, then led me by the hand. "Well, this fortified town of Colmars is very very old and spectacular, and my uncle had a small house where we were going to spend the summer, but the car broke and we spent it with the Dupaignes instead. I was very happy." Patterned iron, painted pale green, framed the curved glass of this corner café, and Per maneuvered us to a tiny table by the door. "Serge and I went to Colmars by train later, the next summer, to stay with him, and it was terrific. A great place for boys, with the mountains and the river and everything so primitive." Per ordered lemonade and sausage, and we watched the street become busy and the sky go dark. We sat so long the school was closed when we walked there.

The Stein "novel" was dense and impenetrable: great wobbling ropes of words, "hims" and "hers" and "theirs" with nary a name or proper place in sight. I lay down before dinner to read it, and this was part of my exhaustion. The book was worn, its spine broken but still holding on, and no price had been written inside. The writing was strangely familiar, like an internal voice that had been overheard, an awkward, private voice. On page 604 (I browsed to get there), for instance, this:

"Loving being, I am filled just now quite full of loving being in myself and in a number of men and women. Loving is to me just now an interesting, a delightful a quite completely realized thing. I have loving being in me more than I knew I could have in me. It was a surprising thing to find it so completely in me. I am realizing loving being in quite a number now of men and women, completely realizing for them, completely realizing in them loving being. I am loving just now beautiful loving, I am loving nice loving, I am loving just now every kind of loving. I am realizing just now very much and quite some kinds of loving. I am thinking now that it is a difficult thing to be knowing without very careful waiting and then a little more waiting besides the waiting that was pretty nearly enough waiting how much any one is, what kind there is in any one of loving. A very great many have very many prejudices concerning loving, more perhaps even than about drinking and eating. This is very common. Not very many are very well pleased with other people's ways of having loving in them. Some are very much pleased with some ways of having loving and not with other ways of having loving. Some are wanting people to be very nice in having loving being in them. Some are pretty well ready to let most people do the kind of loving they have naturally in them but are not ready to let all people do the loving the way loving naturally comes to be in them. A very considerable number of men and women have different ways of having loving in them. I have different ways of having loving feeling in me I am certain; I am loving just now very much all loving. I am realizing just now with lightness and delight and conviction and acquiescing and curious feeling all the ways anybody can be having loving feeling. I have always all along been telling a little about ways of loving in different kinds in men and women. I will tell now a little more about specific loving in some specific men and women."

Louise and I had twin racing bikes at a time when that style of bike, with its ram-horn handlebars and thin, penetrating seat, was novel and sought after. Ours were from Sears, which made them less exotic. I was fourteen. At home I rolled mine downstairs to the cavelike laundry room, stood it upside down on the clothes-folding counter, and "customized" it. With blue house paint I erased the blocky markings of the Sears corporation, and then with decals and stickers I covered up my poor paint job—the red and blue oval of STP, Bardhall's black and yellow checkered flag. I got carried away with the stickers. It became the sort of bike one finds falling over in rows at the drafty back loading dock of a charity thrift store, next to the great tangled pile of a hundred or so beige bed frames.

It was summer, and we rode to the ferry dock to bicycle to our meadow on the other side and come back before it got dark. Louise had packed a picnic in her knapsack, bread and cheese and chocolate and tuna-fish salad sandwiches, plus a bottle of white wine ("white because it's fish") and two or three sodas for me (Dr. Pepper, another badge of my independence). She tied the bundle onto her bike rack so her shoulders could tan while we rode. I brought a set of elegant metal tools, tiny fist-sized tools, mostly picks and hammers, which I'd found in one of Louise's boxes downstairs. They were for archaeology. Margaret Chang-Sagerty had given them to Louise in grad school when she was still planning on a career.

I think I mentioned summer before, summer where I come from. It occupies two weeks of the year and is glorious: bright warm days with dolorous evenings that bleed slowly into long sunsets and then turn black and cold about 10 P.M.; crystal-clear nights thick with stars that disappear in a brilliant dawn sometime around five in the morning. The mountains to the west, across the open salty sea (a mere arm of the sea plied by ferries like the one that took us that morning on our bikes), are sharper, taller, and more jagged during these weeks. They receive the sun at dawn and stand out in such relief before noon one can almost make out the elk and goats that scramble up their rocky flanks. These mountains grow larger as the ferry approaches until, disembarking, one stands at the water's edge in a thin strip of forest, pinioned to the shore by their encroaching steep face.

We bicycled north along this shore until the peninsula abruptly turned and the road bent west and we followed it. Bicycling made my legs ache, especially the fronts of my thighs, and I liked watching the muscles there as I pushed down on the pedals. These muscles were well enough defined to be someone else's, some man's, so that as I watched them working a few feet from my face I had the strange perception that my legs were not mine, that some man was attached to me there. We had our sandwiches on a great bare rock that jutted from a hillside by the road. The sun warmed the rock and I could have slept there, but Louise wanted to get to the meadow and we pushed on, a long winding climb that exhausted me but was forgotten in the euphoria of arriving.

The meadow was heavenly. Deep grass filled its bowl, thick and shimmering where the breeze made it shift in the sun. Patches by the tarn had been eaten bare, but the meadow was so rich with grasses and wildflowers most of it remained untouched by the animals who fed there. I had taken my shirt off bicycling up the hill and now I ran into the meadow whooping, whipping my shirt around like a helicopter blade, and collapsed into the grass. It was unusual for me to be so loud and demonstrative, but I was dizzy from the ride and no one was there to see me but Louise.

She unpacked the rest of our food and put the drinks in a cold stream, and I scrambled over the tarn to the small lake to swim. This was our routine. I knew Louise was resting. She lay in the sun by the wine with her eyes closed and was gone. I climbed over the low ridge, dazzled by the blue sky, then hopped from rock to rock down into the windless hollow that held the lake. It was hot there, and dusty, and the glare off the water was blinding. I stripped my shoes and socks off, pulled my cutoffs and underpants to the ground with a few tugs, then stepped from them and stood naked on the rocks.

I took a single plunge and then climbed from the water onto a flat rock in the sun, numb, clean, and exhausted. The water was unbearably cold. I swam just long enough to wash away the sweat and dirt, to have my skin chilled into goose bumps, and to make my bones ache before climbing out to lie on the hot, smooth rock. The sun was too bright for open eyes. The parts of me that weren't usually naked felt especially good. My belly, the stretch of it from my navel down, presented a series of dazzling sensations. The hollow divot of my chest experienced moods. I was all muscle and skin. My heart raced and I tried to lick my armpit; then I turned over onto my face and lay flat on the rock. Scree tumbled from the ridge, footsteps that frightened me, and I scrambled to sit up, cross-legged, grabbing my cutoffs and squinting into the sun.

"Louise?" She was not supposed to do this. If she did this I wasn't supposed to know, or let her know I knew.

"Hello." A man. A man in our meadow. I was just as mortified as if it had been Louise. I turned my back to him and struggled into the shorts. My underpants lay in a bundle by my socks and shoes, bright white in the sun.

"I was swimming," I said, turning back again.

"Don't be embarrassed," he said. "I'm not looking." I couldn't see him because of the bright sun. His voice came from the top of the rocks. "Tell me when you're ready, and then I'll come down."

"I'm ready," I said. "I mean, I don't mind. The water's really cold."

He appeared, jumping down from rock to rock so the sun no longer obscured him. This man wore shorts with a lot of pockets and some kind of equipment, clamps and spikes. His knapsack was big and nearly empty. "I was just going to have a swim myself," he announced. I pulled my shirt on and tried covering my underpants with the shoes.

"Did Louise see you?" I asked.

"The woman by the bikes?" He took his shirt off and undid his belt. "I think she's sleeping."

"I'll go tell her you're here." I slipped my shoes on, stuffed my underpants and socks in my pockets, and scrambled up the ridge, not looking back.

Louise was not asleep. She was watching the ridge, and when I came to the top of it she waved at me. "There's a man here," I said, calling down to her. She shrugged. "There's a man here," I shouted, a little louder.

"That's okay." Louise's voice was very clear. "He's not bothering you, is he?"

"No."

Louise waved me away with both hands then lay back down. I looked toward the lake and saw the man splashing around as if this were a regular old lake you could actually enjoy. His butt was bright white in the water. I stood for a while and then went to where our bikes lay in the grass and unpacked my little tools. Louise was prone, maybe sleeping. I took a soda from the creek where she'd put them, gathered my shirt and tools then climbed back up the ridge.

The tools were a complete mystery to me. One brass pick was very sharp, and I used it to pry at some loose shale. The heaviest tool was a wedge that could be hammered and I tried this too, making a pile of fragments that I picked through. I had no idea what to look for, but the soda tasted good and this spot on the ridge seemed to be the right place for me. I could see both the man and Louise from here, and I could disappear from the sight of either one in just a few steps if I wanted to.

Louise had opened the wine and was wandering around the meadow with the bottle and a half sandwich. I knew the man was done swimming but I didn't look until I heard some rocks tumble. He was climbing toward me, with his shorts on, thank goodness, and he'd dipped his shirt in the water then wrapped it around his head like a kerchief, which looked very cool. I turned back to the shale and crouched beside it, inspecting the rocks deliberately.

"That *was* cold," this man said, announcing himself. "My hands are still numb."

I looked over my shoulder at him. Anything I could've said was dumb, so I screwed up my grin and shrugged.

"Looking for fossils?" he asked. He crouched beside me. The muscles around his knees looked the same as mine, only his legs were hairy.

"Uh-huh." I swatted a loose shard of rock with the flat of the hammer and it broke, predictably, into a billion pieces, so it was just dirt.

"My name's Larry," the man said. He took the hammer from me and shook my hand. Larry, like the possum who used to come in our house. I grunted, thinking of the possum, and flashed another screwy grin.

"Hi."

"You should use that pick when you're working on shale. Shale's really delicate." He ran his hand through the dirt. "It's like very dry mud."

"I did use the pick." We both looked at the dirt. "I mean earlier."

"Do you have a brush, a wire brush?"

"They're my mom's tools." I nodded toward the meadow where Louise was dancing along the creek, sometimes in the creek.

"A wire brush lets you remove layers from the shale without destroying any fossils that might've been preserved there."

"Mmm." What he said made no difference to me.

"What kind of stuff are you looking for?"

I stared at his shoes, which were also very cool, sandals that he wore without socks and had apparently worn right into the lake; I mean they were wet. "Can you hike in those shoes?" I asked, wanting also to know if I could have them please. I hated my shoes, nylon sneakers that looked like blue lozenges.

"What?"

"I hate my shoes. They're not even comfortable."

He undid the few straps of the sandals and handed them to me. "Try them on. They won't feel right since they're shaped to my feet, but you could get your own and break them in. Of course you can hike in them."

"Wow." What a swell guy. I undid my sneakers and pulled them off. The sandals were furry, soft, and they were smooth where the imprints of Larry's feet had pressed into them—like polished fossils. I put them on and walked around a little and immediately got an erection, which didn't seem very important or weird just then. The sandals were the right size, almost, and the way his foot was shaped felt very cool against my foot.

"We're the same size," Larry said. "I mean almost."

I jumped around a little, making dashes and cuts along the rocks. Larry crouched beside the tools and watched me. I went a little distance toward the lake, leaping down rock to rock and then about-facing to work my way back up the tarn. I made a particularly fine jump and looked up to watch him watching me and there was Louise. She had surmounted the ridge and stood with Larry and the sandwich and the wine. They were talking.

"Look!" I shouted, but there was no especially interesting leap left to make and I simply sprang from one end of a rock to the other like some dumb little kid.

"That's wonderful, dear," Louise said. She handed the wine to Larry, and he drank it from the bottle.

I pointed back to where I'd been. "I can jump really far in these." I proceeded to spring back down the tarn feeling like a bird or Rocky the flying squirrel until I reached the edge of the lake. The shoes felt great. I was hot and wanted to make my shirt into a hat like Larry's, but now he and Louise were a million miles away, laughing and passing the wine back and forth. I ran back up the rocks to them.

"Let's make hats like Larry's," I announced, panting and out of breath.

"You've met my son, the athlete."

Larry and I both made stupid grins. "I'm really hot. Let's make our shirts into hats like Larry's."

Louise glanced at the bunched underpants hanging out of my pocket, but didn't mention them. My socks lay in a small pile where they'd tumbled out. "You're all sweaty again, darling boy. You should take another swim and then we'll eat our picnic in the meadow."

"Larry." I turned. "Show me how to make my shirt into a hat. We can go to the lake. You can come too, Louise, come on." They looked at each other and didn't answer me. I hated that. Louise smiled and took the wine from Larry. "You don't have to *do* anything, I mean just let's go down there, okay?" I wished a helicopter would come along and swoop them up in a basket and dump them down by the lake on the rock that I could see by the water, that nice flat rock where we could all stand if only they would move their feet, one after the other, and go down there.

"It's really easy," Larry said, taking the tied shirt from his head. "You just tuck the sleeves in and make knots at all the corners. Then you dip it in the lake."

I looked at him and then, fiercely, at Louise. They still weren't moving. I tugged my shirt off and gave it to Larry. "Come on, come down to the lake and show me." I crossed my arms over my nipples and could feel them harden against the soft inside of my wrists. Larry tucked the small sleeves of my white T-shirt into themselves and tied the four corners off so that I had a hat like his, only dry and too big for my head.

"There." He handed it to me. "Now you dip it in the water so it's wet and won't just blow off in the wind."

"You really ought to take another swim, dear, you're filthy. I'll show Larry the meadow and get the picnic ready. We'll feast, darling." I said nothing. I stared at them.

"I'll clean these tools off," Larry offered. My shoes lay in a heap between us, and Larry sat down and put them on his feet. Louise picked up my dirty socks, and then they started down the tarn to the meadow.

•7•

Stéphane woke me the next morning astride his bicycle, clever boy, rolling through my room with a tight turn by the bookshelf and a bump against the desk that woke me. He *click-click-click-clicked* past my bed and out the door again. "I have thought you were awake. You will excuse my joke of the bicycle." He stumbled from it, wheeling around to park in the hall. "Per said you would like a guide to visit to the school with you."

"What time is it?" I made a show of stretching, so the boy would know I wasn't bashful. Did I smell? He clattered the bike into place outside my door. "Come back in and help me find my clothes and watch."

"Watch what?" Impertinent. I put a pair of instructive hands on his shoulders.

"*La montre, mon montre*. In English it is called a watch."

He shrugged my hands from him. "Why?"

"Because I would like your help."

Stéphane lifted the slim-banded timepiece from the side table where it had been in plain view all along. "Why 'watch'?"

"Twelve-thirty? I slept fifteen hours?"

"The English is crazy." He tried the watch on his wrist, and it looked handsome, loosely bound beside the colorful braids of cloth he had tied there. "Per made a rendezvous for the school of three

P.M., and I will go with you for lunch and basketball and then for the school."

"How genial. Thank you. I don't play basketball."

"You will watch me."

"You like that?" I nodded to the watch. "You wear it today, see how it feels." The boy nodded and paused. A rush of blood or intelligence flushed through him, mute, barely visible, transforming his placid gaze into pinball-tilting calculations, and then he scrambled away without a word—up the stairs in a leap or two, scrape and bang of pulled drawers—and bounded back with a wadded black T-shirt in hand.

"You will wear this, and I wear the watch." The boy seemed pleased by the symmetry of the arrangement. The shirt smelled and was tight, but I pulled it on. *Metallica* in hideous faux-Gothic script bubble-foamed across my stomach beneath Beelzebub on a souped-up Harley. "It's good, yes? Good fit."

"Lovely." I made beach muscles. "Shows off my nice body."

"Yes. It's very good."

Lunch was *caviar d'aubergine* (smashed eggplant on pita bread) from a snack stand that gave us sticks instead of forks or knives, stir sticks, which Stéphane insisted were superfluous. "These pieces are luxuries," he said. "You put it in the mouth, you see"—he demonstrated the stuffing of the rolled pita into the mouth—"and you eat."

I nibbled at mine en route to the park. Lunch was *en plein air, et mobile. Le plein air* today was mawkish and brooding, indecisively gray but warm as bathwater.

"The spring in Paris, since it has fairly begun, has been enchanting." [This from another book.] "The sun and the moon have been blazing in emulation, and the difference between the blue sky of day and of night has been as slight as possible. There are no clouds in the sky, but there are little thin green clouds, little puffs of raw, tender verdure, caught and suspended upon the branches of the trees. All the world is in the streets; the chairs and tables which have stood empty all winter before the café doors are at a premium; the theaters have become intolerably close."

We took a bus and I watched all the pretty sights while the boy kept his nose in a magazine (Pink Floyd *Les Rois du Rock*) despite my excited reports—"Quick, look, a charming Parisian bistro." We got off at the park. Cars crawled in the dull glare. Stéphane, star student of the Per school-of-blind-street-crossing, cut a clean path to the park gate, lunch in mouth, and I followed. His flapped blue knapsack looked smart and stylish, slung low off his shoulders. The great trees billowed, flaccid and waxen in the day's porcelain air, over pale green chairs and gravel paths. Four days, three visits to this park; I sauntered, I think is the right word, with the grace and carelessness of the habitué.

Stéphane looked smart striding past short-panted boys prodding their boats around the shallow pond with sticks. From the slung knapsack he produced his basketball, his emblem, and it was clear his purpose at the park was anything but childish. Small boys stared at the marvelous orange globe. Stéphane, his big hands all over it, said "scram" to the ones bold enough to step near. We arrived among the trees and the knapsack was dropped to the ground, the basketball spun in hand. An inner-city slouch (transmitted via music television) like some kind of dybbuk bled from gray tin air into this thin French boy's body and, split-second channel-change style, I found myself standing beside a jaded gang-banger (sweet-faced, just guessing really), scopin' for his homies.

"Stéphane?" His wrist, dangling hipside, turned slightly toward me. "Are your friends here?" He nodded at the usual cluster of hand-slappers. "Mmm." A drab cabin/café sat opposite in a gravel plaza of metal chairs. "You know, I'm still a little hungry. I think I'll watch from over there and have something to eat. Can I get you a soda or anything?" Birds rushed from the trees, pigeons, blotting the sky with their dirty flapping wings and soft underbellies. They lifted from the branches above the boys, who swooped and hollered like earthly birds as clumsy and doomed as the ugly pigeons who shit from the sky in parallel descending streams above them. The court was awful, really, cracked and uneven, and the basket was simply a metal ring welded to a sheet of steel. A handful of Africans, regardless of anything else about them, held the rest enthralled.

"Coke, please. In the can." He turned and smiled. I left to take up my primary role as audience.

The boy had brought his kit. He unpacked it solemnly: terrycloth wrist bands, a string for the hair, small immaculate towel, ankle brace (the right), doubled-up socks matching under and over, plus the special shoes, wrapped in tissue, big as cats, which he laced completely (with one circuit around the back) and then tied. Other cooler boys wore theirs without lacing. It took him several minutes (Coke delivered in respectful silence, mid-lace), and he was neither rushed nor bothered. The sun, unlocatable behind dim overcast, made its way through the sky. The waiter was a flirt. He brought me the Coke with a smirk and stared while I fumbled through my poor French for an order.

"*Recommendez-vous une sorte du vin particulier?*"

"*Une sorte du vin?*" He smiled. I nodded, suspicious, even, of *oui*. "*Bordeaux. Ça marche.*"

"*Bien. Un pichet.*" I tried a face I had seen on Serge—bland disinterest—then one from Allan Stein—fierce disinterest, which pleased me more. A drowsy smoker slouched in his fatigue jacket, sprawled on paired chairs to my right. He watched the strutting boys. Stéphane stood to the side bouncing his ball, which was brighter by far than the game ball and gave a pleasant *ping-ping-ping*. The boy feigned cynicism, when in fact he cared very deeply. Eight boys played while mothers ambled past with infants in strollers, common as wind or sunshine on this bland corridor of a day. One *maman* stopped and sat down beside me. She smiled and tended to her hidden infant. Stéphane, cross-court, glared, and I waved at him, happy to be noticed.

"*Ton fils?*" this settling young mother inflected.

"*Je m'excuse. Mon français c'est pauvre. Je ne comprends pas.*"

"Yes, yes, I understand. Your son?" she repeated. Charming accent. The waiter arrived with what appeared to be a half gallon of wine, plus a napkin and glass (a slip of paper beneath the glass). He spat a nasty stream of French at the young mother, and she said something about pigs and flung a hand-clutched arm, and the waiter left. The smoker nearby slid deeper into his chair, eyes closed, bored.

"No, no, he's my—uh, cousin. *Cousin.*"

"Mmm. He's very beautiful." Said like a good mother. This one could have been his girlfriend at a small stretch; she looked barely out of her teens. We stared at the angelic devil/boy, all limbs and equipment, rubbing his great round fetish while the game went on and on without him. He dribbled for a bit, switching deftly hand to hand, then inspected the basketball minutely for flaws. Mother's treasured infant, still invisible amidst woolen wraps, slept silently and deep. "I would offer a cigarette, but obviously you don't smoke them."

"Thank you, no, I don't."

"Americans never smoke. Australians do, and the British naturally, but Americans don't even carry matches anymore." I pulled out a book of matches (*Shackles. Diverse Ales Since 1989*) and struck one with a little more panache than I had intended. Miss International Relations gave a tight smile and strolled to the neighbor table to bum a cigarette. What a marvel, the easy rapport of café society. Tiny roped children, two rows on a great linked leash, marched past with a matron at the helm. A second leash led from her hand to a solitary dog, who leaped and yapped at a bag of treats. The children shuffled forward, silent as doomed Jesuits. Teen *maman* jogged the shoulder of our neighbor and took two cigarettes from him.

Stéphane at last managed to insinuate himself onto the court. In the wake of a victory, the four triumphant lay beneath a tree smoking while the losers argued. Stéphane dribbled out among them and tried some tentative heaves at the rim. His soft blue cotton shorts, baggy and low-slung so they tickled the tops of his knees, reminded me of water.

Last night in bed I had imagined him in shorts like these, piloting a bicycle across "our meadow" of flowers, the delicious mountain sun casting shadows in the folds of the garment. It shaped and shifted with his pumping legs. Mostly I thought of the shorts and the pumping, those long thighs a little warm but not exhausted. No shirt (as per monsieur's request), plus a glimmer of sweat along his heaving ribs. I followed on a second bike. This bedtime scenario got lost before it formed any trajectory. The boy just kept wobbling through the flowers, his legs in motion, over and over and over.

Just this side of sleep, echoes of my vision had gathered, a web of them bursting like carefully planned fireworks. At first these bursts obscured the boy, and then, dimming, they illumined him, brief visions that turned into a dream as I fell into sleep: (1) how intricate the nap of mosses became when I lay down in the meadow, face pressed to their carpet; (2) the poorly sung melody of "Eidelweiss" when my mother sang it wrong there; (3) how I heard the song in my head, always, for many days after; (4) that I could swim naked in the milky blue water hidden by pinnacled ridges where slides made a tarn (the water so frozen my bones ached), then lie on the rocks in the sun since Louise promised she would whistle before coming over; (5) the heat of the sun; (6) my fear of hornets and wasps; (7) the deeper heat, stretched out on the rock, jerking off, eyes closed to the sky; (8) knowing the names of flowers (I have forgotten them); (9) the empty feeling of the car ride home at night, radio catching static and a Sunday hits countdown, along the black road; (10) how trees and animal eyes swept by headlights read like a movie in the dark; (11) my knees cupped beneath my palms; (12) not having to talk to be happy. Which is when I fell asleep.

No game yet, still idle milling, sizing up of some sort. The shorts arranged themselves against the boy's body, his smooth thighs striating with minor strain, legs leaping or muscling along through a gathering of foes. Miss Teen Mother sat and smoked, eyeing my wine, with her silent baby very silent beside her. Mr. Nod stirred and stared our way.

Beyond the boys and the trees, in the listless distance where gravel marked the park's main crossing path, the linked brats had been unleashed by matron and they clamored around a tired old donkey, the Sisyphus of donkeys, whose fate it was to haul cartloads of these tyrants from one end of the arboretum to the other. Unleashed by their keeper, the once docile victims became tiny monsters, aping matron's flat cruelty in shrill outbursts, practice for the grown-up pleasures ahead. In the great psychic economy of the French, the young victim waits graciously for someone weaker, on to whom he may pass the raft of cruelty that is his patrimony (the gift of parents, matrons, priests, and the like). This noble donkey was a practice ground for the young, his abuse and humiliation the child's first rehearsal for a satisfying grown-up life. Alas, the donkey had no easy return trip for the contemplation of his labors. There were always more pinching, poking children, another load to be packed and hauled, which fact lifted this beast's nobility far above the heights of his mythic counterpart. The donkey's labor was continuous, as if Sisyphus not only rolled the rock uphill but also delivered pizza to drunken college pranksters on his way back down, and I felt certain Albert Camus must have sat one day at this very same unbalanced table, with the same half gallon of marching wine, observing the same ancient donkey.

Stéphane picked and pawed at the shorts, mere gestures, but his audience was appreciative. A game was emerging from the on-court milling. The four victors assumed their offensive positions, facing five hopefuls in some disarray. Our neighbor, Mr. Nod, strolled over and asked after *maman*'s little baby.

At the foul line, the tallest of the winners, in bulky sweats and unlaced shoes, complained. *"Qui joue avec vous?"* He held the ball on his hip and his five opponents stared blankly back, accused, looking for one to sacrifice. "*C'est qui alors?*" Oh, Machiavelli could not have written a crueler scenario! It was plain as the bright stars pitched in the vault of heaven that nobility was about to surface and be made to suffer. Teen *maman,* chatting happily, lifted baby's woolly wrap and Nod gazed on her sainted sleeper. Good Stéphane, raised by intellectuals, stepped forward to assert the rule of law.

"*J'attendais,*" he pointed out, claiming rights to the next game with a kind of endearing and archaic respect for fairness. "*C'est mon tour.*" The others would shoot for the privilege of joining him. Mother pulled a little infant arm—no, not an arm, was that plastic?—from her bundle and gave it to Nod (which didn't keep her from hearing the crude on-court reply to my noble "cousin," some French curse that I understood only in the laughs that followed it). *Maman* shouted *"cochon de branleur, va"* at the boy's adversary, winning Stéphane a tidy second helping of shame and a parting shot, in poor English, from the adversary's short bent teammate, his Igor: "No next till this game's over, John Stockton." (A vile curse, I gathered from my boy's distress.) Stéphane slouched to the side of the court, furious, and the game commenced without him. Nod fumbled and a tiny hypodermic clattered to the ground beneath the stroller, which *maman* swooped up neatly and plunged back into her woolen bundle.

"Eh, branleur, t'as fini de déconner?" she shouted at the tall basket-bully. Or was it friend Nod she addressed? Regardless, she gestured universally from her chair at courtside. Stéphane stared at the chaotic play of the foolish warriors on their pitched and cracking court, his perfect shoes still untested, and I went to him, rising from my midday drunk, and said, "Well, fuck them." This both surprised and cheered the boy (a trick I'd learned in school). I steered us away, my arm thrown around him like a pal's.

"Fuck them," he repeated, pleased with the feeling of these words in his mouth.

"They play like children," I went on. *Maman* took my wine and drank it, but that didn't matter; the boy's hip moved so gently in the cotton beneath my hand. What could it matter? We strolled away, away. "This isn't basketball they play, this is beach ball."

"What is beach ball?" He looked at me, cheeks flush, his eyes full of tears, and I became dizzy, recognizing that the boy had come close to crying.

It wasn't anything. "A child's game, a game in the sand. Basketball, real basketball in America is nothing like this . . . this chaos."

"You have gone to the NBA games?" Stephane asked. His nose needed a wipe, but he wouldn't do it.

"Of course I have, everyone goes."

He swiped his wrist quickly, smearing the snot a little. "You see how these are stupid; they don't know the game."

"Mmm." I lifted the hem of his shirt to wipe his nose properly and let my free hand drift onto his belly while I cleaned him. "Mmm, there." Taut, sweet slip of a belly button, finger on the lip of it. This caress could not be called a seduction; there was no hidden algebra, no calculation; the gesture was complete in itself, a habit of my devotion. "So"—my hand to his chest—"come. We'll play real one-on-one." I nodded to a free, more forlorn hoop and the boy said yes.

Any teacher must be ready to play sports. I was graceful and effective in the game simply because I was at ease and I enjoyed the contact. Stéphane tried to guard me but he wasn't very good at it. When I moved forward he moved away and it was a simple matter to get to the basket and make a layup. When he had the ball I stayed close to him with my hands on his body. I have no idea whether it was legal, but it gave me pleasure to feel the shape of his hips and ribs and the way his body moved. He said that I was fouling him. Birds, the pigeons mostly, had settled in bunches around the court, a nattering audience that swooped and scuttled away whenever the game drove us near them.

"American basketball is much more physical," I explained. *Maman*, watching sweetly from my table, enjoyed the last of the wine. "Contact is allowed." We went on playing American basketball, and his hands felt good on me. I pulled my clinging Metallica T-shirt up to wipe sweat off my face and he watched. My clothes stank fully now. Once, he landed poorly and began to fall and I wrapped my arms around his back and held him. "Thank you," he said. I had the ball and I moved toward the basket ferociously. Stéphane reached to poke the ball away and my shoulder hit him squarely on his nose and he started to bleed.

There was a lot of blood. Everything was still—the birds and the day and the distant barbarians, all gray and muted; the boy and I, abruptly silenced, stood in place while the ball rolled away into the pigeons. He stared while blood flowed down his face and into his hands. My stomach felt uneasy because of all the blood. I took his arm to guide him, but he turned his back and hurried from me. Stéphane went to the metal table, where our drunk, alarmed neighbor pulled a diaper from her kit. She held it to his nose and cursed me, caressing the boy. I sat down in a chair near the empty wine while she held him and kept the diaper to his face until the bleeding stopped.

Stéphane had a change of clothes but I did not, so that by the time we arrived at the gate of the École Alsacienne I was not very presentable. He led me—rather, I followed, that is I tried to keep up, I mean to say I chased after him, still not speaking—across the Luxembourg Garden to a toilet where a woman took coins (my coins) and gave him a private stall to wash and change in. He was in there quite a while. I slouched on a bench by the woman. The march across had been painful, past Stéphane's tiny admirers pondside with their boats and sticks, and mothers and policemen, all guessing what crime the mewling heavy-metal drunk had vested on the proud and bloodied French boy. When the boy emerged he was immaculate. His hair was neatly brushed behind his big ears, his face solemn and scrubbed, and he wore a clean shirt tucked into khaki shorts, with wool socks and sandals below. "We go now," he said.

The boulevard bordering the garden ran south to a roundabout. A few dull shops and vendors punctuated the long blocks, and I bought a cheese crepe from one of them. Stéphane wasn't hungry. I felt a little sick now and threw half the crepe to pigeons in the square where the boulevard ended. The rue Notre-Dame-des-Champs led away from it to the school. The boy hardly spoke, although he walked alongside me now, startling, beautiful, and angry.

Language was the least of our barriers. Stéphane hovered behind a scrim, trapped inside a body whose proportions and angularity perfectly expressed something to me . . . "becoming," I'd like to say, but it might have been nostalgia. His posture as he led me, the narrowing shoulders, the lilt of his arms and bounce of his blue knapsack that kept disappearing into the crowd, enthralled me by pointing elsewhere—away from him. The hollow of his back and then the turn at the hips, his long thighs, became abstractions, pure equations, so that he engaged that part of my mind that also loves geometry or angels.

The wind, which was uncomfortably warm and full, picked up, and the great branches shading the square shook and then settled again. Their leaves glimmered silver and gray when the tree shivered, and this made me think of winter or water emerging from snow, or the way a creek, when it is frozen over, still moves beneath its roof of ice. Since the accident the boy had ignored me so that a show of arrogant disinterest appeared to be the only coin I had left, of any value, for buying back his attention. For the last ten minutes I'd been heaping this upon him unsparingly and it had begun to work. A mere glimmer, a peep. "Look," he whispered, stopping sweetly. His relaxing thighs had become goose-pimply along their silky fronts, and he lifted the hem of his khaki shorts high enough for me to see this. "But it's so warm." I ignored him a moment longer, and this drew him out.

"It was horrible," he cajoled, his shoulder bumping mine. "When you hit my nose, I thought it was broken."

I turned to poor, wounded Stéphane and held his shoulders, gently inspecting the "nose area" with my eyes. "Mmm, I know." Eye contact, our first since the blow. "I thought we had done something terrible to it."

"Ouch." He was cross-eyed, hurting with anticipation as my fingers hovered by the sore nose.

"May I . . . touch it?" He whimpered a little, drew himself up, then said no.

A pleasant château was settled in the courtyard, as if the rest of the school and Paris had grown up around it, out of fields, plowed clover, and the forests of Gaul. Stéphane led me to the small anteroom of the registrar, a trim woman who had been assigned to my case. Miss Ploquin, as she called herself (preferring Miss to Mademoiselle), was nervous as a birch mouse in fall. Her supplies—paper and stamps, clips, tacks, glue, books, and twined files—had been hoarded in every cranny of the tiny room. Per must have given Miss Ploquin a line about Herbert Widener; she cooed and purred the good fortune of having *un professeur émérite* pry into the archives and let her eyes skip right past my catalogue of smells and stained garments. Paper was cleared from two chairs and we were invited to sit. The boy was my translator, but Miss Ploquin preferred the cosmopolitan pleasures of her schoolbook English. Stéphane sat obediently and fiddled with his tender nose.

What a pleasure, and the honor of a published scholar from blah-blah (mmm, published?) writing a book about the school and of course it is celebrated in France, even the boy must know this (yes he does) but rarely do the *éducateurs béats* of America (in English there is no word; "Smug?" Stephane suggested bravely; No, no, silly boy, not the same) turn their attentions to France, the cradle of the Enlightenment, America its grave, for examples of progressive education, though l'École Alsacienne has pioneered a singular model for ninety years, God bless Jules Siegfried, you're aware it is the source of Gide's *Les Faux Monnayeurs,* the model of the school, Gide attended at the dawn of La Grande Époque of Siegfried.

"No, I wasn't."

Le Géranium calls it *l'école légendaire,* in his history, and it is he who has divided the periods into La Grande Époque *et*—that is, and—Les Temps Magnifiques, but of course you will have read that; I can set up for you a visit with Le Géranium—you must be patient, he is eighty—and inquire of the teachers whether classroom observation would be appropriate at this point in the . . .

"I'm only interested in a boy named Allan Stein." I put this in sideways while Miss Ploquin struggled after a word or phrase that had, in the instant, eluded her.

"Allan Stein?" She made the first name French and the second German, then looked at me across her paper-pinnacled desk like a wronged dog, that sad look they give when you hide the wanted stick by your thigh and gaze into the misty field where you haven't thrown it. "A boy here?"

"Yes, he was a boy here in 1905 until 1914 or so, at least I believe he was." Stéphane had moved from the nose to the knees; he held his legs out stiffly, cradling the egg-yolk-shaped kneecaps in his long fingers and pulling up. Soft fuzz blessed the shins from the knees down, and it looked pretty in the dim office twilight. Herbert (aslumber now through all my afternoons, because of time zones) fetishized calves, and I'm certain he would have enjoyed these: muscular and rounded, then tapering to fine aristocratic ankles delicate as a bird skull or the wrists of a lemur. The boy's big feet bumped the desk and Miss Ploquin rose slightly to peer over it. "I would like to see anything you have about him."

"You are writing a book about this boy?"

I picked at my clinging shirt where the bubble-foam logo had folded, a tiny bit, into my belly. "Yes, a book." (Why not?) "He might not have gone here at all." Stéphane glanced at me and nodded, very impressed by something. Perhaps he hadn't known until now I was *the* Herbert Widener, writer of books.

"What is it," Miss Ploquin asked, "that is important about this boy Allan Stein?" Oh, where was Miriam when I needed her? Stéphane was still caught in his admiration for me, regarding my profile with new delight and listening, for goodness' sake, and this fact made me doubly anxious to export myself well. But without the Picasso painting as a touchstone, the point I had to make was, at best, abstract.

"Boys have this power, you see." Puzzled, distant, vague Miss Ploquin didn't see. "Over me, anyway, and I'm fascinated that they could be, Gods, which no man can be but a boy could." The spirit, if not the letter, was correct. Miss Ploquin looked at me, one beat, then turned to my translator, who produced an impressive stream of French, peppered with "Allan Stein"s and ending to the marked satisfaction of the registrar.

"*Eh bien,*" she replied, nodding.

I told her the dates I knew and waited. While Miss Ploquin rummaged and culled, Stéphane explained that he'd said Allan was "an American, a maker of D-Day, and a friend of France," which was at least two-thirds true. Smart boy, and quick on his feet. "But I do not understand what you are meaning to say about him," he whispered, enjoying the peril of our subterfuge. "It was confusing. I don't understand how he is *actually* important." I shrugged and said nothing. A chronicle of the day wafted from my person, buttery crepes, pointless soap at the john, the grime of sport, including ghostly dried estuaries of dirt that gathered at my wrists and fanned to outline my palms and fingertips, which were themselves left pink by the moistness of the ball. This effluvia smelled like garden soil, my palms like water, and the shirt simply stank. My knees ached. Miss Ploquin returned with a sour look and a box.

"The boy was here, you are correct." Her verdict was delivered in a somber tone, eyes downcast, as with the dreaded affirmation "we have found the body." "There is very little. Le Géranium has taken almost everything, and I'm afraid he can be very difficult." She handed me the box, and it was indeed nearly empty. Stéphane nosed in at my shoulder as I pawed through the yellowed documents: a few photos, tennis team, boxing club (Allan a rather meaty brute at seventeen but with a sweet smile); list of war dead (eight of twelve boxers); a dry lifeless moth, turned to powder at my touch; curricula for the forms (can these be copied? but of course, monsieur); and Allan's thrifty little script from 1910, an exam in German: STEIN, ALLAN, 16 marks out of 20. (May I have this? Le Géranium must be asked; Oh, never mind, but please copy it too; Yes, of course, monsieur.) Who could read German? Miriam, the boy assured me, reads German.

How the air stayed so warm after nightfall I cannot say, but this night it did, and the bus through the dusk home was like a well-lit bed, firm, broad, afloat in the dreamy streets from l'Observatoire to the Place de Rungis. Serge had hung paper lanterns in the garden where the shelter of the walls kept the warm air still. Denis, Miriam's friend, was coming to dinner and we would eat outside. He worked at someplace called the "Carnival Ay" and wanted to meet me (that is to say, Herbert). I bathed. There was bubble bath and candles on the porcelain rim and incense from Stéphane, who promised silence, so that I fell asleep bathing, which refreshed me perhaps more than the hot water did.

8

It was pleasant to dress well. Pressed cotton slacks, white shirt, and a sweater, with a favorite silk tie (ducks) just for the show of it. How should one dress for a garden party? Per was startling and fantastic in a Ricardo Montalban puffed white shirt with Abbie Hoffman's flag-striped bib overalls (one strap left undone). The man was an idiot savant of fashion, a genius who seemed to import most of his clothes from some American thrift store. Stéphane was our waiter, with his hair pulled back into a ponytail, big blushing ears all scrubbed and clean, white shirt buttoned to the top, plus a black bow tie and slacks. He carried the meal, tray by tray, down two flights of stairs and served.

Miriam and Per were in the garden drinking, and I joined them. I brought the photocopied German with me. We drank scotch; Per sprawled in a great overstuffed chair (American late-forties Levittown opulence, which he'd dragged from the basement), while Miriam and I sat primly on folding garden chairs. There were treats: nuts, bread, and (for me?) a bowl of Doritos. In the window, top floor, Serge batted at smoke with a towel.

"No, no," Per was telling Miriam, slouching in the shadowed corner of his chair. "You don't swallow it, just let it lie there, on your tongue. You'll need a lot of spit."

"I don't have a lot of spit. What about scotch?"

"No, never scotch. Even water has too much of a flavor. Herbert knows this; I'm sure he does it all the time." I smiled and leaned my chair against the brick wall.

"Here." Per pushed the Doritos toward me. "You just lay it on your tongue—isn't that right, Herbert?—curving downward like a shield. It's like a mint or an eau-de-vie, it must dissolve into the mouth." Miriam pressed one onto her tongue and worked it around softly to bring some spit up.

"Ith no woking," she slurred.

"Give it time, dear," Per scolded. "So, Stéphane has taken you back to the school today, has he?"

"That's right, yes, he did. He did a terrific job of translating, too."

"And was it the right school?"

"Oh, yes, 1907 to 1914. Allan actually got his degree in 1916, in Aix, for some reason."

"And what are these pages you have?"

"An exam in German. Allan wrote it in 1910." Miriam peered over my shoulder, breathing across her smelly chip. "Stéphane said you could tell me what it says." The garden door rattled, and Per strode to it. Miriam took the pages and pulled the chip from her tongue, where it stuck a little.

"Sixteen marks out of twenty, very respectable." Bright orange mouth.

"Denis, *bonsoir.*" Per stood hugging a huge black man, maybe a foot taller than he, and they both swayed like dancers.

"He writes about the floods," Miriam went on. "Very interesting story about the floods of the Seine in 1910." Stéphane tore out the door and leapt at Denis and Per, hugging them both midair before falling off and fidgeting foot to foot, belying his somber costume. "He mentions his Aunt Gertrude here, the things they did to help during the flood." I rose and Miriam looked up. "Oh, Denis."

"Denis Oppenheim, Herbert Widener," Per offered. "Though I believe you already know each other." I dearly hoped not! What a graceful man, not lithe but somehow tending upward, as though his feet touched earth only because he willed them down. On his great frame, a linen jacket and very drifty, thin cotton pants (tan jacket, blue pants), plus loafers whose excellence was in their simplicity and the neat fit on his tiny feet (so small for such a giant). Denis glided to the table like a perfume or a trained dancer. I held out my sweaty hand, fearful Denis somehow *did* know Herbert but did not know me.

"Not in person," Denis clarified. He grasped my damp hand. "But of course everyone at the Carnavalet knows of Herbert Widener." I blushed, laughing nervously, as he sang a few praises. The Carnavalet, it appeared, was no carnival, but a museum, and Denis was one of its exhibition directors. His kindness was flattering, creating that ticklish warmth in the viscera which is pride (despite the fact he was describing someone else's virtues and I was an impostor, one whose undoing might be etched in any detail of this man's detailed praise). His litany of all that Herbert had done—in fact, it seemed to have been gleaned from one of those tossed-together art world annuals—pleased me, even while its traps and hazards began to shadow the tiny garden of my stolen delights. A nice little valley, Herbert's, while I dwelt there, but destined, perhaps, for a great deluge.

"It's too much." I blushed the praise away. "Most of this"—two shows Herbert co-curated, Denis calling them brilliant, although he hadn't managed to get a look at them; thank God *I* had and could remember—"wasn't my doing at all, but the museum's. I was really little more than a spectator."

"That's your humility." Per.

"No it isn't."

"Please, everyone, sit." Miriam ushered our guest into the chair beside mine, while Per sank back into his sultan's throne.

"Denis," he wheedled, pushing the chips toward us. "You have to try these elegant American snacks, like a savory liqueur."

"It's funny," Miriam whispered to me, smiling. "I had the impression yesterday you were a historian or, I don't know, a novelist of some sort."

"Well, an art historian, and I *am* writing a book!" Half true.

She laughed, which smelled like cheese powder. "I'm embarrassed. There I was lecturing you about Picasso and *Meneur de Chevaux Nu*, like an idiot. I hope nothing of what I said was terribly stupid." Denis crunched a mouthful of the chips and said they tasted awful, like old sneakers.

"Not at all. I've been repeating exactly what you told me everywhere I can, claiming it as my own." Entirely true. We both laughed.

"You're so brutal, Denis, eating these delicate crackers like a handful of cheap candies." Per took them from him and tried instructing Miriam again.

"Herbert, what a pleasure." Denis drew close and touched my arm.

"Oh, Denis." We smiled circumspectly, glancing at each other a few beats too long, which established a certain faggish complicity.

"You're not at all like your photo."

"No?" I reached for the olives, and Denis watched my hand. "I've never taken a good picture, you know. What photo is it?"

"It is a tiny picture."

"It's probably very old. I'm sure I look like a boy scout in it."

"Actually you look very much younger in person."

"No." Said like a true Herbert. "Well, the camera always lies, doesn't it?"

"It doesn't do you justice."

"Flatterer. Do you have it with you?"

"What are you two on about?" Per interrupted.

"Tell me *everything* about the Carnavalet." I lurched, grinning like the idiot I was.

Denis smiled once more at me, then turned to the group. "Oh, it is terrible, everything is terrible, you know." Hmms of commiseration. "The building is so old and there is no money for anything to do. It is worse than America." He sighed. Idle chuckling. "I mean the French resistance to supporting good work is much more."

"Business," I put in, pouring myself a dollop of scotch, "the—um, industrialists are the *only* hope in America. Our museum depends on the largesse of a half-dozen tycoons."

"They do not meddle?"

"Pfff. It is a conspiracy of interests. They only collect what we tell them to and are well rewarded when the museum shows whatever it wished to in the first place." I pushed a handful of chips into my mouth, then slurped the scotch. *Blech.* "This" (crumb spit stuck on my lip and chin) "is only *my* view." Miriam pressed a napkin into my hand. "None of what I tell you is the museum's position, per se, but I take the liberty, here among friends." Solemn Stéphane, well behaved now, emerged from the doorway with glasses and bottled water. I poured some at once and drank.

"Very much the man now," Denis said, running his hand along the boy's back, praise and hand accepted. Miriam smiled. That is, she didn't smile; she was supposed to smile, as a token of her amusement, her good feelings about Herbert, Denis, and the evening, but she didn't and already the evening was going wrong. First, Denis had ambushed me with his ambiguous confidences, and now I'd looked to Miriam for her scripted smile and in its place was an empty vacancy, like a whitewashed billboard or a plate. I looked at her blank face, wanting the party scene to get back on track. Her failure betokened deeper resentments, maybe, some undertow that had surfaced in the wake of Denis's provocative gesture—the hand on the boy's back—a memory or intuition, so that now I read the blank look as something meaningful or menacing, but this was little more than a fantasy triggered by my desire that she smile in the first place, as a gesture for my scene, my happy dinner scene, when in fact, she did nothing, for no reason, standing for nothing at all, and I saw nothing, and it bothered me a great deal. I felt, for a moment, like slapping her, an urge that rushed out my chest and along my right arm so I had to put the glass down and massage my knee, and as I did, she blinked and smiled. Miriam smiled.

"Not really yet," she whispered to me. "Or a very silly man who still sleeps with his stuffed revenger." Our shared secret: Stéphane's deep and ongoing involvement with his boyhood. I smiled, good actor, faithful to the scene, and soon the meat arrived. The boy hoisted his heavy tray and held it beside each of us. Succulent cuts of beef, sliced rare, fanned in a great circle. Serge, with a silver fork and spatula, lifted them up in threes, and laid them on our plates. The lantern light glimmered on the juices, on Denis's bright eyes, Per's delighted smile, Miriam. The boy fetched a tureen of pepper sauce, thick dark gravy made from the drippings of the beef and a great handful of green peppercorns, threads of steam drifting from it. He sat down on a piano stool at the foot of the table (Per, enthroned, was our king) and Serge produced wine, three bottles, dusty from the *cave*, to complete the pretty picture, and then I relaxed a little.

It's silly to think that a name, even unspoken, could alter a man's posture, but I found I sat differently as Herbert. My head rested on a sounder pivot. I slid down in my chair rather than slumping forward at the waist. I don't mean that I imitated Herbert; in fact, he usually sat up straight and was more deeply uncomfortable at dinner parties than I had ever been. I mean the name Herbert had been emptied out, like a terrific apartment an old friend has abandoned, which you finally see bare and clean, the walls broadcasting memories, but empty and available to you. "Herbert" was a big bare room. The name left space for my new inventions, my ease. As Herbert I turned from conversation to conversation. I ate slowly and didn't finish everything on my plate.

Miriam was going on about the *muladhara* while the boy played with his gravy, making tiny boats with beef, which he pushed across the great brown lake of his plate before swallowing.

"How long do you sustain it?" Denis asked.

"Too long," Per gruffed from his chair. "There isn't a moment of quiet in this house any more." I smiled at Stéphane, with an ease and confederacy that surprised me. Being Herbert had the further advantage of putting me on an equal footing with the boy. If he was trapped inside a constellation of fantasies (mine), I would be too. We'd huddle together behind screens. I could play a role that interlocked neatly with the one I had scripted for him.

"Herbert described to us very beautifully a kind of kundalini of the boy," Per chirped to Denis. "He spoke with some brilliance about the Picasso painting of a boy who has a horse, and the boy's power, which maybe is kundalini; don't you think, Herbert, some of that power is the sex power?"

"That was Miriam who spoke about the Picasso."

"That's right, though I remember as if it came from your mouth." Which was in fact how I remembered it. "You share her view, don't you?"

"Yes, I think she read the painting beautifully."

"Herbert is writing about the boy in the Picasso painting, who was a real boy, apparently. What was his name?"

"Allan Stein," I told Denis. "The late nephew of Gertrude Stein, the American writer."

"The boy who is also portraited by Picasso, isn't he?"

"Yes, that's right." Stéphane, sent to the kitchen by Serge, reemerged with a tray graced by three ceramic bowls and the yogurt crock. There was soccer on television, which most of the neighbors watched. We could hear the announcers' voices, fluid and obscure, like distant birds, through the windows the neighbors left open because the night was unusually warm. The buildings flickered and glowed in bursts, the televisions all tuned to the same channel. Per stared at the boy, absently and without intent.

"It verges on a cult," Denis repeated, touching my arm. I was becoming drunk, and when Denis touched me I enjoyed it more than his argument, which I immediately forgot.

Per interrupted. "The bricks are still warm."

Denis smiled dismissively, then went on. "The Picasso Museum is not interested in the artists around him, only Picasso, Picasso as a God, the creator of everything." He massaged my forearm as he made his point.

"It *is* the Picasso Museum," Serge observed. "What else should they do?" He lifted one of the heavy bowls from Stéphane's tray (long green beans, heavily buttered; in the other two, a smashed sweet squash with a glaze of Madeira and honey, and potatoes sliced thin and fried with pressed garlic). Our poor waiter had been standing by unnoticed for several minutes. Per reached above his head and took a blossom from the heavy branch of the plum tree. "The petals are warm too." He held it to Stéphane's nose; the boy smiled and breathed its odor, then he held it up to mine.

"I hate plums," Stéphane said.

"Every museum is a distortion," Serge argued.

"You used to like them," Per told Stéphane. He rolled the blossom over the boy's cheek. "You used to sit in the garden and eat them until you were sick."

"Did I?" The boy smiled. He was flushed because of the wine he drank. "I guess I ate too many."

"Is that why you hate them now?" Stéphane did not listen, and we were all silent for a moment. Something happened in the soccer game and the noise of the crowd rose, crackling and sibilant, like a brush fire coming near. The buildings flickered more intensely and then became steady and dimmed.

"I ate mud when I was little," Per said. Stéphane began laughing, and when Serge took the last bowl from the tray the boy set it down and put his head on my shoulder to stifle the laughter. "It was very special mud, Danish mud. All the children ate mud." I felt the boy's hand through the cloth of my shirt; he went on laughing for a while. Serge and Per watched in silence until the boy was done. How sweet that he chose my shoulder.

"It was very good mud," Per insisted. "You think mud is just mud, as if meat is just meat. There are families who eat the mud of Denmark at meals."

"How do they cook it?" the boy asked.

"No, it's true." Miriam put in. Denis turned back to me (to anyone who would listen) hoping, soon, to make his point. "They've made a tourist attraction of it, you know. One can buy jars of Danish mud in the markets of Jutland—as a novelty, I mean."

"But that isn't the real mud," Per objected.

Serge agreed. "No, it is like the tourist bakeries in Paris. The plum tarts." He took the plum blossom from Per and smashed it on the table. "These aren't real plum tarts they're serving. They serve the idea of the tarts, the image of tarts, so the tourists can think they are being French. The tourist does not want a true French tart. It is too sour."

"It *is* too sour," Stéphane said, sitting down on his stool.

"They sweeten them for the tourist."

"Like the Picasso Museum and its Picasso," Denis announced, at last heard by all. He made a gesture with his hand, then took the wine and filled our glasses.

There was some kind of special bottle, its dust much thicker, with sediment gathered inside, that Serge brought up long after the soccer match ended, after the beans and squash and potatoes were gone, after the last bread end had sopped the last drops of gravy, and a salad and cheeses had come and gone. We were very drunk. Afghan wrapped (he brought out several for his guests), Serge wobbled with the twin bottles through the chilly end of the evening, to the table where we lurched at each other's comments. I'd finished telling Denis my (that is, Herbert's) minimal plans for the acquisition of the Picasso drawings, and what a torrent of admiration these had unleashed. He was full of ideas, some of which I caught and all of which I applauded, saying yes, go ahead, thank you, you're too kind, by all means you write the widow, whatever. I was expansive. Denis became a friend, and life was very sweet as Herbert. Per and Miriam danced under the plum tree, a slow shuffle to the Chet Baker songs our boy waiter had pointed out the window while he studied. How could he study? It was his job, as legal secretary was Miriam's and art acquisition had become mine. It always helps to have a purpose. He applied himself to it without much fuss, even a little drunk in the late evening while his parents caroused in the chilly garden below.

The buildings broadcast a mix of channels now, flickering in the later night, after the monarchy of soccer had ended and no one could agree on anything anymore. Our garden was an oasis in this desert of dim, aggravated gazes, and we leaned into one another as only new drunk friends can. The dancing pair danced; Serge, Denis, and I sprawled around the table, talking about geography and the peculiar way in which a new place, Africa once for Serge, Paris for me and Denis (he grew up in Marseille), is unable to resist the power of one's imagination—there is too little reality gathered there—which makes it malleable and transporting like a dream or a thin-skinned fantasy that both enchants and is completely misleading to the traveler, who falls in love with it and stays, only to discover that every place is real, its intransigent bulk hidden, the airy island drift of its first appearance an illusion, and that unless he keeps moving he is trapped in a world of stubborn realities, of actual places.

The almanac records that it became stormy late that night, the air stirred by a steep drop in temperature coming down from the north behind a wide band of moisture. The rain managed to skirt the city, while its cold back edge caught us and lingered until the hour before dawn. By morning it was bright and warm again, so that for anyone who had gone to bed at a decent hour, eleven or twelve, and slept through the freeze, spring simply continued in its glorious first flower without interruption.

◆9◆

In the fall of 1912 a young American named Sylvia Salinger came to stay with the Steins. Her romance in San Francisco with a man known only as "the coffee boy" had upset her family, and they sent her to Paris with a girlfriend to end it. Visitors were always coming from America, and Sylvia stayed for almost a year. Allan Stein fell in love with her. He was sixteen years old, and she was twenty-three.

"Dearest family, Paris is such a strange place. After six hours on the train we landed, and Sarah and Mike and Allen [sic] and Gertrude and Alice were there to meet us. Alice and Gertrude got into one cab and disappeared. Our trunks got into another and the rest of us into still another. Then the cabs had a race up to the Hotel Lutecia, where we had engaged two rooms. The Steins stayed here awhile Friday evening, and then we went to sleep in wonderful beds. I have had absolutely no recollection of the steamer and I think that is rather unusual, *nicht wahr*? Which reminds me, I must drop German and take up French.

"Saturday morning we woke up at ten-thirty and had breakfast in bed. Mike called for us at one and we went to the Steins. The first impression of their home was a never to be forgotten one. I could not make out much, but finally decided the thing to do was to concentrate on one painting at a time until I could see something. I have hopes for myself. In several of them I could see what was meant, the object, but in few could I see beauty, and from what I hear that is doing rather well. And I did it all by myself too.

"After lunch Allen took me to see Paris. We did not walk, we ran, just everywhere and through everything, Allen giving me the historical significance to every piece of everything as we ran by. His chief object was not to have me see anything definitely, but just to kind of get an impression, so that I should fall in love with Paris immediately. It was a funny afternoon. I ran through the Luxembourg Gardens, through the Luxembourg Gallery—just imagine it—through the Cluny Museum, through some funny little church, through Notre Dame, and along the river. It was not to see anything, remember, but just to get an idea of the possibilities of Paris. He certainly is some youth. I forgot the Panthéon. Then he rushed me to Gertrude's and he vanished."

Sylvia Salinger was a clotheshorse, an avid shopper who put Matisse and Picasso and all the Steins' arcane concerns out of mind just as fast she could hail a fiacre to the nearby Bon Marché. Her letters home are rife with shopping lists—hats and boas, coats, dresses, and handmade shoes—which betray a covetousness that easily outstripped the Steins' enthusiasm for art. Even at the fabled Autumn Salon, where, nine years earlier, the Steins had made art history when they bought the reviled Matisse painting *Woman with a Hat*, Sylvia had eyes mostly for the decor.

"They are having the Autumn showing just now. The main attraction is Matisse. He has two things that are supposed to be *très* wonderful! I can see the coloring wonder of it, but as far as grace, etc., are concerned, I don't get it at all. Still, I am not supposed to, they tell me. The one interesting thing about the Salon is the display of wallpapers that have been designed just as all the other arts are worked out. Some of them are very lovely. Then, another thing is the rooms—bedrooms, drawing rooms, tearooms, dining rooms, libraries—everything complete, each little room a thing apart from everything else. There was one, a child's bedroom, that was the prettiest I have ever seen. They are completely furnished, even to the books on the shelves. It's a splendid way to get ideas."

Allan, a teenager preoccupied with horses, boxing, and tennis, also had little time for his parents' passions. Sylvia must have been a bracing tonic for him. American, brash, naive, and stunningly beautiful, Sylvia enchanted Allan. Her letters home record the course of his infatuation, and of his escape from the claustrophobic seriousness of his family's salons.

"Yesterday afternoon I went riding with Allen out in the country. It was a beautiful day and we had a glorious ride! There were two aeroplanes—monos—flying up over us the whole time, which helped to make things exciting. They are not allowed to fly over Paris proper. Last night, when I went to my room, I found a big box of all kinds of assorted milk chocolates, with a verse to Sylvia, and a little book with a French story started therein—what the story means I have yet to know, but the verse I could translate a little of. It was very well done, and so well put up. Allen, of course."

While Sarah's little boy was turning into the impulsive, extravagant, woman-chasing man he would soon become, the Picasso painting of the boy, age eleven, remained unchanged, hanging in the bedroom at 58 rue Madame. Collectors had been courting the Steins, some offering upward of $5,000 for Picassos the Steins had spent less than $100 on. Mike sold a few, but they held on to Allan's portrait for the rest of their lives.

In the bright morning sunshine I saw the boy in the garden wearing his worn-out khaki shorts and nothing else. He was alone, staring at the sky above the wall through a branch of plum tree blossoms. I had got up to pee and watched him through the window by my toilet. Stéphane stood facing away, the air full of calling birds, tilting his head like a slow metronome or a boy whose thin neck is sore. Dirty hair tickled his shoulders. Bright sunlight shadowed the grooves of his spine, and feathered outward along his ribs. His shoulder blades this morning were made golden and prominent by the sunshine, and they rose from his smooth back whenever the boy moved his arms. The hollows behind his knees hid in the shadow of his baggy hemmed shorts. Stéphane turned toward the house, toward me, and what I saw verged on abstraction: the hollows of his collarbone, the way sunlight pooled in the slim lip of his belly button, his pale nipples soft as drained blisters, the broad gap between his rabbit teeth, plus the relaxed, arrogant tilt in his hips and neck. He stood looking at the sky, scribbling. I watched from the toilet, and then the boy walked back inside.

On Monday Herbert phoned. It was before noon, and he was very drunk. It must have been the middle of the night in California.

"Herbert?"

"Thank God it's you, I can't remember a word of my French."

"What time is it there?"

"Here? I haven't any idea. Jimmy's asleep in front of some tedious video."

"In the big room?"

"Of course in the big room. He insisted I watch it with him and then he fell asleep, and now I'm stuck with the video and Jimmy, and you know he has me sleeping on the futon, so until I get him out of here *I* can't go to sleep. I started rummaging around in the kitchen and found this incredible coffee, just thick as tar. I'm so glad I have your number, no one on this continent is awake yet."

"What's the video?"

"Some four-hour silent; I think it's *Napoleon*. How *are* you? I've been worried to death, waiting for a card, anything."

"You're drunk."

"Of course I'm drunk. That doesn't mean I haven't missed you."

"Well, I've missed you too. I'm fine. It's beautiful here, as you can imagine. It's been sunny and warm, with pleasant cool evenings."

"I didn't call for a weather report. How *are* you? I mean, how are you, *really*?"

I left a long pause, and the distance was audible in the line, all sorts of intergalactic crackle and hiss marking the deep curve of space through which this phone call traveled. There was no clipped delay, thank goodness; I can't speak if there's a delay, it's just too disturbing. It makes so vividly clear exactly what the telephone is supposed to disguise—that is, how impossible the distance is that separates us.

"Hello? Are you there?"

"Yes, of course I'm here. I was just wistful. I miss you too, you know. It's just terrific to hear your voice."

"Sweet."

"I'm fine. The family is lovely as can be, and they've even got a young son who's a bit of a distraction."

"How young?"

"Oh, I don't know."

"Of course you know. How young is he?"

"Fifteen, I think. Maybe he's sixteen."

"Mmm. You're not doing anything, are you? Because you know I wouldn't, and it's me who's staying there, on the museum's tab no less, so obviously doing anything is out of the question. He must be gorgeous."

"Oh, completely. Of course I'm not doing anything."

"I'm worried about you."

"Sweet."

"Maybe you should come home, come to Jimmy's."

"I couldn't."

"The weather is absolutely stunning. I haven't left the compound since getting here."

"I really couldn't. The drawings have got me very busy already. I've set up something with the widow, Allan Stein's widow."

"Jimmy's got Vicodin, I mean bottles of it."

"I don't like Vicodin, and anyway, Herbert, I'm enjoying myself here. It's a great relief having something to do for a change. You may have been overworked for months but I've just been sitting in my room. The last thing in the world I need now is to be idle, even at Jimmy's, which I'm sure must be heaven."

"You don't like Vicodin?"

"I loathe Vicodin. I'm probably going to have those drawings in hand by the end of the week."

"You really should write to Allan's son, he's got an address in Paris."

"Allan Stein's son?"

"Yes, hold on, I'll get it for you."

"Why didn't you give it to me before I left?"

"Oh, I don't know. I never thought you'd take these drawings so seriously. Hold on a second." Herbert rummaged for a while, and when he returned he recited the address and sighed. "The end of the week?"

"Probably. I mean, between the widow and the son I can't imagine I'll have any problems."

"Then you're coming home?"

"Of course I am."

The phone call left me torn apart, as if Herbert's kindness had obliged me to span the distance which separated us, so that now I felt dispersed, like an aerosol spray. I wanted to occupy myself and so I wrote to the son straightaway, asking for his help and signing the letter with my usual flourish. It was almost one, and I was still completely out of focus. Swimming seemed like a good idea.

According to Herbert's antique guidebook (Baedecker, 1907), an artesian well fed a bath for indigents on the Butte aux Cailles, just a short walk up the rue Bobillot from home. *Une station balnéaire (avec piscine, buvettes, etc.)*, curiously located on the summit of a butte, was promised, though no hours or fees were listed. I packed two towels, my baggy trunks, stale bread and cheese, and left a note promising my four P.M. return (school's end). Dazed by the bright sunshine, I stopped for a coffee at the Café Bobillot. A woman with a purse and a purse-sized dog spooned her way up to the bar beside me and propped the dog sidearm so that his tiny clean butthole was poised exactly at the lip of my *petit crème*. Good Parisian, I pretended it wasn't there. With the broad windowed walls pulled open to the street, the café became littered with blown trash, shouted French, and car-horn honks in the billowy air. I enjoyed another *petit crème*, plus a baguette smashed with camembert and butter. Time wafted away with the odor of this pungent bread and cheese, and I got lost in it, delirious with ammonia and cream and the grim resistance of the chewy bread.

This part of the Thirteenth District was plain and quotidian beside the Paris I remembered from my trip with Louise. I was sixteen then, and we stayed in a small hotel near the Place Saint-Denis, where it seemed like every street at every hour was loud and crowded, decorated with the come-hither blandishments of tourism. Card shops and overpriced cafés punctuated this twisting labyrinth of streets in every direction, and I loved it, thinking this was just like TV, which it was: a constant jumbled stream of pumped-up sensations that left us exhausted and irritable, so irritable that Louise and I decided, for the first time in any place, traveling or at home, to go our separate ways for great chunks of time. We set up rendezvous for certain meals back at the hotel and spent the next ten days like strangers who have met each other abroad, get along well, and agree to share a few dates in the course of their separate vacations. It is clear to me now that Louise, progressive mother that she was, had decided it was time I began having some independence, some kind of adventure, and where better for a handsome young boy to start than Paris? I know that now, but at the time of our trip what I had figured out was exactly the reverse. In Paris, thrust onto my own by my mother's eagerness to "explore" (as she put it), I reasoned that *she* was pursuing sex, or at least romance, and wanted to get rid of me. I was hurt by it, and suspicious. My forced independence became an affliction, and I spent most of the time paranoid and morose, staying close to the hotel so I could monitor her comings and goings as closely as possible.

Our rooms were separate but they shared a thin wall, and I always knew if she was in, and what she was doing when she was. Typically we had breakfast at the hotel and discussed our plans for the day. I improvised elaborate fictions, long walking tours of great swaths of the city that I never actually carried out, pinioned as I was to my surveillance of Louise. Always I had maps and guidebooks to lay over the small table, covering the coffee and stale pastries, as I explained my ambitious tours. Louise was attentive to all this bluster, but it was clear she wished I would just calm down and enjoy myself. Usually she had no plans except to go somewhere in another neighborhood and sit for a while in a café, and, as I discovered, that's exactly what she did. She always invited me to come along, but since my "new independence" was the great victory of this vacation, accepting Louise's offer would clearly have been a defeat, disappointing to both of us. No, I always said, thanks, but I must get ready and be off. In my room I waited, silent, for Louise to return to her room, then I scrambled out the door to an awful Formica café across from the hotel's front entrance, where I had a Gini soda (in a can, no glass, so I could take it with me the moment I had to leave). I waited, hidden behind a mirrored pillar, for my mother to emerge, and then I followed her.

Louise was not a very interesting traveler. She peered in windows but rarely went inside to shop. She stopped randomly (I suppose it was usually warm sunshine that stopped her), and stood like a homeless woman for long moments doing nothing. If I lost her, which was often, it was usually in the metro, where I couldn't risk sitting in the same car and had to lean out at the stops to watch the platform, hoping I would spot her when she got off. I visited a great deal of Paris getting off at the wrong stop and following some other brown head through a crowd, surging along the narrow tunnels and out into the street. Stalingrad, Place de Clichy, Gare de l'Est, Mouton Duvernet, and on one morning of endless mistaken tailings through three train changes, the Porte de Bagnolet, where I was too exhausted to return home and spent the rest of the afternoon sitting in a sandwich shop reading a British sport newspaper. Having lost her, my usual strategy was to return to the Place Saint-Michel and sit in that same Formica café with a soda until I saw her come back to the hotel.

In a way I *was* beginning an adventure, as I now believe Louise had hoped; my new habit of surveillance was tremendously exciting to me, making my face flush with nervous energy, my heart race, and my body become electric with that blood rush of Eros that seems to drift so haphazardly over the hodgepodge days of adolescence—petty dinner-table arguments raising fat erections; orgasms poked, midafternoon, into television-room couch cushions, the cat or dog licking in a backyard hollow, licking just an arm, but nevertheless—and now this top-secret trailing through the streets of Paris, my erection pressed flat against my jeans, until later each afternoon in my room when I beat off. I never thought of Louise, but of trailing her. In fact I thought mostly of myself, and, while I worked my fist up and down in the dim gauze light of the hotel room, what I imagined was me on the subway train, unzipping and doing it there, Louise in the next car clueless while I performed gloriously, naked for all the men and women and children in the bright enamel subway compartment to admire.

Before I could allow myself this pleasure I sat, sometimes for hours, in the café, hoping to catch her return. The man or men I thought she must be chasing never materialized, with the notable exception of one extremely handsome thirty- or fourty-year-old Frenchman who had befriended both of us in the first days of our stay. His name was Frank (which sounded lovely in French with the soft "a"), and it was obvious to me he wanted to have sex with Louise. What gave him away—beyond the touch, the attention, the body language, the great and constant amplitude of joy and strained humor, the wine, always, which he brought to our table asking could he join us—was him palling it up with me, as if *we* could be great buddies. He would show me all of Paris, everything a boy should see. In short, he employed the trick of most men I'd seen showing interest in Louise: buddy up to the son to get Mom. We enjoyed him as we would a fireworks display, dazzled and amused but also very distant. He joined us for dinner three or four times and at the end of each evening, when at last Frank had withdrawn, Louise and I would just look at each other and laugh, not derisively but in amazement.

Frank had appeared twice at cafés where my mother sat but nothing ever happened. "Appeared" is unfair; in fact, Louise told me on both mornings that she was going to meet Frank, who had called, and wouldn't I like to come too? "Frank asked specifically for you to come; really, he'll be very disappointed to see it's just this old woman, and I don't know that I'll enjoy it much without an escort, oh please!" But no, Mother, I absolutely cannot, I have the whole Buttes Chaumont to see today, not to mention the zoo of the Bois de Vincennes, which *Le Guide Bleu* insists should not be missed, so that both times Louise did go alone and I followed with extra vigilance, hoping something would at last happen. Nothing ever did. Frank seemed bored, distracted in a way quite unknown at our dinners together, and they drank their coffees, chatted for less than an hour, kissed cheek-cheek, and I returned to the hotel to jerk off.

On the seventh day, at last, something happened. I had lost her one morning in the metro going north from Saint-Michel and returned to the tacky café, where I found an American newspaper and parked myself in the best spot, facing a mirrored wall that caught the hotel entrance in its greasy panorama. I could read and watch at the same time from there. I was only mildly bored, halfway through a canned Gini, when I spotted Frank standing by the hotel door looking at his watch. So, it had come to this: clandestine rendezvous while the boy hiked the Canal de l'Ourq. All the dreary hours spent in this bright orange café, scraping the flimsy feet of my plastic chair across the tiles, all of my week in Paris spent day after day in this ugly hole waiting, suddenly became worthwhile, like hot bread in the hands of a starving man. I dropped the paper and tore ravenously out the clattering glass door, Gini in hand, to intercept this desirous paramour before he could have his way with my mother.

"Hey!" I called, feigning enthusiasm, rushing up to Frank.

"Oh, hello." From him a flash of distress, with a smile propped up quickly in its wake. "What a great surprise."

"Waiting for someone?" I managed to say, not coy at all, as I sipped the Gini.

"I'm not sure. I mean, I have no appointment with anyone, if that's what you ask. I'm awfully glad to see you."

Uh-huh. "Yeah, what a coincidence."

"Not so much of one, really, I know this is your hotel." Horribly, I thought he might try to confide their rendezvous to me, the man-to-man ploy, demanding my confederacy, and I forestalled him with a quick invitation.

"Come up to my room, Frank. I mean, you haven't seen it yet, have you?" If I could get him there for long enough, Louise wouldn't find him and would leave.

"If you want to," he answered ambiguously. I was silent, petulant, and impatient to get us out of there.

"Whatever," I said, hurrying into the lobby, drawing him along with my sheer momentum. "Come on." Frank looked around anxiously, a last scan for dear late Louise; then he followed me inside.

The charm came back on. Frank smiled now, positively aglow once we got in the elevator. He really could turn it on, and I supposed he was revving the engines to get this whole distraction up and running quick enough to catch his date, but as it turned out that wasn't the case at all. Frank put his hand on my shoulder as I jiggled the key, and when we pushed through the door he slammed it closed behind us and pinned me to the wall of the tiny room. He pulled the buttons of my shirt undone one by one while kissing me flat on the mouth. His tongue found my lips, parted in complete surprise, before pushing past them. My mind fled while my body went straight toward Frank. I pressed myself against him and my erection pushed at the metal buttons of my jeans. Frank pried them undone and pulled my pants down my legs while pushing me onto the bed. Was I beautiful? What boy is not beautiful? He dragged my underpants off, a dirty frayed pair, grabbing and tugging so I got burns along my hips, and then he fell on me. I felt the day come rushing down through the top of my head, raging along my spine, and then, after a span in which he bit me and pinched my nipples until they were sore and raw, it all burst out my middle and into his mouth. And then I slapped him, hard across the face, which amazed and delighted me. I don't know if or when Louise returned, I don't think she did until after dinner, but Frank and I had sex every day for the next three days, and then I left Paris. Sex was terrific, but Frank never acted very affectionate before or after it, and that was fine. It meant I didn't fall in love at all. After we left I hardly thought about him, except when I jerked off and would replay the scene in the hotel room. I still do. It's one of my favorite scenes.

As I say, the Thirteenth District was nothing like that gaudy area of Paris where so much had happened to me, and as I walked through it to the Butte aux Cailles I saw only locals, Arabs, and Asians among the European French, shopping and drifting through their day-to-day pleasures and chores. It was spring, really and finally, I thought, with mild air and so much fragrance from the trees and turned dirt, the car exhaust faded for whole blocks behind the day's fresh breeze. The street rose toward the Place Verlaine. A flock of screaming back-satcheled kids flooded the sidewalk in their haste past me, and beyond them a steamy-glassed brick building held the *piscine*. No artesian well or *buvettes* in sight, just the clank and suck of metal drains, pleasant repetition of laps, wavelets splashing, minor adjustments of steamed goggles, the hothouse air. I felt like a great and weeping orchid going in and a flat drained field coming back out again. I swam until exhausted, showered, dressed, then drifted home along the boulevards. A paper schedule, gratis from the pinched concierge, told me that evening at the pool would be an *ouverture spéciale* featuring reduced admission for teens and sporting play with hoops and balls. Voilà! The boy and I could return for a night of wet fun together. I praised this kind universe that turned its wheels so. And oh, the air felt lovely as the clocks tolled four above the great city. I unlocked the garden door and hurried in to be sure I had not missed the boy's arrival.

No one home. Sweet birdsong from the garden and courtyard, starlings. The mail had arrived and with it a postcard from California: two hideously oversized artichokes whose color was off. *Dear Herbert!* (What a coincidence.) *Thinking of you gallivanting all over gai Paris. Jimmy and I are exhausted: the sun, the hills, the pool. No sign of Tristan, alas. Looking forward to seeing you here, you bon vivant!*

Where was that boy? We'd have to stop at the GoSport! for a proper *cache-sexe* (the sort required by the Minister of Bathing, or whomever). Perhaps we'd get a bite along the way. (Why bother Serge with early meal plans?) Arriving for the 8 P.M. pool playtime seemed easy enough, and, prone athwart the cushions, I anticipated the fun. God, he would be so interesting; that is, interested in the sight of me. Clatter, slam! It was the boy, *click-click-click-clicking* his bicycle along the hall, and I rose from bed, eager to announce my grand plan before his usual exodus to basketball. The telephone rang, loud and final as a school bell. I ignored it, but the boy did not, and in a flash he yelled my name, singsong, down the landing: "Herbert," all *air* and *baihhrr,* with that soft guttural ending I loved so much.

"Got it." I picked up. "Hello?"

"*Allô,* Herbert?" French.

"*Oui, c'est* Herbert."

"Ah, it is Denis, I am happy to hear you again after our wonderful night." The boy could be heard, scuttling his drawers.

"Yes, Denis, a marvelous evening."

"I have done so much today, chasing the Steins for you, I have wanted—"

"I'm sorry Denis, just a second." The house had gone silent, like an empty fridge, so I listened more closely, trolling the air for any clues to his movement. "Water boiling. I just had to take it off the burner."

"Of course, it is your teatime."

"More like cocktails."

"Yes, I am thinking exactly this, if you please. You will be interested with the action on the Steins I have taken today." Probably the boy was in his bathroom, having a quick scrub before setting off to sport. Nothing was very clear anymore, and an annoying car horn honking outside made it worse. These rhythmic tuneless blats echoed in the telephone, all doubled up and tinny. "Excuse me, Herbert, I am just saying hello."

"Yes, Denis, and I am saying hello back." A shout sounded from the upstairs window, the boy, disturbed by the car horn, no doubt.

"No, no, to someone else. I would enjoy this cocktail with you now."

"That's thrilling, Denis, we must make a plan for sometime soon." The phone was wired on a three-foot cord to the wall by the bed, so that I was like a watery-eyed mole trapped inside its cave, pressed into a corner, blind and listening: a soft rumble, like a boy's heavy tread on the stair steps, sounded, and then the telltale *click-click*, severed from its familiar series by Denis's voice.

"A very good time is right now, if you are free."

"I—ouch."

"Are you hurt, Herbert?"

"I'm sorry, Denis, this cord; it's the boy, you see."

"He is startling, isn't he? In two years a Casanova, you will see."

"Yes, of course, but I mean that right now I am supposed to be seeing him off to his sports."

"Yes, yes, I am saying good-bye to him right now." Outside, the awful car honks again, sporty and shrill. "*Bonne chance,* Stéphane, *bon courage!*" This rather forced bit of humor was shouted away from the receiver.

"That's very nice, Denis, but he is here, you see, and I must—uh, see to him, before he goes off to sport."

"Off he goes, and so strong for a boy who is yet so *maigre et souple. Vraiment beau.*"

"In addition to which I will be obliged to be home when he returns, so that this instant when he goes is my only free time, and I know you couldn't possibly get here from the carnival, Carnavalet, but if you have tomorrow free?"

"But Herbert, I am now here, right now as I say."

"Here in the house?"

"I am outside in the car. The boy, I see him, very fast on the bicycle—oh, now disappeared at the corner."

"Have you been honking?"

"What is 'honking'?"

"The boy is gone?"

"Not far, but I no longer see him because of the road turning. I will drive us to catch him and then we have cocktails."

"*Eh bien.*"

Denis, grinning, scarf aflutter in the wind, piloted his little Golf like a jet ski through a crowded summer wading pool. He cleared our path with serial blasts from the awful horn, swept around the bend, and gained rapidly on the racing boy, who tried increasing his speed for the sport of it when he saw us.

"*Quelle vitesse!*" he shouted, heaving for breath as we all slowed, pulling close to the curb.

"Forty-five," Denis reported. "*Pas mal.*" Sweat dripped from the round of the boy's jaw, making a delicate line down his throat. The artery there was pulsing rapidly, flat and exposed, and I watched him swallow, then spit.

"Cool." He said it like a French word with an exhalation at its end. "I'm sorry, but I must hurry where I go." Still he fidgeted in place, leaning against my door. "My best on the track is sixty, but the real street is more difficult."

"Cool. Tonight you go to the swimming pool with me."

"We hurry too," Denis announced, revving the motor.

"Tonight? The swimming pools are not open in the night." I produced the blue info sheet and pointed to the *ouverture spéciale*. This was met by a grim puckered *pfft*. Evidently, not cool. "I must ask my father."

"Eight P.M.," I barked to Stéphane, as my willful driver, already bored by the exchange, began to pull away from the curb. "And we must get a bathing suit, the small kind they require." The boy stayed put, astride his still bicycle, and stuffed the blue sheet in his pocket, then waved and rode off to his sports.

The car seat hummed with our acceleration, and I settled back into it. "We're certainly in a hurry."

"I don't enjoy this street," Denis shouted amiably, above the increasing wind. "We go to a very nice bar. I know you will like it." He pressed a tape into the glowing mouth of his car stereo, and great twin thumping bass lines, entwined like dancers, came booming from behind us. Denis showed terrific skill anticipating "hazards" (including all traffic lights; veering sharply away from one red, he explained, "There is a hazard, I will detour"). He kept us on a continuous unraveling path across a great expanse of the city. I'm not very good with directions, but we crossed the river three times, pursuing the driver's pleasure, which was not economy but speed and motion, and ended up on the right bank. The streets were extremely narrow here. Many a fur or leather, with dog, strolled past. Denis maneuvered the car at a stylish crawl, then swooned with joy (honestly, tears welled up) when a car the exact image of ours pulled away from the curb in front of us.

We parked, and Denis lifted the car's cloth top into place and locked it.

"What part of town are we in?"

"You will forgive me for being so boring, but it is the Marais, the Fourth, which you must already be tired of. There is a bar here I like." The Fourth. Where Herbert had forbade me to visit.

"Just don't introduce me to anyone."

"Of course, Herbert, we'll just 'window-shop,' I think is a right phrase."

"Mmm."

The bar was a café with stools around a high U-shaped counter filling its tiny front room. Tables in the back were full, and the few sidewalk chairs were too, but this counter was a perfect place to sit. The barman stood in the middle and talked to everyone, while outside the traffic drifted past. We snagged two stools, shook hands with the barman, and Denis ordered Armagnac.

"You don't really know my work, do you?" I asked, with the first sip. "I mean, that was just you being friendly the other night, wasn't it?" Denis smiled as he drank, probably glad to get this out of the way.

"I know enough, but of course I've never been to your museum."

"That's a great relief."

"It is in California?"

"North from there." Denis lit a cigarette, and I took one from him but simply let it burn as I held it. "Not to be a prig, but you should know that any flirting will be hopeless. I'm practically married back home."

"I will enjoy it without hope." Denis smiled. "Who is your companion?"

"A Turk; he plays soccer and is really quite talented. I can't tell you his name because of the taboo in athletics, you know. He won't tell anyone, but we've been together—oh, it seems like forever—since he was fifteen actually."

"A 'long-time companion'?"

"Mmm." The smoke in this place was thick and pleasant, like local weather, a whole different season from the breezy spring that continued outdoors. It went well with the fiery Armagnac. The barman was so affable and attentive I thought everyone must treasure him, but Denis let on that he was considered to be an oaf and quite stupid. I suppose the language had dazzled me. A Frenchman in Shackles might think the portly assistant manager charming, unless he understood a little English.

"Do you live with him?"

"No, no, he wouldn't think of it. He has his make-believe girlfriends and all that. I am a secret pleasure. Are you dating?"

"Oh, everywhere." He finished his drink. The barman had set the bottle within reach, and Denis splashed some in our glasses.

"You have a boyfriend?"

"Many, many. When I want to meet a new man I go to the dance. Boy is very exciting, and Le Palace. It's very easy in Paris to find the kind you want, if you know which place has him. Almost like New York. I will take you for the dancing on Sunday."

"What a treat. Really?"

Herbert had taken me to a dozen gay bars back home, disastrous little trips chasing after men he'd met and then chitchatted to the verge of exhaustion, trying to discover their haunts. These men never ever seemed to be in the places they named. No matter, there were always other men, all of them "hideous," and Herbert always swore we'd never do this again. The resolution usually stuck for a few weeks, and then he'd meet someone else. Typically, these bars stank of beer and floor cleanser and were nearly empty at nine or ten when we arrived. I don't know why conservative, drunk ex-husbands in tract houses watching TV news exposés are so easily convinced the gay demimonde is sex-saturated and glamorous. In fact it is just as tacky and crass as the worst G. I. Shenanigans bar in the most sexless highway strip mall of the most forlorn suburban development where *they* go, and if the terrific gains of gay liberation continue apace we'll soon be joining these straight potbellied swingles on the margins of those twelve–lane highways that seem to go on forever and ever into a false dusk of sodium-vapor lights and revolving billboards, that permanent orange glow of America's well-armed nighttime, with its televised cops coursing across their grid of streets blurring the videotaped faces of prostitutes and kids who get stuck out there with straight men wanting dates, all of them clueless about love except for their conviction that it's magical and someone else has it. Gay men have got exactly the same bars, except ours are in enviable high-rent districts of the city, where you can actually see the guy who pulls a gun on you rather than being picked off by the high-powered rifle of a night-goggled sniper. As the Enlightenment proceeds, however, to its final and totalizing end, the bright light of sexual liberation will shine out of the cities to reach the towns and sprawl, and everything will shift so that perversity will be allowed to thrive in that purgatory too, where we can join our brothers, the drunk ex-husbands, at R. U. O'Bliterated Ale House, BlandeWoode Towne Centre branch, 250550 Blande Parkway (old Highway 3). In the meantime, we can drink and get sick at the gay bar downtown.

"Thank you Denis, you're too kind."

"I enjoy it." Denis caught the eye of a man directly across from us and got up, excusing himself to the toilet. He stopped beside this man, kissed, and they walked through to the back together. I took some olives from a shallow bowl placed near the drink and asked the barman for some bread. The café was packed, with many more standing around the tiny bar than there were sitting on the stools. Men and women, mostly young, bombastic, and wildly various in their styles, created such a noise and cloud of smoke I easily forgot that it was only seven or so and the sky still light out. Denis returned with his new friend, who wedged in beside us with a dirty glass he poured full of Armagnac.

"George Humphry," Denis began, "Herbert Widener, the American curator I spoke of to you."

I shook hands with this pleasant-enough, very drunk man and leaned close to Denis's ear. "Denis, I really must insist that you do *not* introduce me to anyone else. This is a matter of some importance to me." I whispered it clearly and with some force, and, as Denis pulled away, he tilted his head, rather impressed.

"Well, of course I will comply with this, Herbert." He was contrite. "But this man you will have to meet in any case for the work you have proposed; I've already told him about you." Now his smile grew at the rim of his glass while he sipped, staring at me. He clapped George on one unsteady shoulder. "Herbert is concerned that we do not reveal his identity, George, so you will please say to no one that he is Herbert."

"I'm having trouble remembering *who* the fuck he is, Denny." George was British.

"Don't remind him," I whispered.

"Have we met?" George tried being civil. "Were you with Denny at that shithole? What was that bar, Denny, the Piano Zinc?"

"You met at a piano bar?" Denis scooted closer to me, paying little attention now to George.

"The Piano Zinc is a very nice bar near here, Herbert. Late at night it is very crowded. I met George there a few nights ago, and then again after I had been with you at Serge's."

"After our dinner?"

"The Piano Zinc only becomes lively around one or two. In any case, I was very restless so I could not sleep well. George looked very hot in these leather pants that he is not wearing now; and of course the light is terrible there." George was now enjoying his drink as he looked around the room.

"How romantic."

"Yes, it was. The night was so beautiful. It was very late and the air was magnificent, ice cold. And you know he is a good fuck." Denis excused himself to use the telephone. I smiled at George, who raised his glass warmly. We neither spoke nor made eye contact while Denis was away.

"Business or pleasure?" I asked when he returned.

"Business—your business, in fact." Denis looked at his watch. "Are you hungry, Herbert? I know a magnificent café near here. I'm sure I can get us a table."

"What time is it?"

"It is half-past seven. If you are not hungry we can simply stay here for a while, but the food is very poor here."

"I told Stéphane to be ready at eight, and I'm sure it'll take us at least a half hour to get back there."

Denis smiled and squeezed my arm gently. "Herbert, the boy won't be going to the children's playtime at the pool; he is not interested in that."

"It is the children's playtime?"

"'I must ask my father' is the way Stéphane has of saying he is not interested in a thing. I've heard it very many times. This water playtime is not 'cool' with the teenagers because they have loved it so much only a few years before. It embarrasses them to be seen enjoying it still." Denis's point made sense, but in its clear, simple light a creeping new worry grew: Stéphane would sit at home, judging my absence as harshly as he had judged the despicable "playtime." I would become, in the boy's eyes, both stupid *and* unreliable.

"I should phone, at least." I patted my pockets for coins.

Denis pointed me toward the rear of the café and offered a battered metal slug required for the pay phone's operation. "And then shall we have dinner?"

"Yes. Yes, of course."

No one answered (thirty-five rings), and I took all my anxieties with me to the restaurant, which was, indeed, a very nice place, tucked into the passageway of an old arcade that took up a great block of land in the middle of the densely built Marais. Clay elements wired into the stone pavings gave heat to the courtyard and we dined out there, under the clear night sky—all three of us. George, a little sobered by the air, became quite chatty. His French was impeccable, and the fact that we'd brought a "good fuck" meant the last spot on Denis's implacable dance card was filled. George occupied a vacancy that otherwise might have loomed over me all evening like some kind of black hole, a motive force I would imagine shadowing Denis's every kindness. In fact, Denis was simply kind and enjoyed flirting without hope or purpose, as he had promised. George got bathed in a steady, serious gaze, while ornate compliments, warmly held glances, and light massagings of the arm came drifting my way like stray droplets, the pleasant mist nearby plants receive while the gardener is busy overwatering the huge root he means to pluck and devour.

It is redundant to tell you how drunk I was (it can be presumed throughout the rest of the evening). Magnified by the warm Armagnac, thirty-five hollow, unanswered rings echoed and rolled dolefully in the great bath of my consciousness, a toll of sad afflictions. Denis and George bantered the sommelier about like a mouse before settling on a Côtes-du-Rhône that he promised would support everything from tongue to pork medaillons. I just sat and watched, not because I was ignorant (though I was) but brooding felt good, like repose to a wounded priest, a Franciscan, for example, shot by thugs while interceding in a crime against children. It drew me into its sweet gravity like a nap.

"Herbert is frequently in New York," Denis told George, trying to engage me in their mirth. "He does not like Hellfire and will not tell me the secret clubs he goes to." I smiled, wan, still expiring from my wounds.

"Christ, Denny, that Hellfire is an awful place, a wet wick for disease. You might as well fuck your way through a morgue."

"You enjoy the bright light for sex, I remember this."

"I like to see a man's face."

"I think Herbert also prefers the more social clubs?" It was a question. I shrugged, still resisting. "And conversation." Denis was being so sweet to me, I'd have to be an awful heel to ruin the meal brooding.

"Mmm. I do prefer social activities, and a younger crowd." A tendril of cold snuck down from the black evening, embracing me; then it shifted away.

"Oh?"

"Yes." Denis raised his eyebrows and smiled. Something about him was so encouraging. "Much younger. Like junior-high school. I'd prefer a junior-high pool party to the Hellfire any day." This admission, even after many years of giving it, raised a shiver in me.

"That's O-levels, isn't it?" George looked a little troubled by the thought of O-levels.

"Mmm."

"Oh, yes." Denis brimmed with insight. "I am understanding now your mood of this evening. You mean the boys of Stéphane's age."

"Mmm-hmm, exactly his age." Denis's curiosity was a tonic, and in bright contrast to the pinched and puzzled frown of George.

"And in America, your Turkish soccer player, he is maybe not much more than the fifteen of when you began to love him?"

"That's right, not much at all."

"Oh"—Denis, now stricken with concern—"what a torture the home of Serge and Miriam must be to you then, with the boy so close and your marriage which you explained to the Turkish lover." He held my hand.

"You're fucking a fifteen-year-old?" George asked bluntly.

"You're such a jealous man, George." Denis laughed. "I see you're mad that here is someone who has sex without you." He touched both of us on our arms with his great, well-manicured hands, so that his rather cutting accusation came across as pleasant chitchat.

"Actually, he's fucking me," I answered. Then I hid behind my drink, savoring a few clean swallows. I was certainly making a fine show on Herbert's behalf, ambassador to the world of European art museums.

"Yes, yes," Denis added. "I have understood from another friend that it is typical for the boy to fuck and not, as in the North African countries, for the man to fuck him. But, Herbert, can a boy really be very skilled at this in any way? What is the pleasure in this for you? Is it as a teacher of the boy?"

"These Picasso drawings are very interesting," George interrupted, silencing us. The wine arrived, to George's grim satisfaction, and we toasted my visit. The wine was peculiar, like seawater and blood, but I liked it more and more as the evening went on.

"The nude boy," Denis observed, of the Picassos. "There is so much about you that intrigues me, Herbert."

"Right, right, Denny, but these drawings won't be erotic in the least," George corrected. "I suppose the *Boy Leading a Horse* could be seen that way, the surfaces are so perfect and nuanced, but these sketches could not be very distinguished in any way, or else they would never have disappeared."

"Do you like the smaller cock?" Denis asked, still pursuing his subject. "I mean, that is an advantage of the boys that would distinguish them."

George silenced him with a loud phlegmy cough, then leaned in and caught Denis's eye. The cough became a question demanding some response.

"I think you are right, George." Cordial Denis. "Nothing of Picasso's that was at all finished or very accomplished in any way would have disappeared from us for this long."

"That's right, but I'm still intrigued by this little constellation that could be built linking the Stein nephew to the *Boy Leading a Horse*. You know the gouache at the Hermitage? A Picasso from the same time as the Allan Stein portrait?"

"Actually, Denis, a boy's cock can be quite enormous. You'd be surprised."

Kind Denis smiled, then turned to answer George. "Yes, in fact I've seen this at the Hermitage and the material is horrible, like pieces of garbage."

"It's a nude boy, and interestingly enough it's exactly the same pallet and materials as the Stein portrait. It could be from the same sitting. I'm sure Picasso smelled money from the Steins and agreed to the portrait, then scraped whatever he could find off the floor of the studio—he was dirt poor then, they all were—cheap old gouache and cardboard he'd probably been standing on for a year."

"Is it falling apart?"

"Oh, they both are, though I think the portrait is being taken care of. This nude is in awful shape."

"Mmm."

The *découpeur* arrived at our table with the roast bird, severing its meat from the nest of bones with the rapid application of his knives. He did not pause, so the serial slashes became a single extended gesture, like a *plier*, performed on the bird, which wilted when the knives withdrew. The waiter placed it on Denis's plate. I had the pork medaillons and George the cold sliced tongue.

"These missing drawings look like a good bit of fun." George slipped a nib of tongue into his mouth with some wine and swallowed it all at once. "Denny said there's a bill of lading that describes them as studies for Allan's portrait."

"That's right. I can get you a copy."

"So then, why do you think they're nude studies?" I had no idea. Why *did* Herbert say these might be nude studies?

"I think it is Herbert's wish, George." A smile with a great draught of wine; then Denis turned to me. "Is Allan Stein erotic for you, Herbert, I mean in the way a boy like Stéphane or your Turk can be?"

"Got to use the loo," George offered. Leaving must have become attractive for a number of reasons. Denis smiled, watching him go, then grasped my hand where it lay by the wine bottle. He squeezed my fingers complicitly. "I am wondering if the dead boy is interesting to you like the living one who might talk and be touched."

"Why?"

"For example, if you think of him in that moment, standing nude, watched by the painter."

I poured some wine. "Denis, I can't help but wonder what it is you're after." He shrugged, then shrugged again. "I do have a kind of longing."

"It is erotic?"

"Allan is erotic, but there's no scenario involved. There's no sex."

"What happens?"

"He's just standing very near and he's silent, staring at me—like in a photo, actually. The proximity is all that 'happens,' so I could touch him, though I never do. He's always poised there, but then nothing . . . proceeds." Part of Allan's appeal was his complete indifference to me. I liked the way he stared and stared, neither resisting nor responding to anything. In this way the dead are doubly fascinating. While the capture of them is impossible, they are also unable to defend themselves against our efforts to try, which means the delight of the struggle will go on forever, if that's what one wants. The fantasies I have pursued with the dead are inviolable; they can neither be realized nor resisted.

Denis leaned closer. "I have this too, with my father, a photo of him that I look at. He's standing, staring, but he can't move. His distance is permanent, 'poised,' as you say." I picked food absently from my plate and listened. Something like this was the case with Louise; I mean, even when she was with me, there was an impossible intimacy she promised that I could never have, and this fact presented itself over and over in the incompleteness of holding her, like trying to hold a torn-open body closed. "When the boy's cock is in you," Denis asked, "have you cried?"

The atmosphere was so unstable, the night air—that is, the cold which had pushed down from the sky (perhaps the heating elements in the stone were turned off)—that I shivered and pressed my legs together. A chill rose up my back and drew my eyes to the stars, like certain painted saints who gaze upward. This circumstance made tears in my eyes, and that answer was all Denis needed.

He squeezed my hand and laughed, recognition, not derision, and I laughed too, but the cold air had gotten in me and the laugh felt like wind from the river, which had laved between buildings and naves, cradling the grotesque statuary, the gargoyles, and, spreading wide above the roofs, come to us in small downward gusts that blew through me and then whispered away into our silence. It's odd, describing this exchange, for the more meaningful it became, the less there was Denis and I had to say, and the less we spoke the more powerfully the night ruptured, so that the billowing places where, for example, Allan or Stéphane came rushing in—that is, the idea of Allan or Stéphane (for they dwelt equally in these uncharted interstices between the pleasantries of conversation, those silences and sighs where crushed thoughts could breathe and become huge)—these opened up, and we had only to be still and courteous to allow them to inhabit us or be inhabited. This is not a critique of language. I could have recorded every idea that was said or implied. It is a critique of "normal conversation," that pinched and narrow grid in which we take refuge every day. George desired it, "a decent conversation," as a barrier to our monstrous desires and all the deranged echoes their articulation might bring. What a gift, by contrast, to find Denis, whose appetite for this peculiar vertigo was generous and keen.

George returned and what was there to say? We laughed, which he took as a private joke, and now, as the evening ended, he sulked and I was at ease. Denis produced a fat cigar. We had had our way with the food, and now the sweet and bitter froth of a rich mousse was all that was left congealing on our plates. Amidst empty porcelain cups, laced with the tan filigree of dried espresso foam, and three snifters of *prune*, Denis puffed great sickly clouds of smoke into the air. The widow's "secretary" (Denis's word) had left a garbled message with Denis's friend at the Musée Picasso. This was the phone call at the café. The Allan Stein drawings might be available, though the attendant wasn't at all sure which drawings these were. The widow was nevertheless interested in finding out more, and if the American, Monsieur Widener, wanted these mysteries, and they belonged to her, of course she would entertain any reasonable offers. How swift and clear and pleasing everything seemed to be just then, as, in the chilly black night, Allan Stein wavered and grew, emerging from the folds of someone else's history.

•10•

Allan Stein's family left Paris every summer, usually to go to Florence, where they shared their vacation with Gertrude and Alice. The summer of 1913 they were going to Agay, a small fishing village on the French Mediterranean, and Sylvia Salinger was going with them. Sylvia and her friend Harriet Levy had taken an apartment by the Jardin du Luxembourg, just one block from the Steins. Allan saw them three or four times in a week, but always in the midst of exams and papers, boxing and tennis—everything about Allan's life in Paris showed Sylvia that Allan was still a schoolboy. He did what he could, acting as Sylvia's tour guide, impressing her with his French and his riding, but next to her tea and shopping and concerts and shows, Allan's schoolboy concerns were a constant reminder of the gap that kept them in separate worlds. In Agay there would be no gap. Sylvia and Allan became part of "the group," a self-absorbed crowd of young Americans, four women and Allan (with Mike and Sarah Stein to take care of them). That summer at the Hôtel d'Agay was like an episode from the pages of some early Henry James novel. Sylvia recorded it in her letters:

"The trip down was delightful—we felt like regular Cook's tours—Mr. Stein kept the tickets, reserved the rooms at Marseilles, where we stayed overnight—did all the tipping—just everything—

that's what I call traveling! And he is so nice to everybody that they do anything for him. Even the conductor on the train helped with the luggage when we changed at St.-Raphaël. We got into Marseilles too late to see anything there, so we are going to stop over on our way back, for a couple of days.

"The Mediterranean is blue—just like it tells about in all the books—we go in swimming every morning about ten, and spend the rest of the time up till lunch swimming and drying in the sun. I have arms that are as red as coals, and I tried awful hard to be careful. The water is the kind that is so salty it just holds you up whether you want to stay up or not. You can float for hours, I am sure. The whole place is wonderfully like Carmel, only so much nicer. The food is wonderful—everything so well cooked—and all fresh—vegetables, fruit of all sorts—such peaches—fish—everything raised right here.

"The climate is perfect—just warm enough, and not too warm! The rocks are all kinds of red and beautiful, and most important of all, we eat on the verandah over-looking the sea. When we take walks in the woods we get the most delicious odors imaginable—all kinds of wonderful smelly flowers and pine trees and things. And yesterday I heard my first nightingale—the woods are full of them, and how they sing! I don't remember of ever having had such a feeling of perfect calm as you get here—there isn't one thing to complain of, not one. We have a little store just across the road, where we can buy all the regular country things, the maids are all pretty and sweet—everything is spick-span clean, and all the washing is done by the Italian women, in a river about a block from the hotel. I am trying to tell you all the details, but they seem to be slipping away."

In Agay, Allan bloomed. Photos show him content, sprawled on the lawn, surrounded by the four women of "the group." They depended on him for his French, his muscle, his constant joy and initiative, while Allan thrived on pampering them. He organized day hikes, bicycle tours, tennis tournaments on the one weed-infested court, taught them to swim, and tutored them on the peculiarities of the food and drink. There is little romance in Sylvia's letters home, despite the fact that Allan had fallen completely in love with her.

Sylvia was a good sport all summer, taking pride in a kind of tomboy fortitude Allan demanded and the other girls could not muster. When they toured she rode her bicycle with Allan and Mike, while the other girls took a carriage. On hikes, she walked the extra miles with Allan to fetch wine and food from the nearest village. She was physical and brash in a very American way, and she was becoming cosmopolitan:

"We have discovered something new about making our bathing comfortable. I have a big heavy bathrobe which I put over me, after taking off my wet suit, and sit in the sun. It feels so good, all the difference in the world; then we don't have to bring our wet suits up into our rooms at all. We just take them off down at the bathhouse and hang them on the line."

Notably, Allan never took time to write that summer. The letters he had habitually sent to Gertrude whenever his family took him away stopped in Agay. The earnest little boy who'd written long letters to his dearest Auntie Gertrude, bragging of his prowess as a reader and a boxer and a sportsman, had no time for that now. His life had begun to become his own. The formation of his pleasures, his satisfactions, became private and autonomous, unavailable to the adults who had treasured him.

His perfect summer went on and on, drifting toward its end.

In the early morning the boy stood in the garden again, shirtless, shoeless, his attention drifting from the warm blossoms to his small yellow pad of paper. He wore the torn khaki shorts. The wooden toilet seat was cool and smooth against my knees, and I rested my elbows on the dusty windowsill, staring out at him. Was it homework? He was making lists, that much I could see, but what he saw or listed was swallowed in the clear morning air. Maybe it was flowers, or feelings for some awful creative writing class. (No, that would be an American affliction.) No one else was awake at that hour when he emerged, and I wouldn't have been either, except the soft shifting stairs he crept down past my door squealed, so that I woke these mornings to pee when he woke.

Sleepy, wearing just boxers, I ambled toward the door. The boy turned in the sun and smiled at me. Deep pleasure, the sunshine on my body warm so my nipples lay soft and flat, armpits a little dank with sweat, knees weak. I smiled too and was quiet, shuffling barefoot along the short stone path to stand by him. Really I wanted nothing more than this just now. The intensity of my pleasure was so great it required this silence, this spaciousness of intent, to even be bearable at all. His pad had names of birds, and we listened for a while without speaking. We heard a call so that he wrote another name down. We watched the trees of the park shift in the slight breeze beyond the garden's brick wall. The shadow by the wall was damp and cool, so the turned earth there gave out an odor that twined about the garden path, vaporous, and lifted to our nostrils with the warmth of the morning.

"The birds," he whispered. "I list them." He lifted the pad and smiled, and I said nothing but touched the pad with my hand, and then his shoulder, where I left my hand cupping the round of his muscle in my palm.

It wasn't long, two days, before a letter from Allan's son dropped through the slot with the junk by the toilet. It was addressed to me. I mean to say it was not addressed to Herbert Widener, as it should have been, but to me, using my real name, so suddenly I knew that in a flash of sloth and carelessness I had signed my given name to the initial letter. Allan's son wrote to me to say:

"Thank you for your letter relating to your current research about Allan Stein.

"My father died when I was barely twelve. He had been ill, and our relationship had been—to use a euphemism—very limited and infinitely remote from the Steins' artistic and literary splendor I have only heard of in books.

"I have no document about my father beside some correspondence relating to his service in the U.S. Army during World War I. If you are interested, I'll try to find it and mail a copy to you.

"I regret admitting there is absolutely nothing else I can contribute to your investigations.

"I believe, however, my half-brother Daniel may have some pertinent items or recollections.

"Sorry to be of no help. I am sure I have everything to learn from your publication.

"Best wishes for the completion of your work."

The letter was bleak and discouraging. It read like a bloodstain showing the last known location of the missing body. Had Allan disappeared so completely? The sad trajectory of his life from a charmed boyhood into grim dissolution—an adulthood his family despised and turned their eyes from—became disturbingly complete. If his own son could tell me nothing, what trace could there be? I wrote a second letter, asking again for anything, and signed my given name, a little nervously.

I have said I tend to become what others think I am, I gravitate toward their vision of me, and this happened again in the stalled languor of the days after dining with Denis and George. Denis's questions about my "love" for Allan Stein had resonated, growing louder and louder, like a great struck bell that sets the rest of the carillon to ringing in its particular tone. His interrogation gave shape to a set of desires that had been, until then, somewhat haphazard. I don't mean that love or erotics had never been at issue with Allan. I mean that when Denis asked was Allan erotic to me, the neatness of the question resolved every aspect of my interest into this thrilling and singular tone. It set an eroticism (nascent in every aspect of my pursuit of Allan) humming. This wasn't new per se, obviously Allan had aroused me, but now it became powerful.

Equally, the name Herbert was beginning to sink in, like a garment I'd worn so long it had shaped me. "Herbert" was a mask that trapped me at the same time as it made me visible, so that I felt a little like the bubble boy (my first boyhood crush), who could only interact with others from behind the complete shield of his enclosure. "Herbert" was the shield that let me get near the boy, where I wanted to be. Every flasher needs a trench coat, and mine was "Herbert." When I was fourteen, I would sometimes get out of bed at night, very late, and sneak through the apartment tugging on my dick, arriving at the open door to Louise's bedroom, where I trembled in the doorway, naked and pulling on my dick, banging the carpet softly with my foot, wondering what would be enough to wake her. I was a kept bird in a cage of hallways and bedrooms, my heart racing like a sparrow. I'd keep pulling and pounding, a little harder with each beat until the instant when the nightstand light came on and bathed me for a single pulse, and I ran, naked and almost coming, to my bed to hide. I flourished in the moment of her regard. And I think it is the same for Allan, as it is for me, or for Stéphane. It is the fate equally of the boy, the character, and the dead to blossom in the instant of our apprehension, in the moment of being seen, and in the next instant to disappear. Pinned to this flickering edge where there is the possibility neither of merging nor of giving up, we are all unreachable. Allan, dead, begs to be watched. He stands just out of reach, frozen at the entrance to the bedroom, unwilling to run until we wake and see him. The house is not his. Art or death trapped him here in a foreign architecture that has fashioned him one position: poised. He can neither disappear nor ever step forward to join us.

•11•

Miriam and I went shopping in the district east of here, on a morning when the sun was still pleasant, ruling brightly in a violent sky of wild gusts and great towering white clouds. It seemed unlikely that now, more than a week into my masquerade, any of them could believe I was a scholar or curator at all. No one cared that I made no progress with the Steins, nor that my methods were so lame and haphazard. Not that it was any of their business, but we had taken an interest in each other's business from the first. I suppose Denis let them believe it was his doing; he was a very protective and giving helper.

Miriam brought canvas carrying bags, hung from the handlebars of our bikes, and I was happy to find she lounged on her bicycle, rather than racing like Stéphane. She had a marvelous dexterity and performed a near decathlon of unrelated tasks as we rode east along the rue Brillat-Savarin, toward "Chinatown." She might have been sitting in the living room rather than traffic, given the ease with which she changed batteries in her small camera, snapped a shot of me, then rolled a cigarette and smoked it, all the while pedaling and keeping up her end of the conversation.

"After the Germans starved the Dutch, you see," she went on, kissing her lips to the first cigarette at rue Kuss, "they took all the bicycles, I mean while in retreat. They'd been defeated by the Canadians, and in retreat they took the bicycles from us, and this is why we say, for example at a restaurant where a German is perhaps being rude, "*Godverdomme Duitser*, give me back my bicycle!"

"I didn't know that."

Miriam pointed to the left, where a narrow break between buildings opened onto a great common yard. Waist-high boys swarmed after a kicked ball, tumbling in bunches where scruffy grass broke through the paving. "Stéphane used to play here."

"When?" I brightened at the topic.

"A few years ago, when he was little, I mean as big as those kicking the ball there. He had friends here, from the school, and Per would bring him over in the afternoons to play." A man on a yellow moped cut in beside Miriam and pulled his helmet off, *putt-putting* along at bike speed. Gray smoke billowed from the tailpipe and filled the road's edge, rapid cars slipping past like fish, so that I was overcome with nostalgia, merely for an instant, for the buses back home and the winter air with its glorious cargo of fumes. I breathed it, deep and greedy, through both nostrils (a last farewell to Dogan), feeling hungry. I was always hungry, since arriving, and getting skinnier and skinnier, despite eating a great deal of everything I was served. Rich, exquisite meats and sauces, amalgams of diverse fats, really, melding threads of garlic and herbs and salt in their thickened splendors. I didn't feel sick at all, nor worried about the trim result of this lipidinous bacchanal. It happened whenever I traveled. Travel made the world erotic, and this increased libido raised my metabolism to adolescent heights so that I could devour everything—food, sleep, company—and burn it all so fast I became slimmer with each bonbon chewed and swallowed. Miriam wobbled along, rolling a cigarette for the boy on the moped. He caressed her arm in taking the cigarette, and she pushed him away, a farewell fuck-off gesture. The boy revved back into the rapid stream of cars and disappeared.

"Silly boy," she laughed. "They flirt with anything that breathes. I think it is all they know how to do."

"I noticed that. Everyone flirts here."

"Or else they find you useless. It's like the British being polite. They've been raised to do it, they have no choice." Miriam blushed, from self-consciousness or maybe the exertion. The gap between our bikes narrowed in the wake of the boy. Empathy pulled us together, and we rode side by side like drunks on a couch.

"Denis is an awful flirt."

"Oh, no, he's wonderful. I enjoy him very much."

"That's what I meant."

"Yes?"

"He's so warm and he enjoys it so much. I react to him like a flower to the sunshine."

"You like it, then?"

"Yes, of course, it makes him so happy." Which of us was speaking? It could have been either, but it was Miriam who praised Denis's attentions. He probably flirted with all of them, he was such an ardent practitioner.

"I enjoy it too." Our shoulders bumped lightly. "I was worried that he'd be frustrated if it came to nothing, but actually he seems to like it."

"Denis is very patient."

We had come to a fat boulevard crowded with people and slow cars. Tiny trucks, some on three wheels, were pulled onto the sidewalks, burdened with splintered crates, vegetables, and sacks of rice. We rolled across the big street to an ugly plaza full of people.

"My favorite grocery," Miriam said, handing a bag to me. "Tang Frères."

A knot of women filled the counter of a tented snack stand where *shu mai* steamed in faulty glass boxes. Three boys directed cars across the littered plaza to be parked in a cavern behind the store.

It stank of rotten meat and hot sesame oil where we stood, but then a breeze cleaned the air and the sun was warm.

"Denis tells me you will stay a few weeks longer to finish your project with the Steins."

A few weeks longer? "Mmm." My tenancy in this place had become so unstable. In the last few days I'd lost control over the shape and trajectory of it, so that the particulars of my time as Herbert were beginning to rupture and shift. We already know my mind gives in to suggestion.

"Did Denis say how long, exactly?"

"No. What should I tell the City University?"

"It's hard to say."

The store's cold interior was big as a warehouse, packed with carts and children, shelves, bins, stalls, and barrels of ash-covered eggs. Shoppers maneuvered past one another in their focused pursuits. Miriam led me into the flow of aisle one, and I pressed myself against her to stay close.

"There is a kind of bean I get for Stéphane's digestion," she explained over her shoulder. "A naturopath told me of it." Wet, aromatic bunched cilantro brushed my nose with the plastic-edged basket of a woman pushing past us. She used her burden as a wedge to pry a path to the canned bamboo shoots behind Miriam's long legs.

"Is his digestion a congenital problem?" Maybe a leaf or scrap got left on my nose, for I kept smelling the perfumy herb, together with a snapped root of ginger Miriam broke and held up to me before dropping it in her bag. Frilly blond cabbage, long mat beans, fuzzy to the touch, and a cucumber as veined and throttled as an old man's dick (sealed in plastic) got tossed in with the knobby ginger. We paused by the ash-blackened eggs.

"He's always been delicate in the stomach." The floor was sticky with spilled juice and my shoes tacked and snapped each time I lifted them, a light percussive rhythm to the vocal rumble around us—multilingual shoppers' babble plus the shouted broadcasts of fishmongers tossing great black eels and crab from tanks to the wrapping men, who bound them, still squirming, in paper at the cold back end of the store. A fur collar, ermine, and the shoulder that pushed it past my face bumped between us, and I lost Miriam, pressing my hands to this billowing new fur and the soft nap of cashmere in the coat beneath it. My hand brushed down the coat's great backside, found a tough button (gut braided to make a lozenge large enough to slip into the belt and fasten it), plus dental floss, a short string left clinging to the coat, but this woman would not move. Rounded flesh inside the coat, brightly lit dirt-specked beets in a great bin (viewed through the ermine), clouds of lavender perfume and a cigarette (clove, sickly sweet), my feet stuck in place, and now a man jammed up behind me (unseen but a man for certain), I watched Miriam turn left past a great mound of porcelain teapots stacked in straw. This man pressed, poking, so that I got pushed against the cashmere, all round and forgiving (but unbudgeable—she browsed through the eggs, shaking them, dusting her fingers off between tries), and impressed with the growing prod in the prow of the man's pants behind me, evidently his purpose although I could not, would not, turn to ask him. Traffic kept me pinioned. I smelled the eggs when she lifted them, musty, sour, like basement storage. To my right, bent rustlers rummaged through bottom bins of cellophaned ramen, crackling red, pink, blue, yellow, green (lime and forest), tan, brown, and beige-bordered boxy packets (marked for promised flavors), their hands flashing in and out of the metal-caged bins. This hidden man's fingers found my hips, firm, like a good handshake, and I got a hole punched in my look of concentration by the pressure he engineered with the twin hip holds. A whole lack of concentration, in this shifting drifting frozen in-store air, slight and heady puffs of clove smoke, widened my eyes beyond noodles, cabbage, dirt or eggs, beets, flack, floor gack, bulb roots, bin splints, dry-wrap fungus packs, green peas, cracker snacks, brine slime, fish powders, tiny paper clothing pin dolls, red and golden dragons, sleeve emblazoned, ruby candles (packs of forty), ginger candy, wrinkled tasty-wrapped rice paper; fancy fabric (cashmere) felt, my fingers fell on piled Pokey chocolate straw packets, feeling packet, packet, packet, and my butt got backed up, feeling prodding poker on me, some aroma from the fur, rain-fresh day, as if it had been winter out—last winter, hail blown down from the gray pigeon sky, trash carried up by the cold March wind—because this man kept pushing. I saw it all, every item in the list (but through the fur), and felt this grand expanding man, this catalogue he pressed on me, fecund and swollen, poking me like a noun, any number of nouns, all fattened so the room was full of them. He left me standing by the sugar beets.

Miss Cashmere placed an egg in her purse, napkin wrapped, then made her getaway into traffic. Mr. Prod was gone, unseen. I shifted my pants up a notch, stone-faced like the drunk who struggles dignified from the fountain, and smoothed my hips where he'd held them. Miriam's head was visible, ten yards away, above twin metal shelves of sake. The incident made me smug, knighted by the sword, so that I bumped my way through the crowd now with greater bravado, slipping my hips through gaps thin as paper and leading with my generous hands. It was remarkably easy to reach her this way.

I've been in love with women more often than men, I think because they're linked to boys in a way that men are not. Herbert complains that I'm not a true homosexual, as if my attractions were some kind of treason, and he's right, though I certainly don't think of myself as bisexual or anything ridiculous like that. Once he said that actually I was straight and a boy, to me, was just a woman with a dick. "You look at a boy and you see a woman with a dick," he complained one evening at home viewing slides. "And you think, Oh, heaven, a woman with a great big dick, the most perfect creature imaginable." Herbert annoys me because these flippant asides get stuck in my head as if they were correct somehow, which is what happened with this notion. He was wrong, of course, but the collapsed image engaged me against my will, I think because the truth was smashed in there somewhere. A woman with a dick scares me, but a woman with a son is magical. I have swooned for this pair often enough for Herbert's crass reduction to ring true. Not only is the great dick kept right there on center stage with the mom around to admire it, but the boy's usual disappearance into brutal, ugly manhood is halted by her too. With Mom holding on, he stays a boy. Their relationship is sufficient: She loves him, and he loves her loving him. I like to get involved in this sort of thing, loving him with her, or loving her for loving him, or loving him as her, or, most pleasing, loving him and having her love me *and* him as a kind of two-headed dick. Miriam was still Miriam, not simply the boy's mom, but there was the ghost of an echo of a thought lurking, an inkling or a memory.

"Do you know sake?" she asked, as if nothing had intervened between us, no man, no hip handling, no thoughts. "Serge will make a teriyaki with fish, and he has asked me to bring home sake." I smiled, nodding no, and scanned the crowded lines of bottles. Their labels were all in Japanese, except for the repeated word "sake."

"Buy the most expensive one. My friend Herbert does that."

"You have a friend named Herbert?" She asked it absentmindedly, still fingering the tall bottles.

"Yes, odd, isn't it?" I shrugged and took a sake from the shelf. "Not a close friend, really, but he buys expensive wines, in any case, when he doesn't know the labels."

"I suppose they *are* expensive for a reason."

"Mmm, exactly." We picked the second-highest priced, a great elegant two liters of clear rice wine, and put it in the bag with the boy's special beans. The broken ginger and a paper sleeve of Chinese five-spice were pungent in the bags, and I pinched a spray of green chives to get the sharp onion smell on my hands.

"The law clients think this way. The more they are charged the better they feel about the service."

"Is that typical of the French, do you think?"

"Nothing is typical of the French. Though I do remember Serge chose the most expensive teacher of tantra, by this same method as your friend Herbert with his wines."

"You take lessons?"

"We did, with this very expensive, brutal German."

"He must have been the toast of Paris."

"She. There's certainly a cult of excellence in Paris, of finding 'the best' and paying a lot for it, but in fact this woman's students were mostly foreigners."

"Mmm."

"Serge was the only Frenchman. I guess there aren't that many French interested in paying to learn sex. Except, of course, the schoolboys."

"There were schoolboys?"

The density of things relaxed and the air became spacious in this long receding wake of my encounter. Tins of green tea filled a shelf at our hips. My hand caused an avalanche of shrink-wrapped dry fish bumping a bin we passed, and Miriam laughed at the great stream of them sliding to the floor around us. The fish were skeletal or like leather, beige and crusty with salt or brine. "Migrating home to spawn." Miriam smiled at my joke and helped me pick the packets up. "Has Stéphane got a girlfriend?" I asked suddenly, breathlessly. A period of time elapsed, less than a second, in which my eyes moved, darting like caged birds back and forth in their prison.

"Stéphane? His guitar and his basketball I think are his lovers. He's very much a boy, you know, even as old as he is."

"Mmm."

"You're very silly."

"Yes."

"He's my boy."

"Yes."

We hung the bags on our bike handles. The plaza was packed with people and cars stuck in lines as if on a stage set waiting for scene two to commence. Sunburst, lights, cue wind and rain, blustery breeze, wet trash under tires, another cigarette; we rolled north along the Avenue de Choisy, east into a tangle of streets, and under a lofted metal trestle where the subway train rode, bright strung boxes of light in the washed-out sky. The rain was soft, as diffused and ubiquitous as the dull light from the sleek bodies of passing cars. Misty green heather bush, black iron fence, colorful garbage spilled into the street. The rain felt good on my face, bicycling home in the queer light.

"Herbert?"

"Who else would it be?"

"Are you drunk again?"

"Well, 'hello' to you too. What on earth is going on over there?"

"Hello. I mean, of course it's nice to hear from you."

"You're not sleeping with that boy, are you?"

"Wait."

"Wait? Wait what?"

"Everyone, I've got the phone," I called into the house. There was no answer. "I think it's okay."

"You're keeping secrets from them?"

"Of course I'm keeping secrets, my name to begin with, and no, I'm not sleeping with the boy. I have no interest in him."

"*Pfft.* That's an enormous lie. If you're not sleeping with him, why are you still over there?"

"I'm getting you the drawings; that's why I came in the first place."

"Forget the drawings. I don't even want them."

"I want them. And I'm on the verge of getting them, just a few more days."

"Come back tomorrow, come to Jimmy's. I'll pick you up at the airport."

"I can't come back tomorrow. I'd be lucky to get a flight, even in the next few days."

"I'm not asking you. I'm telling you I can't stay away longer. I've got to get back to the museum, and I can hardly return while they're still paying for me to stay in Paris."

"When do they expect you?"

"Monday."

"I'll leave on Saturday."

"One day at Jimmy's? That's ridiculous."

"I can't go sooner. I'll fly straight home and meet you there."

"Jimmy will probably never speak to you again."

"Tell him I'm sorry."

"I'm not speaking to you."

"Herbert."

"Tell him yourself."

Per was raking garden compost into the flower beds, wet and silent in his ragged shorts. Miriam was on the porch, and I went out and stood with her in the rain. It was nearly dark, the last light draining out the edge of the sky, that narrow westering edge, and we were quiet for a while, which was a pleasure to me. The silence left the air uncluttered so I could see farther beyond the dimming horizon, smelling the turned earth of the garden, while my mind stretched over the fat dusty hills where Jimmy and Herbert, doubtless, walked now with a straw basket, getting stoned so they weren't sure if they'd gone miles over several hours or just a few yards in the moment since leaving the door. I couldn't be there, and I couldn't be here entirely either, and so I went back inside.

Serge cleared the kitchen table and let me cover it with my work (Allan) while he pared artichokes by the stove. He had a whetstone in a cloth on the cutting board and kept sharpening the knife he used to pry the tops from the blossoms—*swack-swack-swack,* like a predictable sword fight, and then his contented humming, punctuated by the occasional thump of a severed stem falling from the artichoke when he cut it. Stéphane, bored by his homework (which turned into a nap at the desk, face pressed to the pages of *L'Idiot* that had put him to sleep), scooted onto the bench beside me and offered to help. A crease marked his flushed cheek.

"And how is *The Idiot*?"

The boy shrugged. "I help you." He pawed through the papers spread across the table, registering nothing.

"What can you do?" In the gray light by the living room window, Miriam arranged herself on the couch with a book. Serge smiled over his artichokes.

"I will make a time line." The boy sat with his leg against mine, and that was enough. It didn't matter what he did. Music billowed from below. Per played jazz records, which turned the evening's repose into a cool nightclub sexiness: Serge the proprietor, DJ Per, plus a smattering of guests (three) taking shelter from the rain.

"In Santos they use the severed paws of dogs as charms to bring luck," Miriam said from the couch. No one answered her. The boy's plastic tackle box of art supplies was fetched from the cupboard, and a swath of white paper got pinned to a board. Per bounded up the stairs and settled in the kitchen with Serge.

"*Artichauts fourrés.*"

"I will need the photos of Allan," the boy announced.

"Stuffed with what?"

"*Des noix, du beurre, et du foie gras.*"

"A light snack."

"The photos can't be glued or anything, I've only borrowed them."

The boy frowned at my objection. "I draw him from the photos."

"The paws got passed from father to son. I guess they were more valuable than houses." Theolonious Monk broke into dissonant bursts, fragments of the galaxy he'd been constructing, while Per danced his hands along the countertop. The pages I held were meaningless, billowy fields of text on which I couldn't focus. My gaze relaxed into a blur, so that I saw paragraph shapes and margins but no words. A raw green smell, the artichoke stems, cut through the old tobacco, and I smelled rain from the window.

"*Né en 1895?*"

"Mmm-hmm."

"His face is very ugly as a man."

Talk is screwy, like machine welds that tack a sheet of metal to a frame. Per and Serge drank *kir* in the kitchen, knee-to-knee on stools beside the stove. Serge peeled beets and smoked. Steam from the boiling kettle of artichokes threw up a scrim between us. Thelonious Monk kept me from hearing anything but their murmured laughter. The boy scrawled a great ugly brute on a horse in the box above 1914. I peered over his shoulder, letting my arm rest on his back, and admired the poor draftsmanship. "What dates have you marked?"

"The birthday, then Paris 1903, the painting of Picasso 1906 when he is a boy, the École Alsacienne beginning 1907, and then the World War in 1914, when he is still eighteen years old."

"What about his teenage years before the war?"

The boy frowned at me. "He was in school, you have said, which is very boring."

"You might include their trips to America and Italy." Stéphane glared at my suggestion. "In 1906 and 1910 he and his parents went to San Francisco. For six months after the great earthquake, and for almost a year in 1910." The boy wiped his nose again but made no note of what I'd said. "And they went to Italy every summer between these trips."

He raised his eyebrow at my trivia. "This is not important for a time line. I do not include vacations."

The artichokes, by the way, were delicious, plump and slightly braised on the outside, soft as butter in the middle, where Serge had stuffed them with walnuts and goose liver; the beets were exceptional, boiled and then caramelized (plus, also, the usual excellent wines), so that I got lost in the details again, especially the metal tang of the second wine, like running my tongue over a sheet of steel, and the sweet dissolution of burnt sugar in my mouth with the flesh of the ruddy beet, a great red doll's head, forked and maneuvered toward my teeth. The boy stared at me over the lip of his watered-down wine with no intent. I glared back, fixing my gaze on his collarbone, where the stretched neck of his oversized T-shirt left a glimpse of skin visible. It sometimes bored me, this constant awareness of the boy, his body, and the possibility of sex with him (a monotony equaled only by Stéphane's perpetual unawareness, his complete disregard for the scenarios tumbling in my head), but there we stared, I through him and he through me, while the conversation burbled on around us.

"Apparently, there are no birds."

"Now or ever?"

"Ever, at least that Lévi-Strauss noticed. I mean, that's not really forever, but there is no record of birds."

"Of course not, he had no interest in them."

"Listen."

We paused and watched Per listen—the hum of the refrigerator, sibilant traffic and rain, Miriam's indigestion, the cold dropping down from the clouds (so cold, frost had begun to frame the windowpanes). The sky streamed high above us, black or invisible, breaking up into daylight somewhere above the ocean, between here and Herbert and Jimmy and Dogan on the far edge of the next continent, where it was still morning, Dogan struggling from sleep, Herbert swimming laps in the pool. I listened, hearing them, and no one spoke at the table until the boy asked if we were done and could he leave.

The sky was so interesting then, in the days before Stéphane and I left Paris. It broadcast conflicting reports—one day a languid summer haze dispersed by a wall of freezing air, and the next angry winter storm clouds dissolving into a muggy, cloying afternoon. The city and its parks became leafy, billowing green even while morning frost clung to the windows. A lazy stroll in the warm sun of the Jardin turned bleak and forbidding upon crossing into the narrow treeless streets around it.

Sandblasting spread from the Parc Montsouris to the graffitied walls of the Cité Universitaire, where Stéphane led me through a labyrinth of fences and gates to an empty concrete basketball court perched beside a glade of chestnuts. I sat on a stone bench admiring the view while the boy trotted up and down the court, practicing his fast breaks. I did my part, watching. The boy seemed to glisten and swell, held in my sights. His skin was wet with sweat and his cheeks blushed red. Below the court and the trees a half-dozen women raced around an oval track in the cold sun, passing batons and clearing hurdles. The wind or air or distance made them inaudible, so the race became melancholy, like scarred footage of boats unloading soldiers from the Great War. Around and around and around as the sun disappeared into thick clouds and then trees and then the horizon.

It began to rain again. Stéphane continued, and we both became soaked. The women left when the rain broke, slowing down to a jog, hands on their wide hips as they gathered and stretched by the track before leaving. They were gone, everyone was gone, and finally the boy stopped, having reached a hundred.

"You don't need to stretch?" I had no idea. Stéphane ignored my sentence and led us through the gates. "I could massage you." Again, nothing. Car traffic was grim and slow, lurching along the wet boulevard, and we simply walked through it to the park. It was night. At the mouth of the metro, commuters filled the sidewalk.

The boy spoke. "Do you know *Nostalgie,* the film of Tarkovsky?" He stopped at the bright lit news kiosk to buy a comic book that I paid for.

"Is he French? I saw a movie called *Passion,* but that was in Japanese."

"You will see it with me, if you want." We joined the rope of commuters trailing into the park.

"Tonight?"

"This week after my school. Tonight I sleep."

"Right after dinner?"

"There is not dinner. No one is home."

In the dark house Stéphane hurdled upstairs to the shower. I laid my wet clothes on a rack in my room and stretched out in bed beside the drainpipe. The soapy water flowed on and on and on, warm and cascading over him, and I listened until it stopped; then I put my boxers on and lay back down.

I supposed he would sleep but he knocked on my door and I said come in. There he was, bundled in fresh cotton, a big white T-shirt, corduroy pants, and thick socks, wet hair brushed and tied back, plus a guitar in his big clean hands.

"I have learned the Pink Floyd."

"Sit here."

"It is very difficult."

"I'll listen." I lay back, drowsy, mostly naked, as he arranged himself on the bed by my feet. The curve of his back as he bent over the instrument, thinly clad in the white cotton shirt, was exact, religious, nearly Pythagorean.

"I play."

Stéphane played the Pink Floyd song. When he made a mistake he would stop and begin again. I moved my leg so it pressed against his hip. The pressure there and the movement of muscles in his hip made a sweet sensation in me. My heart began to race, and I breathed more deeply, like a dreaming sleeper. We were together, alone. The room's warm air touched me along my nipples, my bare stomach and thighs. It seemed to breathe under the elastic hem of my boxers, shifting the hem against my skin. My cock grew so that it brushed the loose cotton, turning itself around as it pulsed, and the head pushed against the elastic. Stéphane watched me. He'd begun repeating one phrase of the song over and over.

He twisted toward me, still playing, and stared at my belly, the hollow under my arm, my chest and sternum, then down the line of hair to my navel and past it. His look slipped along the frayed hem of my shorts into the shifting folds of cotton, and I pressed my leg harder against his hip. Stéphane kept plucking at the strings. The touch of his look brought the blood through my back and legs, pulsing in my balls, which I felt fatten and become sweet. The hem of my shorts was pushed from my skin and my erection swelled so the sewn cotton slipped down off the head and along an inch of the shaft before stopping. Stéphane watched, hitting a few notes. It was slow like this, and detailed, marked by the diminishing music, so that these few minutes had the measured exactness and clarity of a paragraph. I closed my eyes, and the world became nothing but the force of the boy's gaze. He was hitting just one string now.

The air on the swollen head of my cock made it feel sweet, and I worked the pulse of it so the hem slipped farther like a dry tongue running slowly down my erection. The boy's hand struck a constant note and the weight of his body fell on his elbow by my side. Was that the air or his breath across my belly? The air, or a hand? It touched me, roughly, and the light felt substantial, raking across the shaft so strong a broad hollow sensation gathered suddenly in my balls, and then it burst through me and cum leapt out into the air. It was a miracle, like a wooden saint that sheds tears on Easter. It fell, warm and liquid on my belly, and I smiled and gasped once for breath. Cum pulsed again, over the glans, and dribbled in runs down the shaft. I could feel the weight of the boy's body pressing down on the bed beside me. His face was near my belly and he leaned on one elbow. I felt his breath, which was irregular, like mine. He'd stopped playing.

Stéphane put his hand on my erection and let it rest there, brushing a few fingers through the cum. I didn't move or speak, but enjoyed the warmth of his hand. We lay there like this until my cock had become small and Stéphane took his hand away. He rose from the bed and I opened my eyes.

"Come to my room again," I said, "and I'll do anything you want." Stéphane did not answer but just walked away and left me.

The next morning I followed him. I hadn't planned on doing it, but at seven-thirty the sound of the boy's leaving rattled me awake and I sprang from bed, dunked my head in a sink of cold water, and got out the door, so that suddenly I found I was tailing him. The pleasure of it surprised me. This gap became charged, like the slim space between magnets, as when I'd tailed Louise. Stéphane set out while I was still maneuvering my bike from its place in the hallway. The morning was misty and cold. Miriam watched me leave but said nothing. She stood in the casement window above the garden, tired and unattractive, and watched me wrestle with the gate. A lurching green Fiat got in my way, a boxy little car whose driver tried pulling around stalled traffic and forced me to the wall while he passed. It put some distance between me and the boy. I mounted the pedals again and got the bike up to speed. The boy was purposeful. He came into sight, crouched low over his bike, aiming it through traffic. Where gaps opened, he traversed them. At the stoplights he kept ready, bent over like a stalking cat, and then he sprang when the light turned green. He was even less interesting to track than Louise, whose aimlessness had at least been unpredictable. The boy cared only for speed and economy, and we arrived at the rue Saint-Jacques within a few minutes.

I'd never known the streets were so crowded in the morning. At the corner of the rue Royer-Collard, Stéphane rolled through a crowd of boys and chained his bike to a battered metal rack. He swatted the hands of a few friends and stood with them in the cold. His self-involvement and the strung-out knots of walkers streaming between us kept him from seeing me. I stood with my bike, twenty or so yards away, watching. Why were these boys locked out? More arrived, girls too, but the gates remained closed. Stéphane had his spot by the bikes, and it appeared he would stay there awhile.

From a café on the corner I could watch. A table came free by the window and I left my bike outside and went in the café and sat. I had sweated from the ride and felt clammy. There was a rack of newspapers and I took one, a French paper I didn't read. Even from this distance the boy was elegant and remarkable. He occupied a center around which his friends spun like minor satellites. His posture alone held them, that pliant slouch I'd seen in the garden, communicating his ease, his native superiority, even through two shirts, a sweater, and a thick parka. His friends puffed nervously on cigarettes, jostling around him, but he didn't smoke. I thought they all must want to suck his cock, but I'm sure that wasn't true. It seemed inconceivable that anyone could stand near him, near to the battered pucker of his fly, and not be overwhelmed by the gravity, the transcendence, of this need. Every one of them stood swallowing the wet morning air in great greedy mouthfuls, hungry for the life of it, and to me the boy's cock was exactly the same. How could they not reach for it?

A woman at the next table asked me a question. She gestured to the newspaper and I gave it to her. Cars moved past, blurred in a uniform light that seemed to issue from nowhere. Colors bled in the mist, which had become brighter. The school's concierge, a tall young man with a great ring of keys, shuffled from a small booth and undid the lock, and the sidewalk emptied of kids. They drained through the gate and into school. Within minutes they were gone and the gate was closed.

The trees of the Luxembourg Garden billowed in the cold air only fifty yards away, and I could see the mist breaking up beyond them. The sun would be out soon and the day would be warm again. The café was pleasant, so I caught the waiter's attention and asked for more bread and some Camembert to spread on it. The hours passed. My attentions drifted, and then I left, circuiting the boulevards on Serge's bike until it was afternoon and I could return to the same table at the same café and watch the school let out again. The interval had been flat and featureless. Birds shook from the fences and made a blur across the sky, that part of the sky I could see. A man at a table near me also watched the school. He'd been nursing a coffee—letting it go cold, rather—and the pages of the magazine he'd propped on the table went unturned while he stared across the street. I thought he might be some kind of predator, lurking near the lycée to victimize kids and lure them into films. My school back home was in a constant uproar about this kind of threat and had organized a block watch of parents and staff to harass every unknown man who lingered near the school. Any man who paused, or was not in some kind of uniform, would at once be assaulted by a concerned and furious den mother shooing him away, which is why it was so handy to actually be a teacher there.

Dismissal time came, and the children flooded out the gate and filled the street. Traffic was closed where they loitered, and this gave room for the boys to swagger and pose. A lot of them ran around screaming, and some got their knapsacks tugged until they fell to their knees. Stéphane was nowhere to be seen. The man near me waved through the glass, then went outside and kissed a boy, a boy Stéphane's age, and they walked away together holding hands. The children dispersed until the street was nearly empty and then at last, as if in a coda to this brief symphony, Stéphane reappeared. He had been sitting in the booth with the concierge and they emerged now, still arguing over the plastic-sleeved cards they had exchanged. He looked up and grinned. He saw me.

What was I doing here? The boy shook hands briskly with his uniformed pal, then trotted across the street to the café smiling, though not so broadly as to look foolish. We also shook hands and he dropped into the chair opposite, knapsack squashed between the chair back and his parka.

"You will come to my basketball?" he asked, drumming the tabletop.

"How strange to see you here."

"It is my school, right there." He pointed out the window. "I thought you had come for my basketball."

"No, I'm just here. Your school team is playing?"

"The school has no teams. My basketball club is playing, very soon. We are at the École Normale, in their gymnasium." The boy pushed his parka sleeve up over the ample hump of a lovely watch (my watch) and gazed at the scratched glass. "It is one-half hour, and then we play against the club team of Boulevard Kellermann."

"I'm afraid—one-half hour—I think I cannot. There are meetings this afternoon." I gazed at his rabbit teeth and dissembled. "It's my last week, and the meetings are becoming so much more important now. Where is this École?"

The boy frowned his disgust and snorted succinctly. He reached into his parka for a pen. "It is very near. If your meetings do not prevent you." He drew a map and left it with me.

I let him go, feeling foolish because I hadn't simply said Yes, I've come for your sports match. My surveillance was supposed to be clandestine. When he saw me, I was caught and I quite naturally tried to hide my mission. He trotted—sauntered, I guess—to the café door and out onto the crowded sidewalk. I was left alone with just my crumbs and cold coffee. As I watched Stéphane disappear down the rue Saint Jacques a terrible sadness welled up, and this abruptly gave way to bright contentment when I realized that now that he was gone it was possible to follow him again. Anyone looking at me would've thought I had terrible gas, so swift was this transformation from puzzled distress to surprised relief. I took the napkin with its scribbled directions and went to the toilet. No point tagging along too closely. I already knew his destination.

The boy's map was economical, featuring only three streets and a great smudged star to mark the École. I got there easily, but the building was neither star-shaped nor obvious in its design. A woman in the concierge booth received my repeated question "*Le gymnase?*" with a hard, flat stare and her own repeated "*La salle du gym?*" "*Le basket,*" I finally tried, mimicking the postures of basketball. She simply pointed. Nothing looked like a gym, no boxy freestanding structures, no great aluminum-sided wing sporting plastic windows around its top, no arched I-beams or grossly enlarged Quonset huts. The École was just a great sprawling stone building with windows and doors. I went in one, sniffing for sweat or the diesel smell of gym towels. Talk and some music drifted in the halls, but nowhere the echoing *ping-ping-ping* of the ball against the hardwood floor.

I wandered downward; these places are so often subterranean. A helpful girl pointed me along a musty hallway of iron plumbing and stored boxes. I found the lockers and then a room of toilets and showers. The boys of the Boulevard Kellermann walked by with their kits, dangerously close. I stepped into a dressing room and then a toilet stall and closed the door. It was a tiny stall with just the toilet and a very few inches of air between the door and the ceiling, and this gap looked out on benches and lockers. I squatted on the seat.

I'm not the sort of person who generally does this, so it was difficult to actually look out at anything. The room was silent—or, rather, it hummed with all the hidden machinery sealed inside the walls. Then voices, a voice, *his* voice, emerged from the dull rumble of the building's hallway and the door opened and slammed repeatedly. They were here, my boy's club team, shouting and swatting, unzipping kits and coats, parkas and pants (excepting those with steel buttons to be pried loose). I quivered on my perch, gleaning clues from the air—the rustle of a dropped pant, belt buckles clanging to the tiles, the snap of elastic pulled off or on, fabric shimmying against fabric, or the click of a joint bending to let a tight sleeve slip off. Boys babbled in French and there were song lyrics and accusations, and then one voice came to the fore, a strutting shout, boastful, answered by some needling question that was murmured into submission. A long silence. A prolonged silence broken finally by a whoop, scuffling and laughter, ripping cloth, and bodies banging against the empty metal lockers. Blind, crouching, overwhelmed, I cobbled together a million scenarios. The stall door shook as a boy caromed off it, and then everything settled. I could smell them through the gap, sweaty and breathing, tangled on the floor, my head full of X-ray visions.

Gradually the boys left. Or some of them left. A whisper persisted, a whispering handful of them diminishing so that I thought they must suspect me (or, rather, the toilet stall) and be concealing a plan of attack. It wouldn't do to be found crouching. From beyond the walls the clean*ping* of balls echoed, bouncing on the hardwood. The game was under way, or maybe just warm-ups, each team beginning their choreographed weaves. A great spasm of the building's machinery shook the walls and pipes, swallowing the nearby whispers and the reports of their drilling teammates out on the court. The toilet rattled. Tiny waves mottled the water, tracing the disappearance of this huge sound, and then it was quiet again. I took a deep breath, flushed the toilet, and stepped out. The room was empty. A bench lay on its side, strewn with clothes. The distant hiss of steam heat mixed with the crowd's watery conversation from the gym.

Per and Miriam sat in folding chairs by the court, laughing and smoking. I strode into the gym, said hello, and we kissed and Per pointed to the bright lit scoreboard: 12 to 3, only a few minutes left in the quarter. The boy glanced over, adjusted his sweatbands, and showed his indifference.

"Has he scored?" I asked Miriam.

"I don't think so. Per, has he scored yet?"

"Yes, he has, dear, he made that basket, that layup"—this was a bit of jargon Per was proud of—"when he took the ball from the other boy."

"He had a steal?"

"Yes," Miriam said. "He stole the ball a number of times."

"Stealing is his specialty."

"Defense is his specialty," Miriam corrected. "Stealing is just one facet of it." This surprised me, given the ease with which I had abused the boy in the park. But as he resumed his position it became clear he could prevent any of his opponents from scoring. There was some kind of tactical fussiness, a sort of elaborate diplomacy about the other team's offense that made their progress to the hoop slow and uncertain. Every movement forward seemed to be negotiated, like the visit of a foreign head of state, so that Stéphane's refusal to move when the other team wanted to kept them from getting to the hoop. Their game simply stalled out somewhere between midcourt and the foul line, until the boy finally took the ball away from them.

"Bravo," I shouted as he snatched it from the weak grip of his smaller opponent. "Slam-a-jamma baby." This exclamation brought Per to his feet and Stéphane abruptly to a halt, as he stared at us and grinned, losing any chance for the breakaway layup I had anticipated. Time expired and we took a small hamper of fruit juice and yogurts to the boy's bench. The crowd was in fact not a crowd at all, but extra players who preferred to sit on chairs. Per and Miriam were the only "parents" in attendance. At the break these uniformed boys swarmed the court, dribbling and maneuvering in great bunches while the sweaty heroes milled around the sidelines with their sports drinks and juice. Stéphane shook my hand and described the four steals I had missed, plus the layup, which was acted out with Per playing the part of the defender. Everything was normal now; I was normal, where a few minutes ago I had been so creepy. I glanced at the rafters. A running track hung there, riddled with cracks and great holes where its plaster had rotted and fallen. It was unlit, hovering in the gloom, so that a man might've been up there now, a sniper or voyeur, without giving any sign.

"Creepy place," I said. "Are all your games here?"

"Not very many," he said. Miriam tried pushing the boy's fallen hair from his face, but he swatted her hand away and scowled. "Our practice is at Kellermann, where the gymnasium is very new. There are glass backboards."

"Hmm."

"The shooting here is very difficult." He gestured to the score. Miriam took a brush from her bag and stood behind the boy, arranging his hair in a ponytail, brushing it for some time, and he accepted this.

"Lousy backboards?"

"All the equipment is below the standard. The floor does not grip." A basketball bounced against my leg and I heaved it at the far basket, where it went in. The amazed boy stared at me, at my dumb luck, awestruck. I thought it might be worth tacking some pithy lesson onto this completely random event, but no serviceable ones came to mind. I just grinned and the boy stared with a new look, something like total admiration.

When the game ended Stéphane and I rode our bicycles on a long route home. He led and I followed, keeping silent so the glow of my famous basket would not be diminished by any of the usually stupid things I might say. The boy seemed to like the silence. He was at ease. We coasted along the rue Pascal and the air was soft, perfumed with exhaust and flowers, as on the first evening when I arrived and saw him in the garden. I watched his strong legs, his slim back and shoulders, and saw everything I could ever love contained within the encyclopedic completeness of this solemn angel leading me into the evening traffic. The boy was a portal, capacious and transporting, so that with him I had no sense of loss. I missed no one, not even myself, my real name.

12

Allan's son sent a second letter:

"In response to your reply, I believe my father died at the Grand Hotel (near the Opéra) where he had been living for months (maybe years . . . I don't really know). He was buried at Père Lachaise cemetery.

"Where he went to and when he left his parents' home I know nothing about."

A few incomplete anecdotes followed, and the letter closed, "I doubt very much whether this can lead you anywhere today. Yet it is all I can dig up from long-buried impressions."

I went to Père Lachaise with Denis on Wednesday, a bright, sunny, cold morning. We met at the Café Bobillot, which Denis thought was charming. "So typical," he said, as we hurried through a plastic sheet the barman hung to keep cold air from coming through the door. The place was empty and we sat at a table by the heater, a clattering toasterlike box with a jet-engine whine, which glowed and shook. The barman was not impressed with us. He fiddled with his syrups while we sat for a while.

"So typical," Denis repeated.

"I like it here. I bring my work here sometimes."

"The Beaubourg would be much more interesting for you, Herbert, the Café Beaubourg."

"The Bobillot is so close. Stéphane, you know, comes home this way, when he takes the bus."

"Ah, the boy."

"Mmm."

"Your life is very simple in Paris, Herbert, very clear. I could never be so focused as you are."

"My work is simple."

"I am impressed with your dedication, your discipline."

The barman polished the last of his syrups and shuffled to our table. Denis dispatched him with a swift sentence, and he returned with bread, twin sealed plastic tubs of jam, and two large bowls of hot chocolate to warm us.

"The widow wants to meet you, George has said. But she will only speak in French, and George worries that won't be suitable."

"What would I talk to her about anyway? She hasn't found the drawings." Denis sipped his chocolate and said nothing. "How long will I need to stay for this, Denis?"

He shugged and looked bored with me. "How long would you like to stay?"

I had no answer, but blew on my chocolate for a while. "I don't see why George is devoting so much attention to Mrs. Stein, except that he obviously enjoys it. He should refuse to see her until she coughs something up."

"With some people, Herbert, there is a great deal of socializing to make possible a very little business. George has good reasons to indulge her. He would like to be her confidante."

"My mother did that, I mean with a man." This bright aside puzzled Denis as much as it intrigued him. "She was sort of an art consultant to him."

"Was she with your museum?" Museum?

"No, she didn't actually know anything about art, but she had impeccable taste, certainly better taste than he did. This man's car was hideous. He had it lined with this plush fake fur, hair really, petroleum hair that turned into molten plastic droplets if you set fire to it. I always got tossed in the backseat with the purchases so I burned a lot of the hair while they laughed and drank in the front. Louise knew I did it and she kind of like it. She liked keeping secrets with me, especially from her boyfriends."

"Louise?"

"My mother. I always called her Louise."

A bum spare-changing by the entrance to Père Lachaise said he'd guide us to all the famous graves if we paid him (two francs per grave). We didn't answer and he turned to the next man.

The bright sun lit bunched flowers laid on tables up and down the sidewalk so the street was garish and carnivalesque. Denis loaned me his gloves, which were warm and too big for my hands. He smoked the way a habitual walker might savor the fresh air, sucking it down in great greedy mouthfuls, smiling broadly and saying nothing as we strode through the gate to the guardhouse.

"I will say you are the grandnephew of Allan."

"Why?"

"It is easier. They will show anything to the family, but possibly the records are not open to a stranger who has walked in." The walls of the guardhouse were drab, cracked plaster whitewashed and stained beige by cigarettes. Chill air spilled through the open door. The guards had disappeared, but Denis was content waiting. He was so big and elegant, so commanding, that when the guard finally came we had no trouble getting what we wanted. Allan's name was entered in a massive hard-bound ledger, which the guard dragged from an upper shelf. The entry in loopy ink was smudged so that it read *Alloon Stair*, with the number of the plot in some difficult code. (97, 9–2–77).

Along the potholed walk, between boxy gray mausoleums littered with garbage and dead flowers, the city's bright green dumpsters caught my eye, gay and spotless where the sun shone on them. The Dumpsters were big as graves. Black plastic wheels made them portable. I thought if someone snuck in at night they could hide there, if need be, and I told this to Denis, who wasn't listening.

"Do you know how he died?" Denis asked, strolling past the uninteresting Dumpster.

"Overeating, I think. He had some kind of intestinal problem. He died alone in the Grand Hotel, near the Opéra."

"I adore the Grand Hotel."

"Mmm. I think it is very sad, don't you? His children barely knew him. I think two marriages had failed. His parents hardly spoke to him, I mean, they even took his ex-wife in as a kind of permanent house guest."

"He must've looked awful. He was fat, wasn't he?" The bushes beside us shook and rattled. Birds maybe.

"Yes, probably." Denis's distaste annoyed me. What did it matter if he was fat? "I understand he was quite handsome, fat. Josephine Baker pursued him, I believe."

"I wonder how they dressed him?" Denis smiled and took my arm. "I would like a sleeping gown for burial, a very expensive cotton or silk."

"What an idea." Hippies struggled from the bushes and staggered past us, drinking wine from a bottle, laughing.

"It is my mother's idea."

"You buried your mother in her nightgown?"

"Not yet. She would like to be buried that way." We started along the path again, which emptied when the hippies turned downhill, away from us. Beyond the next grave, a great carved marble dog had sunk into the ruins of a collapsed tomb. His head and fore-paws could be seen, but the rest had fallen in with the roof. "What a peculiar day." Denis sucked the air in, marveling at the broad blue sky and the trees against it. I felt weightless, knowing the ground was full of bodies. The graves were pretty, dappled with cold sunshine, overgrown but contained by the paths and avenues. LOUISE inscribed on a tomb caught my eye, but moss obscured the family name and dates. Two collapsed trees by the tomb left a hole where the blue sky looked empty, as if something were missing from it.

"You're leaving Paris soon?" Denis asked. I didn't answer him.

Allan's grave was awful, an overgrown plot of weeds atop a shallow marble box. I didn't think it was his because the names were misleading: ALEXANIAN HAIGAZIAN STEIN. Was this his given name? Apparently the widow buried her other relatives in the grave with Allan. I presumed she meant to join them someday, making at least four in a small plot. Allan and his in-laws must have been cremated first, or somehow reduced. Herbert had told me that Allan's hair is kept locked in the vaults of the Beinecke Library at Yale, a thick golden curl from 1899, when the boy was four. Gertrude had kept it all her life and passed it along to the Beinecke with her letters. This particular library is a monument of twentieth-century architecture, a great translucent marble cube, fully four stories high, enclosing a glass chamber that seals its treasures in a vacuum (in case of fire). Allan's hair rests in acid-proof paper, curled like a fetus in the bed of its own impression, and can be inspected by anyone requesting it. Guards patrol the vault. A receptionist transmits requests to messengers, and the hair is retrieved. Surveillance cameras cover the room where the hair can be inspected. Why should Allan's childhood curls be treated with such greater pomp and care than the remains of his tired dead body?

At home I sat in the garden alone. Per called but I didn't answer. I might have slept or drifted; in any case, time passed. It became dark and I sat on the bench beneath the plum tree. The stone wall stayed warm a long time. Serge had watered the flower beds, so the garden smelled like rain. There was no moon, and the garden was lit by the buildings around us. I was still on the bench when the light in Stéphane's room was turned off and replaced with the flicker of candles. Someone—Miriam—opened the window, and I could hear their voices. I was cold enough to feel sleepy, as after a long hike when it's pouring rain and the fire can't be started, but I sat up and watched the shadows on his ceiling.

The walls of the garden kept the street noise out. Stéphane spoke and Miriam went to the window and closed it again. I couldn't see them, which frustrated me, so I climbed partway up a tree near the window. There was a branch near the top of the wall, and I sat there and watched. Stéphane lay in bed with no shirt. Miriam leaned over him, massaging his back and sides. His hair fell in tangles around his face, which was pressed into the pillow. His arms were stretched out, over his head, and hung off the edge of the bed. Miriam put oil on her hands and rubbed them together to make the oil warm before touching him. She put her hands on his shoulders and moved them in circles; then she ran her palms, flat, along his spine to his hips. Moving her hands out from his spine, she traced his ribs with her fingers spread and then pushed her hands under him, under his hips, to rock his body back and forth. Because I'd seen his stomach and hips bare in the garden when he stood watching birds and I knew the skin and the shape of the bones where she held him, I could feel his hips and the weight of him in her hands. Stéphane turned his head on the pillow and Miriam kissed the nape of his neck. She reached under him, below his stomach, and he laughed some; then she pulled his pants off by the legs. His boxers got pulled down too and the waistband turned under halfway down his butt, which was lighter than the skin of his back. Miriam leaned over him, blew the candles out, and went upstairs. "*Bonne nuit,*" she said from the door as she left. Stéphane didn't answer.

I thought of climbing through the window, or knocking on it somehow, but I wasn't supposed to be out here sitting in a tree watching. I wanted to flip him over and have the other side to myself. I went inside the house. Miriam lay on the couch in the living room, above the sleeping boy, with a book and a pillow tucked up to her chest. I sat by her feet and she just smiled and kept reading. A magazine beside me had pictures of Germany, and I flipped through them for a while. I yawned and stretched, making a grimace as I rolled my shoulders a little. Miriam did nothing. I rolled the shoulders again and then turned my neck and cringed, so that she looked up.

"Are you all right, Herbert?" she asked, noticing my theatrics. "You seem discontent."

"I'm just very sore. In my neck and shoulders mostly." I made a show of my pain, then sighed and looked out the window. Miriam pouted to show her sympathy, then returned to her book. "I think I turned too suddenly. I suppose it's nothing."

"It can't be nothing."

"I mean nothing terribly important. I'm sure I'll be fine if I can relax enough to get some sleep." I looked at Miriam purposefully, and she looked back for a prolonged moment with an amused smile.

"Eat the bananas; they are very good for the electrolytes that help sore muscles. I think a little wine is a good idea too."

"Wine and bananas?"

"Mmm. And Serge can give you his heating pad."

"That must be a very good book you're reading."

"Yes."

"What is it?"

"It is Nescio, a Dutch. He reminds me of my grandmother's street in Amsterdam. I read him every year, the same story." She handed the slim book to me and I looked, but it was in Dutch and I understood nothing. I got up from the couch, took a few bananas from the kitchen table, and went to my room.

◆13◆

In September, 1913, Sylvia Salinger sailed to America and Allan went back to school, impatient to be done with it. The following summer, the Steins returned to Agay, alone with Allan. They'd booked rooms in the same hotel, for the same months as they'd spent before with the group. Sylvia's absence was everywhere in the small village: on the terrace where Allan had sprawled at her feet, on the empty clay tennis court, along the path by the river where they had walked and seen the horses. This summer, for Allan, was a last good-bye to a romance that had failed and a childhood that was ending. He arrived in July of 1914, impatient to get on to his final year of school and move forward into life.

Allan had brought some of his books, and Mike was still game for adventure, but mostly Allan did what he'd done with the group the previous year, only now alone: he swam, lay about on the terrace, took the same walks into the hills, and waited for summer to end. In August, with only a few weeks left before school, news began to circulate around Europe, the import of which was reflected in Mike's letters back to Gertrude.

August 8, 1914: "My dear girls,

"How are you and where are you? We are here and shall remain for the present as the train service to Paris is irregular and difficult, 48 hours at least. I have not heard from you or Leo. Please answer. Mike."

August 21, 1914: "My dear Gertrude,

"Just got yours of the 15th. Strange you did not hear from me, I wrote twice. We are very comfortable here. I have not heard from Leo or Claribel, have you? I guess the only way is to draft postals frequently, as the mails are so irregular. Love from all, Mike."

September 8, 1914: "My dear Gertrude,

"In the *NY Herald* of the 4th there was an announcement from U.S. Ambassador Myron T. Herrick, 5 rue de Chaillot, asking all Americans having apartments or houses in Paris to register their residence, whether occupied by them or not, with view to issuance by the embassy of proper certificates to safeguard their property. I notified him of our apartments and you might want to do the same. With love from Mike."

War broke out in Europe, and Mike Stein felt his family had no choice but to stay on at the small hotel in Agay.

December 23, 1914: "My dear Gertrude,

"Enclosed you will find a check for 1,000 ff. When you cash it, will you please ask them how much more I am entitled to according to the terms of the moratorium, and I will then send you another check when you let me know what answer they give you. We are thinking some of coming to Paris after the New Year.

"I'm rather glad to get to see for myself what it is like here in the winter, as I had often thought of breaking the winter with a trip down here. The nights are cool but the days are sunny and we take long walks and bicycle rides. I see the sunrise every morning from my bed, and the cloud effect at sunset surpasses anything I have ever seen. We practically own the hotel. Someone drifts in for a while and then another, but we are practically alone and the landlady caters for us *en famille*. Her son is at the front and her husband is in barracks at Antibes. The troop trains all stop here as do the Red

Cross trains, as the engines all have to take water from the rivière d'Agay.

"We sent to Paris for the books for Allan's school, so he has been able to keep at his studies. I guess that's all. Affectionately, Mike."

Mike's attempts to get back to Paris, or to get his family out of Europe altogether, were halfhearted and unsuccessful. The family remained in limbo, always poised to leave Agay but never leaving.

January 4, 1915: "My dear Gertrude,

"We expect to arrive in Paris Saturday the 9th at 4:15 A.M. We are having lots of rain here at present but had a homey Christmas and New Year with a wreck thrown in. A little schooner was thrown on the rocks, and the men came here drenched and chattering and we fixed them up. Claribel is still in Munich. Chilly mornings and evenings. We had a log fire in our room. Affectionately, Mike."

January 5, 1915: "My dear Gertrude,

"No we are not coming this week. After staying through all the storms, now that radiant sunshine has come, I could not pull myself away and decided to see for myself what the wonderful January was like on the Riviera. Enclosed please find a check for 1,000 ff. Love from all, Mike."

Mike, Sarah, and Allan settled in for a long stay. Allan pursued his schoolwork alone in the deserted hotel. In Paris, Gertrude tried to put things in order, though she was deeply reliant on Mike for advice and finances. Eventually she left with Alice Toklas to Spain.

February 12, 1915: "My dear Gertrude,

"Enclosed you will find a draft for 2,000—will send you the other 2,000 in the early part of March. For the present the pictures had better remain at your place, as it's covered by your policy. Should you want to leave earlier, let me know and I'll send the second draft to you in Spain. Do you plan to leave your Cézannes in your studio when you leave? If not, put the *Femme au Chapeau* with them. Yours affectionately, Mike."

March 23, 1915: "My dear Gertrude,

"Here is your sheet to fill out for income tax. I got a couple of sheets at the Mairie at Cannes and am enclosing a sample filled out for you to copy onto the real sheet, which M. Dursonoy sent me from Paris. Then you want to mail it at once registered mail to: *M. le Controleur des Contributions directes à la Mairie du 6ième arrondissement, Paris, France.* The joint is that should by any chance the sheet not reach them, you can prove by your register tag that you had sent it within the prescribed time. We're now having the equinoctial showers here and it has rained more or less for a month, but it is not cold. The traveling to America seems to be getting worse instead of better, but it may change soon, let us hope so. My love to Alice, Mickey."

Another year passed, and the war got worse.

May 17, 1916: "My dear Gertrude,

"We shall surely be here until Allan's exams are over, the last part of July; then it will depend on the conditions of ocean travel. I have written for your insurance bill. I guess that's all, Mike."

June 17, 1916: "My dear Gertrude,

"So you are back again. Well, Allan's exams take until the middle of July, and then we may come up and begin packing. Here all is quiet and one day is like another. Au revoir, Mike."

July 24, 1916: "My dear Alice,

"The magazines came. Thanks. Allan came back from Aix with his degree after a very serious cram. With love, Mike."

Allan had passed his exams, a year late and hundreds of miles away from his classmates. He went on to Paris and joined the U.S. Army, adrift now in the world. Somewhere in this last prolonged stay in the hotel at Agay, Allan Stein's only real life drifted away. His boyhood disappeared and he emerged as an inconsequential man, a man whose family preferred their amusing stories about his childhood to the stubborn, dissolute adult he had become, a man who would be eclipsed by famous paintings made of the boy he had once been. The track forward from his youth disappeared in Agay, and by the time his adulthood spun out of control in Paris he was a lost, untraceable soul. The final thirty years were little more than the working out of a failed equation. Alice Toklas said, "He was the natural reaction of an exaggeratedly cultivated home—quite an abnormal atmosphere for a child who had no proper childhood."

I went with Stéphane to see *Nostalgia*. The movie theater was in a deceptively small-looking café with enough black walls and mirrors to make its real size inestimable. Stéphane and I sat at a glorified picnic table, somewhere midcenter, by a mirrored wall that had cracked across the middle so that a line went through him when I watched him there. I could see a half-dozen views of Stéphane, because of the mirrors, and these occupied me for a while. He flipped through a newspaper. Rain pestered the windows, reminding me of home and Shackles.

The simplicity was starting to wear me down. The boy. My desire. The gap between us. Our knees touched beneath the table. "What is the film about?" I asked, but he was taken with something in the paper. I went to the bar and got a mint soda, bright green, plus a Coke for the boy. At least Shackles had decor, even if it was fake. The ticket girl sat near the front, smoking, reading a dog-eared play. There was nothing on the walls, I guessed so they could clean by just hosing the place down. The air was blue with cigarette smoke. Tiny spotlights clamped to metal tracks on the ceiling made pools of light on the tables, and my soda shone green as a Christmas lamp when I set it down there.

"What's the film about?" I asked again. The boy returned his knee to mine beneath the table, though it probably meant nothing to him. His hair was wet from the rain and he'd slicked it back, which made him look about twelve and very handsome.

"Serge said it's very beautiful. I think it is a man and a woman in Italy. They're looking at paintings."

I pushed my leg forward a little. "Would you go somewhere with me?"

"The movie starts soon, in a few minutes."

"No, on a trip."

The boy stared. "Why?"

"I don't know. I need to see Agay, the Côte d'Azur." A crowd poured into the room from downstairs; the movie had let out.

"What is there?"

"Oh, it's hot as Spain, I'm told. You know, beaches." He smiled like a boy with a Coca-Cola. "My French is so poor, I need someone. You know."

"I would miss school."

"Of course you would miss school."

"I could do that." Here he stared again, as if adding up figures. "If you want to."

If I want to. The phrase echoed somewhere in me. The boy got in line for the tickets, and I finished his Coke and my soda. It was never clear what he knew. Making him talk about sex was out of the question, more absurd than actually having sex with him. The boy got the tickets and beckoned for me to follow him, and we filed downstairs into the theater, where we settled with our wet coats piled on the seats beside us; then the room became dark.

There was a valley with a path leading down it past trees and a pole and a horse. The people who walked away into the valley kept turning to look at us, which was disturbing. The film made shadows over Stéphane's wrist and the bend of his arm on the chair beside mine. His arm was bare and I stared for a moment, but, strangely, the film was more beautiful. I put my arm across Stéphane's shoulders and he let me.

The film moved slowly, laterally or sometimes away. I couldn't tell if the valley was real or the construction of a set designer. The woman and the man drove across an empty pasture in a Volkswagen. When the woman's face appeared in close-up, Stéphane sighed and shifted his body. Did he find her beautiful? She looked like the women in the paintings of Botticelli. The picture had the hollowness of a painting. Stéphane fell asleep when the veiled women entered a shrine bearing a statue of the Virgin on a bier of wood. His head was on my shoulder. They knelt before the Virgin and prayed while candles filled the wall behind her. The candles flickered, and I saw them reflected on Stéphane's mouth, which had opened while he slept. One woman bent forward and parted the gowns of the Virgin. Birds, hundreds of tiny birds, poured from the gash in her dress and filled the air above the praying women. Their noise was tremendous. My heart raced, probably from fright at the birds. Stéphane stayed sleeping and his hand dropped to his belly. The light and sound of the birds filled both rooms, both the vault of the shrine and the darkened room of seats, of folded coats, and people hiding from the afternoon rain, where I sat with the boy.

How could he keep sleeping? Noise and shadow cascaded over him. I watched his face and arms in the dim light. The light was beautiful, and I brushed my fingers across his cheek to feel it. He was soft, like water. I slipped lower into my chair and let my head rest against his. I turned my face toward him so I could smell his hair, and he slept beside me like that. I reached again but did not touch him. The film was empty and beguiling, like a series of paintings inside of which photographs moved.

There was a pleasant scene of rain in bottles. The poet was deserted by his translator. He drank vodka in a ruined church filled with water from a fresh spring and trees in which birds nested. He told stories in Russian to a little girl who looked like the woman painted on the wall. In the end the man fell asleep by the fire, and the book he'd been reading caught flame and burned. Stéphane turned closer to me and let his hand lie against mine on my lap. He might have been sleeping. His hair smelled like rain. Nothing startled me after the birds, except a terrible event at the close of the film when a madman made a speech and then burned to death.

This is what he said:

"Our heart's path is covered in shadow. We must listen to the voices that seem useless. Into brains full of long sewage pipes, of school walls, tarmac, and welfare papers, the buzzing of insects must enter. We must all fill our eyes and ears with things that are the beginning of a great dream. Someone must shout that we'll build the pyramids. It doesn't matter if we don't. We must fuel that dream. We must stretch the corners of the soul like an endless sheet. Where am I when I'm not in the real world or in my imagination? What kind of a world is this if a madman has to tell you to be ashamed?" And then he called for music. The "Ode to Joy" began to play through a broken speaker. It faltered, surged, then faltered again. He poured gasoline on himself and lit it. The music became overwhelming. Then it stopped and all we heard was his screaming.

When the lights came up the theater filled with voices. I was silent for a while because the movie upset me, but Stéphane said he liked it, although he'd seen very little. We walked up the stairs, emerging from underground, and the crowd waiting for the next show parted to let us through. It was night and the street was busy. A bakery had just opened and people spilled out its doorway. Two men shouted in a Laundromat, which was ugly and too bright. I saw them shoving, and one threw wet clothes that thudded against the heavy glass window. In the cold wet air we walked toward the metro. I asked if he thought the woman was very beautiful, and he nodded but didn't speak. I said too bad she was insane, but he had missed the scene where she lost her mind and grew impatient when I recounted it.

His mouth when he frowned was Miriam's. The pouting lower lip turned down at the corners, with its firm ridged upper lip, elegant and clean as the wing of some early modernist duplex, all long lines and weightless, perfect in its geometry. He parted these lips, wet them with his pink tongue, which circled to taste the skin, to take the evening air, then closed them firmly and grunted his objections. The boy kept bumping his shoulder against mine so that oncoming walkers had to part like water as we passed. I worried the small ticket stub between thumb and fingers, hidden in my pocket, until it was lint. "You'll be sleepy tonight?" I tried. The boy frowned once more and squinched his brow. We made our way home, silent and verging. The evening air, public clock, metro station, then home again through the park.

I was relieved to hear Miriam's laughter rattling down from the top floor when we got home. It drew me to her like a stone to earth. I squeezed Stéphane's shoulder bye-bye and bounded up the stairs. Pink Floyd, top volume, burst from the boy's room a moment later. Per lay across the cushions in the alcove, reading out loud to Miriam and Denis.

"'Completely enclosed by its seventeenth-century walls, this curious little fortified town makes an unusual holiday resort.'" Denis made room for me on the bench; the spy had come in from the cold. I was absent, fundamentally, still caught in the labyrinth of my own espionage, but it was nice to sit on these fat cushions with friends (Herbert's friends). "'The name Colmars comes from a temple to the god Mars, on a hill. The Fort de Savoie, which lies to the north on the hillock of Saint-Martin, makes a pair with the Fort de France to the south and recalls the time when this market town guarded the Provençal frontier, the Duc de Savoie having annexed the Barcelonnette Valley and Allos at the end of the fourteenth century.'"

"Colmars," Miriam whispered to me. "Per has an uncle there."

"Yes, he told me."

"I mean that Per has an uncle who is buried there." The music from below diminished, becoming all dull thuds and rumbles, which blended nicely with the pot of boiling eggs on the stove. The boy was tired, that much was clear. He might have been asleep. I liked to think the day had been obliterated from his mind already. There were quite a few evenings he stayed in his room, studying, while we ate dinner without him. He had a refrigerator full of yogurt and snacks in a vestigial kitchen (mini-fridge, cold-water sink, a shelf of bowls and glasses) directly below the one where we sat talking.

"'The visitor will enjoy strolling through the narrow little streets, which come out on minute squares bright with fountains, realizing that he has reached the south from the atmosphere all around.'"

The book had a map, which Per spread on the table between us. It was marked with pale red checks and arrows, the residue of a waxy pencil used a half century ago. "How did you get there?"

"Train. But then we rode the last ten kilometers in a cart along the river to Colmars." Denis strained a bundle of eggs from the pot on the stove and put a fresh dozen into the boiling water. "We scaled a cliff to get from the road into town. I remember climbing with our bags and feeling very weak."

"Are we having eggs for dinner?" Denis brought the cooked eggs to the table in a bowl of cold water and began peeling them. I took a pair from the water and rolled them under my palms.

"No," Denis answered simply. "I need them peeled." What a benign mystery. Denis was like a hot spring, an unending supply of warmth, of easy sensuality, with no apparent source or end in sight.

"Armand, my uncle, was lame, but he made a wooden cart the right size for a dog and his dog pulled it. At the top of this cliff we had scrambled up, at the Porte de Savoie, he met us, and the dog pulled our bags in the cart from there. He had a radio with a battery, in the cart, and kept it on very loud because he was deaf also, and this way we paraded across the Place Gireud to his house."

"You were teenagers."

"We were boys, so this was very exciting." Steam from the eggs fogged the windows, and Miriam opened one a crack to clear the air. "Armand had dozens of these radios with their Edison batteries stacked in the room of Serge and me, all packed in wood boxes, which he meant to sell to all the houses of Colmars. He was an evangelist of this battery radio. He wanted to broadcast to them."

"Serge said you went as far as Allos with Armand and these radios, trying to sell them."

"Or give them away. I was very small and the boxes were heavy. The dog cart never left Colmars. I stopped by the river on one trip to sit on my box and rest and I fell asleep there in the sun. Serge and Armand didn't notice I was gone until they stopped for lunch."

"You were how old?"

"Fourteen. Serge was much stronger than I. I called him the squirrel, because he was very slim and wiry, and you could see his heart racing and racing for many minutes when we'd get out of the river and lie on the rocks to dry. We were so brown from the sun. The altitude is very high, and everything we did was exhausting."

"I want to take Stéphane there," I announced, crushing an egg. "I want to take him to Agay."

"Agay?" Miriam asked. "Is it near Colmars?" Denis stared at me, smiling; he took the damaged egg and rescued what he could of it.

"I don't know. I think so."

"He'd like it," Per said. "It's a little early, but the valley leading to Colmars is stunning."

"Agay is on the coast."

"It's only a few hours," Per guessed. "The train goes to Nice, and from there it's very near."

"I want to go Friday." My resolve startled me, but it was a perfectly plain suggestion, like taking the boy to soccer, and they treated it this way.

"Not Friday," Denis objected. "George has arranged Friday dinner with the widow, Herbert. It will be very posh and it is already arranged. You cannot disappoint her."

"Saturday. We'll go in the morning."

"He'll miss school."

"Only a few days," Per said. "It's very generous of you to ask, Herbert, I think he would love it." Miriam left the table and went downstairs, and when she came back up she said yes the boy would like it very much, and yes she thought it would be fine, and I took it all as a kind of blanket permission. I was taking the boy.

Per retrieved a brown cylinder from the freezer, some kind of bottle that was icy and looked like it would be effective as a pipe bomb. On a white label in red, obscured by frost: OUDE JENEVER. Four shot glasses came from the freezer with it and Per filled each of them to the lip.

"Prost," Miriam said, rolling the *r* and lifting her glass to me.

"Prost."

It got late. The others went to bed drunk. Alone in the darkened alcove, I phoned Herbert. He had the cell phone in Jimmy's garden, where he'd fallen asleep.

"What time is it?" he asked.

"God, two in the morning, three?"

"But it's still light out."

"I meant here."

"The sun is just gorgeous. You know those huge hills behind Jimmy's? They're absolutely golden right now."

"Mmm."

"You're not coming home, are you."

"Herbert."

"You're fucking that boy every morning, noon, and night."

"Don't be ridiculous."

"I don't care. Better that you do it in France than here."

"Herbert, I'm coming back. I'll just be a few days late."

"Monday at the museum should be interesting. Did Hank call you?"

"Why would Hank call?"

"I don't know. He left a message at work; he said he'd try calling me in Paris, which is fine since apparently I'm never leaving Paris."

"I'm leaving the Dupaignes' Saturday. You'll be gone on time, officially. I'll fly back home next Wednesday."

"It doesn't matter. How's your dear friend the widow?"

"Of course it matters. I'm trying to be decent about all this."

"Thank you very much."

"I'm seeing the widow Friday; with any luck she'll have the drawings."

"Where are you meeting her?"

"I don't know, someone's house."

"Is it her house? Find out what else she's got."

"I don't think it's her house."

"She must have a million little treasures. Don't say anything, just smile a lot and laugh at her bon mots."

"I'll be charming."

"Uh-huh. What is that boy's name, anyway?"

"Stéphane. Stéphane Dupaigne."

"Mmm."

"I'm not doing anything with him. It's all fantasy, you know how I am."

"Not really."

"I'm leaving in a few days, why would I want to get involved at all?"

"Mmm."

"There's no point in it. He'll be five thousand miles away."

"Mmm-hmm."

"I've got to get out of here, Herbert. I can't wait to get home. Save Wednesday for me. We'll go somewhere."

Things fell apart. It was Friday. My resolve either collapsed or it accelerated to the point where events overtook me. At a time when I should have been supremely relaxed, on the verge of leaving with the boy, the nearness of it made me panicked and impatient. I strained to look bored. We ate *caviar d'aubergine* at his favorite snack stand and I said to him, Why don't we go to the park? In the pinched margin of this last day my mind had got stuck on the Elysian court, with its glittering promise of sweat and spilled blood.

The rain kept all the players away, except for one small boy with his multicolored shoes. He dashed around the puddles and made inexpert layups as the late-afternoon sun broke through and the court steamed where it shone. I joined this little boy, which looked predatory and awkward, but the inequity of it forced Stéphane onto the court. Clearly he and I were a more proper match. The kid gladly yielded his ball to the tall boy with the catlike shoes and his American friend, and he was content watching. We had scored only a few baskets when I took Stéphane by the waist and dumped him into a large puddle. It was almost dusk now, and the sun illuminated the trees, casting long shadows across us. The boy was soaked, and mud stained his prized T-shirt and pants. He was livid. He swore in both languages and slammed the ball to the ground before storming away. I could barely keep up with him and was lucky to board the same train in the metro station. At the Parc Montsouris, where night had fallen, he kept his silence and his pace. He wouldn't look at me. At home, he slammed the front door shut and went straight to his room and the shower.

I could barely keep myself still. I listened to the water run for two or three minutes and then took off my clothes and went upstairs in the dark. Steam billowed from the white tile bathroom, and I reached in and shut the light off. The boy swore again. "Who is it?" he said, in English because he knew who it was. The steam tingled all over my bare skin. I felt my way past the sink, parted the plastic curtain, and stepped into the shower beside him. Water poured over us. He said nothing, and I ran my hand down the center of his slim chest to his navel and then to the wet tuft of hair below that. The boy stood still. I paused, then he pushed my hand down farther until I found his cock, like a slug under a rain spout, and I squeezed it in my hand so it fattened and moved against me. Stéphane had his hands on my shoulders now. Water splashed off his back and arms. I worked my fist over the shaft of his cock, which had become quite large, stroking it as he pushed me against the tiles. There was a certain mindless symmetry to the beautiful gap of his open mouth and the great fleshy head of his cock that kept emerging from my fist. I stumbled backwards and he didn't catch me but pushed me down farther so I was flat on my back in the tub. I held on to his erection, pulling it down as the boy stood straddling me. Water haloed around him, spraying the curtain and the tile wall, running to where I lay in his shadow. He wasn't smiling. The boy stuck his foot on my crotch and rubbed it up and down my cock and then he knelt, his knees in my armpits, and started fucking me in the mouth. He was still angry, and he fucked me that way. The boy grabbed my head and pushed it back and forth onto him, driving his body into me as hard as he could. He grunted and squealed like a pig or a dog rooting out bones and became more furious until he came in my mouth and collapsed in the water beside me.

It wasn't the kind of sex I had imagined. If he'd been a weapon he might have killed me. Obviously there was nothing to say. I don't think his impulse was violent, but rather the territory of our exchange was lawless and immoderate, unspeakable. Our bodies were dumb, irreversible. We lay there for a long time, folded over on each other, until I felt his erection stir again and move against my leg, and then he got out of the shower and went to his room. I don't know what connects anyone to anyone. My body felt like an accident, a wrong turn.

I lay in the dark for a while; then I turned the shower off. Music drifted from below, Per's jazz, muted by the walls. I dried myself, pulling on my dick a lot, which was still very hard. What was tonight? Denis's dinner? He might be here already. Anything could have happened while we showered. I dropped the towel and went to the boy's door and walked through the beads. Streetlights from outside showed his scattered clothes, his guitar and comic books, and then the boy himself, still wet, lying on the bed with his hands behind his head, watching me. His cock lay up against his belly and sometimes lifted from it. It breathed like some sea creature that draws great streams of ocean water through itself, heaving a sigh and dropping back down again. His torso was pale and luminous, marked by the slim divot of his navel and the twin blisters of his soft nipples. I got on the bed and knelt over him, then lowered myself down like a man doing push-ups. I slid back and forth over him. My cock felt ticklish, driving through his soft thatch of hair, and my chest and belly grazed his. Stéphane wrapped his hand around our paired erections and I spit there. While he played with this twin-headed dick, rolling it around in both hands and inspecting it, I ran my fingers over his chest, pinching his nipples and then soothing them with my thumbs. I traced his collarbone, cupped his shoulders in my palms, ran my fingers over his wet lips, and then dipped them in his mouth and traced spit along his throat. I pushed the head of my dick against each nipple, blessing them, and then the hollow in the middle of his chest, which fit nicely. I inched up and touched the head to his lips and then his eyes, so the shaft rolled over his face, pressing down first on one cheek, then the other, and he let his mouth open and licked me. He put his lips in a round, tentative O and took the head of my cock in so his teeth tickled along its underside. I pulled back and sat on his hips, and simply stared for a while at his beautiful puzzled face. Leaning down, I kissed him on the chin and left his room to dress.

• 14 •

Denis wore a jet-black jacket of some thin elegant fabric, like rayon, only it had none of the brassy sheen of rayon. It drifted and lay limp on his racklike frame so that one might have taken photos of him lounging in the chrome chair to advertise almost anything: cigarettes, automobiles, real estate, liquor, the new Europe, anything at all. His skin was luscious and smooth, like hard milk chocolate, and his mood was gay.

"The widow, Herbert," he exclaimed, grinning when I came in. "The widow at last." Per was naked, retrieving a bowl of ice from the freezer, and he rushed past me to the stairs with just a quick smile.

"It's very exciting, Denis." I'd chosen a soft white shirt and khaki pants, very plain and undistinguished but redeemed, I thought, by the peculiar gray-check jacket I wore with them.

"We are due at eight, which is the time now, Herbert." Denis was in no hurry. He slouched farther into the chair and sipped the small glass of scotch Serge had poured him. I didn't want a drink. My body was all undone, like a deboned hen under the *découpeur*'s knives. So much had been undone. I sat on the edge of the couch, perched with my weight settled on the twin bones of my butt. I smiled weakly at Denis, and he smiled back. "You are looking very smart."

"Thank you, Denis."

"Dinner is at the apartment of Harry Pym-Gardner, a very rich Englishman who collects nice things."

"Will there be many people?"

"George, of course, and Sir Harry. One or two others. Do not fear, Herbert, you and I will sit together, with the widow between us."

We caught a cab because there was no point trying to park on the Quai Bourbon where Sir Harry lived. The Ile St. Louis was an impossible place, its narrow streets clogged with tourists and taxis and the occasional car circling eternally, scouting for a place to park. There were none. The cars simply had to be abandoned, driven into the river, left in the street, given up to thieves, or taken to another district and parked there. Our cabby nosed across the crowded Pont Sully and traversed the island, depositing us at Sir Harry's door.

Denis performed a series of codes which got us through a battered wooden door into a great stone courtyard. "Harry will like you, Herbert. He's always hungry for new people."

"That's sweet of him."

"George is constantly supplying them, like a pusher of drugs." Denis pressed a button at the elevator's gate. "He finds young men at the clubs, I mean well-bred young men, and brings them to Harry's for dinner."

A butler arrived in a glass elevator as tight as a phone booth, shut us in, and launched it, then walked the stairs, spiraling around the box, keeping pace so that he seemed to be circling like some grim creature of the desert until he passed the elevator door a fifth time, as we stopped, and let us out.

Denis pointed and there was our host, some distance away, surrounded by his "nice things"—paintings, statuettes, antiquities, and a drinks cart. Sir Harry might have been a stage actor, with features as huge and exaggerated as his frame, so that one could read the slyness of his grin, a twitch of the mouth, even across the great distance of his living room. He was a little drunk and sat waiting for us, patting a small shampooed lapdog.

"Scotch? Pimm's?" Harry offered. "Bombay? Denis tells me you like gin." We had still not made it halfway to him. "You're looking fit, Denis, spending all your time in that gymnasium, aren't you? You must be strong as a colossus by now, with all that iron you keep pumping and pumping."

"I am weak with pleasure, Harry. It makes me dizzy just to walk so far."

"You didn't walk here, did you? It's a madhouse, you could've been killed." The dog started yapping when we arrived, and Harry swatted it on the head and it stopped.

"Harry Pym-Gardner. You can call me Harry."

"Herbert Widener." The name had gone a little sour in my mouth, so that I offered it in a mumble. I used it less and less now. At the park or in libraries, anywhere that Herbert's business didn't have to be mentioned, I simply went nameless rather than producing this token I'd prized so greedily. It was like a Christmas toy that falls apart before New Year's. I had used it cavalierly and for everything, banging it around on the airplane and the bus, in conversation with strangers, cabdrivers, clerks, and with every acquaintance I'd made, so that it finally just broke and became depressing.

"Herbert," Harry repeated, still holding my hand. "George has told me so much. Where is that awful man? He treats me like dirt."

"He treats everyone like dirt," Denis assured him. "That is why we're so fond of George."

Harry walked us around the room, giving the inventory of his nice things, while the dog yapped at our ankles. Small torsos and heads on metal rods were antiquities and I enjoyed them, but didn't appreciate their rarity as Herbert would have. The paintings were famous. I knew the names but could not have distinguished one from another. They were minor works by great painters, except for a broad swath of shriveled birds nailed to the wall in a sort of grid, each one sporting a tiny knit muff or sweater. "It's a Mensonger," Harry told us. "Pepper Mensonger. George had it installed today." He scooped up the dog. "They look like dried vomit to me, but George says she's very important." The view out was exquisite, looking out over the sluggish river and rooftops to the dirty walls of the Hôtel de Ville, brilliantly carved from the night by the klieg lights of passing tour boats.

The dog sprang from Harry's lap as the elevator arrived again, replete with George, the widow, looking awfully young and spry, plus a very old man. "Ariel," Harry scolded, "No bite, no bite," even while the dog nipped at the new guests and the widow kicked him away without breaking stride. Who was the old man? "You're late, George. Obviously you know Denis and Herbert." The trio labored their way across the great expanse. Harry stared at the implacable woman on George's arm as if she were a mere appendage of this unfavored friend. "And who is this you've brought me?"

"Mrs. Stein." I stepped in. "It is my great pleasure to meet you at last. George has said so much—"

"Harry Pym-Gardner," George interrupted, "I'd like you to meet Pepper Mensonger. Pepper, this is Harry. I'm sure he won't mind in the least if you call him Harry."

"Charmed," our host whispered. Pepper cast her glance proudly, possessively, over the freshly nailed birds.

The silent old man was Le Géranium, scholar of the École Alsacienne, and he looked older than I had ever imagined, more frail and distracted, and with both feet already out of this world. He was well over eighty. "He was hell-bent on meeting you, Herb," George said. "Six is fine for dinner, right, Harry?"

"George, I would give you anything. He speaks English, doesn't he? *L'anglais c'est la langue de la maison, non?*"

"Yes, of course."

Was he named for a flower? I caught George's elbow on the way to the dining room and scolded him. "I've stayed an extra week to meet the widow, George. Where is she?"

"The widow?" Harry asked. He had Ariel in his arms now and was kissing the dog on its exposed teeth. "Matchmaking again, George?"

"The Stein widow, Harry. It's business. She wants to meet us later at Boy."

"After dinner?"

"After dinner." George squeezed out a little turd of a smile. "Boy's a fabulous club, Herb, you'll love it. She has some Picassos Herbert wants."

"Why didn't you tell me this, George? You know I would just die to have some of her Picassos. Or were they all snapped up ages ago, I mean before you tried to pick me up at that horrible bar?"

"She's not selling, Harry. Herb's just having a little look-see. And I did not try to pick you up."

"I recall Picasso," Le Géranium whispered. "When my father and I called to visit in Montrouge." No one seemed to hear him.

Harry got us all seated except Pepper, who was unhappy about being placed next to me and hovered, going on about the widow. "Everyone wants her Picassos, but in fact she has none." In the attentive silence this bold claim triggered, Pepper gestured to George to give up his seat and she took it. She brushed some imaginary crumbs from the chair and settled beside Denis. "She sold them all, years ago."

"That's just a crock of shit, Pepper." George unfurled his napkin. "You were drunk, Harry, and tried to give me money.

You thought I was a trick, and we all had a good laugh about that."

"An innocent mistake."

"I know they are sold, George," Pepper continued. "I met an awful Swiss who owns twenty or thirty of them."

"You were in Switzerland?" Travel seemed a promising topic.

"Zurich. I hated it. The Swiss are barbarians. My dealer kept me there four months."

Harry proposed a toast to the missing widow, and we drank our wine.

"Are you a collector?" Pepper asked, fishing.

"Herbert is the curator of contemporary art at a very important museum," Denis explained. "His was the famous 'cut sleeves' show, you certainly read about it in the *Art Flash* magazine." Cut sleeves? "His opinion is sought after." I had no idea what Denis was talking about, but Pepper evidently knew and, voilà! Cinderella was transformed into the queen of the ball.

"Herbert *Widener*?" She reached across the table to squeeze my hand (too bad she'd already switched seats) and relaxed into a grand smile that was like glorious summer after the spring monsoons. Le Géranium smiled too.

"I'm so hopelessly behind." Harry sighed. "I've never heard of this 'cut sleeves' show, though it is obviously à la mode, Herbert. Do fill me in." Pale string beans were laid on our plates by an astonishing young helper, fresh-faced, whiskerless, and nattily trussed in a short-waisted coat to indicate his inferior station. The butler followed with a roast.

"Denis explains it well," I demurred. "I mean, it's perhaps better described in French, don't you think, Denis?"

"No, I don't think so, Herbert. It is a show of garments, Harry, that have been damaged—not the literal garments, but garments of all kinds, metaphorical, conceptual, and also some clothing. This 'cut sleeves' was a piece by Jeffries, where the Beuys felt suit has been slashed with knives."

"He's brilliant," Pepper said. I smiled bashfully. "Jeffries is brilliant. He paid hundreds of thousands of dollars for that Beuys, and then when he slashed it the value more than doubled. I think he made back two or three times what he paid." Ariel took a slice of meat from Harry's plate and dragged it to the ground. She had it trapped between my chair leg and shoe, where she growled and mauled it before swallowing.

I smiled at Pepper, wanting to say something, anything, worthy of a true Herbert, but all of that had deflated, collapsed like an old balloon, and I could only murmur "delicious beans," to no one in particular, and watch my plate.

"I find Jeffries to be nihilistic and derivative," Le Géranium announced, putting a stress on every syllable. "He has done nothing but turn Duchamp into pornography." We all turned and stared, as if the window had blown open and no one knew who should get up and shut it.

Pepper spoke into the silence. "Isn't that interesting. He has an opinion about Jeffries." Rather than engage that opinion, she was content to just point it out, as one might point out a child's constipation.

"He's absolutely right," George put in. "Jeffries is a dull opportunist. He hasn't had an original idea in his life."

"When Duchamp was a young man," Le Géranium went on, "he painted all of my clothes in a brilliant gold paint. He was Midas. He ruined all my clothes."

"Is he all right?" Pepper murmured. "George, you are simply bored by what is beyond you. You work in a glorified department store."

"I cringe to think what you'd say of the Carnavalet." Denis. Pepper only smiled and shrugged.

"Oh, Denis," Harry consoled, "we all know you've done marvelous things there. Have you seen it, Herbert? But of course you have. It's all Denis; everything good about that musty old building is his." I looked past Le Géranium to the dull passage from which the young bean server had once issued, but saw nothing. Only grim, static shadows.

"I'd like more beans," I whispered to Harry, and he rang his little bell. The butler again. I excused myself. Denis engaged Le Géranium while George and Pepper fought, to Harry's amusement. The dog took some meat from my plate as I left, and the butler quickly replaced it. The apartment went on and on for a great distance, with rooms opening up off a corridor hung with etchings and prints. Beyond the kitchen door was a bathroom and a toilet, and I went past these through a closed door into a huge dressing room. It was a mess, with little rawhide dog treats, all gnawed and soggy, scattered among an explosion of clothing (Sir Harry's experiments preparing for tonight's guests). A far door, propped partly open, invited me and I went through it. Here was Sir Harry's bed, a great canopied Louis XIV with a bolster and scattered shams, plus a small basket of toys beside it, clamps and collars and such; things that embarrassed me. I went through the drawers, which weren't very interesting.

The door swung open behind me and there was Sir Harry. He might have been annoyed or perhaps so drunk that his face went out of focus, as if he couldn't calibrate the right degree of severity for my crime and so his expression wavered. What was I doing here? He snorted, or maybe sighed, and walked toward me while I pushed the drawer back in.

"I thought I'd find you here," he finally said.

"I wasn't taking anything, you know. I'd never take anything."

"Oh, Herbert, I know that. Don't be so defensive." He reached me and ran his fingers up my buttons. "I knew you'd be in here. That's why I dragged myself away from that lively table as fast as I could."

"Yes."

"We could barely keep our hands to ourselves, could we?" He planted his great beef-tinged mouth on mine and dragged my shirt-tails out while we fell back on the bed. He was really very big, and I got kind of crushed beneath him for a while as he humped and thrusted at my crotch. A little breather came when Harry propped himself up to pull our paired pants down and turn me over. With his left hand up to muzzle my cock, he reached in the drawer with the right, unleashed a condom, and rolled it on himself in a gesture as practiced and swift as the butler's pour, and then he buggered me for a few riveting minutes. He made noises like the boy, pig and dog noises, but was really very gentle for a man of such size.

"Thank you," I said, rather pathetically, when Harry was finished. "I mean that was very nice, Harry, very well done." He lay beside me like an abandoned mattress, red-faced and exhausted. I kissed him chastely and put my clothes back together.

"You go first," he exhaled. "They'll be wondering where you've gotten to. I think you can say that I showed you the Renoir. It always takes me a little while to put the Renoir back and set all the alarms."

The dining room was empty when I returned. There was only the bean boy, trussless, wiping down the table's glossy top. His circumspect pucker and pert motions were enchanting and I asked for a glass of water, which he fetched from the kitchen. The boy gestured politely toward the living room and I went there.

The French doors had been thrown open so that cold air rushed in. Le Géranium sat on the couch with his coat pulled up around his throat. The others were on the balcony, smoking and arguing. Ariel had pulled the bottom row of nailed birds from the wall and they lay scattered around the room, stripped of their muffs and slightly chewed. She sat on Harry's chair holding an especially fat one between her paws and growling at anyone who approached. I sat beside the old man and offered him my glass of water, which he refused.

"You were curious about *La grande époque de l'École Alsacienne,*" he whispered, a little rosy from the wine. "I would like to tell you about it." Here he took a deep breath and glanced past me toward the empty dining room. "Our host has retired, so I am certain it would not be rude to speak French now that he is sleeping." I smiled, saying nothing, and rolled the drinks cart near. "*Et il est vrai que le vingtième siècle s'est ouvert sous le signe de l'optimisme.*" There was port on the lower rack, and I took a glass of that. "*Certes, les catastrophes naturelles et accidentelles ne pratiquent pas de parenthèses dans l'histoire de la misère humaine. La violence des hommes, les agitations, les conflits, les scandales ne s'éteignent pas d'un coup, et particulièrement l'anticléricalisme en France va attendre son apogée dégénérant en affrontements irréparables, mais le progrès technologique semble promettre pour tous des lendemains meilleurs.*" The argument on the balcony was much louder than Le Géranium, but distance kept it quiet so the two blended evenly, like crossed conversations on a telephone wire, and I couldn't make sense of either one. The sounds were pleasant though, especially Le Géranium, who spoke in a mellifluous rumble and formed his words carefully and slowly, like a river polishing stones (without thereby making them any more meaningful to me). "*Déjà l'amélioration de certains aspects du mode de vie, l'éclairage, l'eau courante, la rapidité des transports, également la multiplication des distractions offertes à ceux qui ont les moyens d'en bénéficier, paraît devoir balayer le pessimisme de la fin du siècle précédent, pessimisme qu'un écrivain hongrois, Max Nordau, qualifiait de* degeneration."

"Mmm," I pondered. "Degeneration. *Exactement.*"

He was delighted. "*C'est le mot juste, n'est-ce pas?*"

"*Oui, certainement.*"

"Donc. Paris, le Paris de l'Exposition est devenu le centre du monde. Cette dernière spécialité va profiter de la mort opportune dès le début du nouveau siècle, de la reine Victoria, monumental archétype d'une morale castratrice —"

"*Castratrice?*"

"Oui, castratrice. Je ne sais pas en anglais. Mais son successeur, Édouard VII, se charge de faire connaître qu'il est désormais permis de s'amuser."

George and Pepper had returned and now scavenged the room on their hands and knees, gathering birds, which Ariel took as a game and joined, barking. Denis smiled from the balcony and walked toward me.

"Denis." I sighed as he sat down on the couch. "What is *castratrice?*"

"Where is Harry?" he asked.

"Locking up the Renoir. What is English for *castratrice?*"

"Castratrice, peu importe," Le Géranium objected. *"Donc. C'est à l'intérieur de l'image d'Épinal d'une vie Parisienne, le style même du second Empire, ressuscité . . ."*

"The Renoir?" Denis seemed to know something about this Renoir. "Don't mention the Renoir, Herbert."

"—sensibles aux apostolats pathétiques en faveur d'une paix universelle, va goûter la séduction des sirènes de l'illusion."

The birds were fixed back to the wall with the small rusty spikes. Only the chewed muffs and one missing bird posed any difficulties, and Pepper and George pawed blindly beneath the couch, searching for the bird.

"Already starting the party games?" Harry bellowed from the doorway. He was in pajamas and a robe, an exquisite silk robe with dragons and a velvet belt that wasn't tied but whose ends hung from cloth buttons at either hip so that it looked like a great draped swag across his front. "Getting into the port, are you, Herbert?"

"It's terrific, Harry."

Pepper freed her arm from the couch springs and now looked up. "He's got a Renoir locked up in the bedroom? How boring." She took my glass of port and sniffed it, then handed it back distastefully. "Is there any cognac, Harry?"

"Is there any cognac, she asks. What are these greasy feathers doing on my chair?"

"The port is excellent, Harry. I've only ever had the cheap stuff before and it tastes like floor cleanser."

"Ariel!" He called for the missing dog but she was out of sight, yapping ineffectually on the balcony, beyond the closed curtains and the closed French doors, beyond hearing, where George had placed her.

"Maybe in the kitchen," Denis speculated. "Dining on scraps."

George butted in. "We're late for Boy, Harry. I'm sorry, but I've got to take Herbert and Denis immediately, or the widow will have my scalp."

"I want a cognac," Pepper whimpered. All the bending and scrambling for the birds had taken its toll.

"The lady would enjoy a cognac, George. Surely you have time for a cognac."

We enjoyed the cognac. Le Géranium went to his satchel and retrieved a photograph of Allan boxing, 1909, a gift he'd brought for me. Allan was handsome and very chunky, a big boy with a round chest and biceps like great flabby cod. His opponent was tall and wiry, so that the weight evened out. Le Géranium's generosity touched me, and I was both sad and gratified when he left.

* * *

The entrance to Boy looked awful, an armored doorway in the flat black face of a wall. Grim applicants crowded around the door, huddling like junkies. George's sour mood brightened as we approached the barrier. Denis was already dancing, a sinuous little walk that was at odds with my melancholy. The burly guard was kind. He kissed Denis on both cheeks and lifted the velvet rope from its stanchion, letting us slip past the knot of disappointed men. It had been a long day, and this step through the portal, rather than energizing me, felt like a last punch in the gut. Inside was an affliction, a wall of heat and darkness pierced by strobing lights, plus a mass of shirtless souls who must have been eternal residents of the place. In bursts of light, two hundred men strobed freeze-frame for a split second, then got swallowed by darkness.

At home the actual boy lay upon his bier, attended by a virgin silence, dumb and rustling in his sleep—his nipples, soft as goose-down, occasionally pressed beneath a pulsing thumb, the thrum of blood through his neck and wrists, hips akimbo, boxers pushed down in front for a hand that holds his cock while he dreams. I was very tired. Denis took my hands and sort of waltzed us through the crowd until he saw by my sad face that I wanted to sit down and meet the widow and just be done with it. No widow in sight. We sashayed on and on until we reached the bar and—a small miracle—two stools.

"Please!" I shouted inches from his ear. "I'd just like to sit and rest for a moment if we could." We could. Pepper and George were gone. Somewhere in the strobing darkness, in this sea of men, they laughed or argued. A cloud of mist snaked from grates in the floors, swallowing dancers. It stank of chemicals. I fell asleep in a VIP room. George chatted on one of the slim telephones the club left scattered at the tables. It was the widow. She was still at dinner with, as George put it, "some rich wanker chemical tycoon" who'd swept into town looking for Picassos. "She sounds delighted with him. She'd like us to stay put until this cowboy finishes his steak and they can join us."

It was hours. I fell asleep, as I've said, on a leather chesterfield that left marks on my cheek. Denis danced while George and Pepper bickered at a table. Denis kept returning at intervals with less and less clothing. He woke me up and pulled me from the recliner. "It is our last evening, Herbert, you should have a little fun." I was an awful dancer, but there was no room to make that obvious. We simply churned around in place like some stubborn wad of dough being pulled and processed in the narrow spinning bowl of a Hobart mixer. The song never ended or changed tempo. My shirt was soaked with sweat and Denis glistened, radiating contentment. I wiped the drops from my brow and looked through the mass of dancers and there, freeze-framing toward me through the strobes, came Hank, Hank Richard, with an elegant old woman, flanked by twin bodyguards trailing behind. I jerked my hand up, as if it held some TV control, to erase this charging rhino of the Discovery network and return us to French Disco-TV-3, but Hank had seen me and grinned as he cha-cha-cha'd toward us a step faster. Denis looked up too, past Hank at the old woman, and shouted, "Herbert, the widow!" top volume into my ear. I turned to flee, but there was nowhere to go.

I could simply return home. With Herbert's credit card and passport I could be in my apartment within fifteen or twenty hours. There was a long lost moment then, hidden in the crowd, when time fell apart and—was it regret?—something bitter and delicious like regret blossomed inside me. It had a pleasant texture like laughter and a generous amplitude that grew to encompass everything—me, Denis, the sweating men, all of Boy. The room quieted and became light. The dancers were still for a moment, kind enough to pause for me while I thought about Hank and Denis and Herbert and the inevitability of my unmasking. Denis wouldn't mind. He might have guessed it already; he would think I had been amusing. Denis stood now, a few feet away, arrested in his dance, observing me, concerned but really unconcerned, because a bedrock of pleasure had been laid down in him so long ago that something as trivial as this masquerade could hardly be a reason for distress. We'd take a cab to La Coupole and drink to my real name. At dawn we'd wake up Serge and Miriam to announce it like a christening or a birth. I feared the widow unreasonably. Having never met, I imagined her beating me into the ground with disdain or, worse, pity and then burning the Picasso scraps Herbert had wanted, as an object lesson to me. She looked like she already knew the truth and had come back from the grave to tell it. Her face was hard as teak or stone, and she had it aimed purposefully toward the VIP door. It was clear Denis would have to scramble after her to catch up when the bright loud night resumed. The walls and roof of the building dissolved to let the night in, and with that the boy, floating from his bed, appeared. He worried the border of the sky, and then he spread like dawn. The boy encompassed Paris, he blossomed like a shroud or a mask, like a book or a face or a cluster of names. By what accident had he arrived in my life? I wanted only to get home to the boy and be gone with him, but just then hell resumed. The widow strobed away and Denis turned and went after her. Hank had lost her but not me, and a path opened up, so that in a flash his neat collar and suit were upon me.

"Hank," I shouted, grabbing his arm. He grinned, pumping my hand. "Hank, I can't tell you how it feels to see you here."

"You're a sight for sore eyes," he yelled back. "Where's Herbie?"

"Outside, Hank. He's a little nervous about the widow. You actually got to her before we did."

"Outside?"

"I'm supposed to go get him whenever you show up. He's anxious to find the drawings and head home."

"Well, I'll be happy to see him. Imagine the three of us and Mrs. Stein in Paris. I'm really enjoying this trip."

"Does she have the drawings with her?" I asked, rather stupidly.

"Roubina? She doesn't have the drawings at all. I thought you knew that by now. Some dealer bought them ages ago. Have any idea where she went to?"

I turned him around and pointed to the VIP door. "She's in there with George and Denis. You go introduce yourself. I'll go get Herbert."

The street was empty. I slumped against the wall of Boy and could feel it pounding away. It might have been dawn, or predawn. In any case, the sky was gray at one end of the boulevard where it opened onto the Place de la République. Above me, the sky was still black and some stars were visible. It would be smart to wake the boy early and go before the news of my unmasking made it home. He had his knapsack packed and ready. There must be trains in the early morning. I wanted to believe he would be sad if I just left now, flew home without seeing him, but really I had no clue. No cabs came by. There were taxi stands at the Place de la République, and I got up and walked there.

The morning air was fresh with a tang of diesel when a truck passed, lumbering along slowly as if it were lost or hobbled. The sky was light at the edge. The scope of the globe, its great curve and the fact that life was scattered across its face, all of us turning in one direction, became clear to me, viscerally clear, as it always does at dawn or dusk, when the sun slips over the lip of the earth, blossoming into day, or disappears, draining its light from the sky as night comes on. You could see how far we'd all traveled then; and that nothing was stopping, that nothing was ever going to stop. Louise was still pins stuck on a map, but, as I watched this particular dawn, the map became, at least for a short while, pleasingly big and real.

15

I got a cab and rode to the Dupaignes'. The boy was confused when I roused, him, but he had no problem with that. He didn't even wake up, really. We shuffled down the stairs and out the garden door and were driven to the train station.

Everything about our remaining time was singular, unified, like in a dream. They made us get off the train in Créteil. The station was hideous, and they did something to the train. Orange plastic chairs had been broken by hoodlums. The shallow fragments of them left bolted to the metal rail were shit on by birds. The birds still nested above the rail. Every life has its own necessities, and mine had delivered me to this empty platform. We waited most of the morning, then got back on. We had plush seats by a window. The boy slouched against me and I got drunk on good wine and slept too.

France flew by outside the window. A cow, dogs, kids in parkas exhaling clouds into the bright sun, a milkmaid out of Proust. Our train kept lumbering along without stopping. Brick houses encroached and mountains rose in the east. The boy woke up and looked at me. "I'm not Herbert," I tried, simply to feel what I felt saying it. He leaned forward to look past me at the view. "I said I'm not Herbert." The boy wrinkled his eyebrows and exhaled, then pressed his face to the glass again. He asked me what time it was. It was afternoon, and we ate together in the dining car. Money was not a problem. We ate on fine china with linen napkins and were treated well. The boy drank a lot of wine, and we slept in our seats through the afternoon. We got off in Grenoble and found a hotel.

The next morning we didn't talk. The boy seemed happy. We watched cable TV in bed. Outside it snowed a little. I wanted to stay several days, but the boy objected. The TV had two dozen stations. They sped by in French, German, English, and the universally tedious language of pop music. The boy squeezed the remote, which made these channels supersede one another with such speed and ease they formed a kind of buddhistic nullity, a flickering gap that kept emptying itself in the millisecond before comprehension. I lay on the comforter smelling the boy's odor. He smelled like oranges, or rather a book that said boys smell like oranges flashed in my memory as I lay with my nose pressed to his ribs. The room was strewn with clothes and half-eaten minibar snacks. I thought of Miriam and Serge and Per. By now Hank and Denis had surely hacked through the underbrush of my deceptions and discovered who I was.

The boy lay undressed on the bed with his indigestion, suckling a bottled Coke while he stared at the busy maternal screen. His skin was beautiful, like polished silver or hard cheese, or a meadow from the air, or flat granite warmed in the sun. His skin was like a boy's warm skin in the flat gray light of day. The spooned contours of his back and hips invited my hands, and I ran them over his ribs to his spine, down into its shallow curve, then onto his butt and thighs. It was alarming that such an exquisite surface could contain all that flatulence. He paid no attention to me. Shrouded in mist, Grenoble looked like an old movie projected on the screen of our hotel windows. Fog blurred the buildings and hills into a pleasing stage set, so that my situation became more theatrical the longer

I stared out at it. The boy. The elegant hotel. The simplicity of the plot.

"What time is the train to Digne?" I asked.

The boy stared at the screen, even while the answer issued from his lips. "Nine-thirty. There is another at eleven."

"We could stay another day, then get an early start tomorrow morning."

"No, I would like to keep going." He turned to look at me.

"Isn't it a rather long trip?"

"Digne is only two hours. Colmars maybe two or three hours more." The boy turned over, and his cock was large and half hard. "Suck me," he said, leaning back on his elbows and pouting like a man whose dinner is late.

"The rails wound over high ground heavily laden with fruit trees," [one of my books] "quince and pears, looking in their rich gold very strange amongst the snows, immense valleys of rock with almost no sign of life between villages, rivers that were beginning to be torrents, snow-clad peaks, and through continual turnings so the compass would behave like a dervish."

The train to Digne was identical to the first train. We sat in the same seats by the same window drinking the same wine while the same country flew by outside. The mountains had grown and now surrounded us. The boy had his tape machine and was lost to the world. The slim earpiece broadcast a sibilant hiss as the boy stared out the window. I had my books. "Nothing could have been finer than the changing panorama of the mountains, silent and slumberous amid the gray cloud drift. Across their broad bases floated detached masses of vapor, sometimes in heavy billows, sometimes in formless mists that grew or dissolved . . ." ". . . As we proceeded the clouds lifted higher, the rain grew thinner, and there were patches of blue sky and faint gleams of sunshine. But still the mountains were wrapped in uncertainty. How high they were you could not guess, though you had glimpses of their rocky buttresses so far skyward that you might fancy they were the pillars of heaven."

Digne, capital of the Lavender Alps, was bitterly cold, and the boy hurried us to a café on the Boulevard Gassendi. A strong wind blew along the river, so that my cheeks ached and then burned when we stepped from the bridge into the relative shelter of the town. We ate but did not stay long. The boulevard was thick with walkers mingling beneath the famous plane trees. The boy and I slept on the train to Colmars. I woke every now and then, jarred by some lurch or turn, and was alarmed by the nearness and severity of the chasms. The boy was pale and his hair was stringy from not being combed properly. For a long stretch the train had run beside a river. Sheer granite rose from the river's edge, forming canyon walls up which our train then climbed, switching back upon itself. As we turned, the view disappeared into low clouds and we came out onto another valley, thick with mist and more tranquil.

It was extremely cold. The train stopped at Thorame-Haute and we got off. There was no one in the station. It might have been the time of day, or the time of year, but the small town was empty, its windows shuttered against the day. The boy had a map and Per's guidebook, and we began walking. The cold air let us walk briskly without sweating or feeling hot. The valley was unnervingly beautiful. Steep granite rose into the clouds. The river and the rock and the clouds were gray, but different grays. The cold air was full and smelled of water and pine, though I couldn't see any pines. The boy was quiet and didn't wear his tape machine. I thought he must be awestruck or at least interested in the view. He held the map and pointed to vistas, which he named.

It began to snow a little. The roar of the river swelled or diminished, depending on our route. "I saw streaks of snow in the high mountain hollows. The snow did not look cold, and I could not help fancying it was some colorless powder that had been lightly sifted over the heights. The sight of it gave me a rare thrill of pleasure—I was really among the Alps—and the clouded mystery of these lofty precipices with their deep clefts whitened by the eternal snows seemed to me superlatively beautiful." Snow gathered on the scrub trees in the clefts of the rock. The boy looked at me and smiled. The river was hidden from us, and its sound was muted by a spur of granite that diverted our path. In the cupped hollow between the spur and the canyon wall, we paused and ate my last breath mints. While the snow drifted lazily around us, sideways and up as much as down, like blown floral tufts filling a summer meadow's air, the clouds broke and opened onto blue sky. I watched the split seam, the ragged canyon made there, and pointed so the boy looked up.

A jet passed. It was tiny, so incredibly high it might have been a satellite. The glittering speck traced a straight line, a soft white trail unfolding in its wake. We heard nothing but watched the jet make its line, splitting the sky, slow as a surgeon's knife, before the clouds closed again and it was swallowed. And then it came, the sound of the jet, so thin and fragile it might have been the sound nerves make in a body before it dies or the rush of blood through a victim's wrists, thin and persistent, not at all like the sound of a jet that intends to land but like a satellite fixed in its orbit, permanently assigned to the sky and its custom of surveillance, marking a path to remind us that something is up there. I like the sound of jets and the feel of a good book, so distant, so unreachable.

We continued along the road. When the clouds shut they lowered and the snow fell steadily now. We'd walked more than an hour and had seen no one. I was glad I'd eaten heavily in Digne and worried that the boy might be hungry. He kept pace ahead of me and showed no sign of slowing. Birds, I don't know what kind, sang from the rocks where they picked at the grasses and brush. A dozen flew from their place and crossed the river to a stand of larches and this was an odd sight for me, these rather small gray birds flying in the snow. The boy named them in French. His cheeks were red from the cold. He looked around us and then dropped into step beside me.

"If this were rain," he asked, "would it be pouring?"

I was so impressed by the sound of his question and the muted silence that swallowed it, I quickly forgot the question. "What?" I asked back.

"If we were some place warmer."

"Would this be rain?" The way my head rattled and itched when I spoke made me realize I was becoming delirious. "Of course it would."

"Would it be pouring?" He gestured broadly at the snow.

"Where exactly do you mean?"

"Anywhere warmer. It's snowing so much now."

"It can't be far. Are you very tired?"

"No." He looked at me like a hurt dog, sheepish and determined. "I'm very cold and also very hot. I will sleep good when we are there."

"In the wide gorge down below was the frozen flood from the mountains, streaked with dust and dotted here and there with great stones. Seen from where we stood the ruder features of the stream were subdued so as to make it seem an exceedingly simple matter to walk across its gentle folds to the opposite side, the high walls of which, with a serrated fringe of trees along the top, was now in plain sight. But when I clambered down the slope of loose grit and stones to the bottom, things had a different aspect . . ." ". . . The river rushes and rushes; it is almost like Niagara after the jump of the cataract. There are dreadful little booths beside the bank, for the sale of photographs and *immortelles*—I don't know what one is to do with the *immortelles*—where you are offered a brush dipped in tar to write your name withal on the rocks. Thousands of persons of both sexes, and exclusively, it appeared, of the French nationality, had availed themselves of this implement . . ." ". . . The river, beneath me, reaching the plain, flung itself crookedly across the meadows like an unrolled blue ribbon. I tried to think of the *amant de Laure,* for literature's sake, but I had no great success, and the most I could do was to say to myself that I must try again."

The valley became picturesque. Snow covered the rocks and grasses. Pines, now visible, were outlined in it. Dusk had come and turned the gray sky grayer. What light there was suffused the wet air and seemed to issue from nowhere. A sign that said COLMARS appeared by a bend, and we scaled the path it pointed to. I could hardly imagine Serge young and thin, brown as a squirrel, sweating his way up this incline. The boy was delirious. He bounded up the path, laughing out loud and turning at every bend to look at me through the snow. However miserable he had been along the way, he was now that glad.

We stood at the Porte de Savoie, looking back through snow and darkness. The swift river, hidden below, could be heard rushing along the rocks. The paving was slick, and ice had formed in the archway. Snow covered the Place Gireud and the small church that faced it. The town was shuttered. There was no light except across the square, where one bright bulb burned in a store, casting shadows through its latticed windows onto a stand of tired fruits and vegetables. With snow in his lashes and bright red from the cold, the boy traversed the square to this sad little grocery where Per kept the key between summers. Uncle Armand's place was just a few doors away. The grocer gave us the key, together with some curt instructions and a canister of gas.

I carried the heavy canister. We found the right number, and the boy maneuvered the oversized key until the door fell open. It was a stone cave, really, with no light or warmth. Stéphane found the right switches, and a bare overhead light revealed a small room with its various appliances arrayed beside a counter, three shuttered windows, and a great stone hearth. It took up most of the back wall. A wicker couch and chairs plus twin beds made up the decor.

"There is also the toilet," he added, sensing my disappointment. "And a tub if we are to bath."

"There's a bathtub?"

"No, a tub for the bathing." (This rendered "bath-ing.") "A metal tub. It fills with the hot water, and it is big enough for sitting."

A low door beside the hearth opened on a dry chamber full of wood, and I struggled with a hatchet to make kindling and get a fire started. The boy went back to the grocer's and brought home chocolate, a chicken, vegetables, bread, milk, and a box of Cap'n Crunch cereal. We ate some chocolate immediately. I complained that he forgot the wine, but there was good wine in a second chamber, near the door. The fire defeated me, several times. I couldn't make the kindling small enough. I crouched over the stone hearth, breaking splinters from the wood, and made a small tepee from them. The flame caught where the splinters leaned together, and I put a broader piece on that.

The boy was feverish. We hung his wet clothes from the mantel, and I wrapped him in a comforter. He took more chocolate and bread, and I set up the gas water heater according to his instructions. The boy huddled in hot water in the tub and said he felt better. I put the chicken in a pot with vegetables and a lot of wine and hung this pot off a hook in the fire. The hook swiveled. The boy's clothes were dry. The room became hot from the fire, and I found candles and a small lamp to put on the floor so the light would be pretty, which it was. He dressed and sat with me.

"Where's the phone?" I asked.

The boy smiled, and I knew there was no phone. "The post office has phones, which can be used tomorrow. It smells very good, the chicken and the fire."

"Yes." The boy had a fever but he looked fine. I dried his hair meticulously, patting and squeezing it in a towel, and then I combed it back into a ponytail. His blush might have been a sign of good health. "According to Galen, wine is very good for a fever. It counteracts the bile."

"The wine is very good. Serge has this wine sent to Paris especially." With the fire so hot, we unshuttered the windows and could watch snow blow against the glass. I couldn't tell how much had fallen, but a thin drift gathered on the sill. The fire crackled and snapped like a man chewing sticks. The stone walls, no longer cold, were reassuringly solid. We ate the chicken by the fire, then dragged the beds there. They were low and, pushed together, made an island in the flickering light. We traced our route on Per's map: nine miles. It would be nice to walk along it in the hot sun, there were so many vistas we had missed because of clouds. The boy undressed a little as we talked. I enjoyed his pleasure undoing his pants. He pushed his boxers down where the pants opened, proud of his swollen cock, and he smiled. "It is my dick." He laughed, trying out the strange English. I think he was drunk with power. I held it, that fistful of heat, and smiled too. I let go and unbuttoned his shirt, lifting it back off his shoulders so it fell. He was very patient with me. Our shadows on the ceiling billowed and collapsed with the flames. The boy's dick stayed hard up against his belly. I kissed it and then kissed his navel. He pushed me down so I was on my back and he pulled the clothes from me, tugging my pants and shirt off, then lay down flat on top of me, where I held him.

Have I ever stopped describing the beauty of this boy? There was no path away from it; the image kept turning back in on itself.

It was not enough to say that his ribs moved like birds lifting off as he breathed, or that his heart thrummed beneath his skin. He reclined beside me. I put my hand on his chest, meaning *stay*, and poured his bowl of dinner juice and wine in a stream from the divot of his chest down to his navel. He arched his back up from the bed, lifting from it, spilling the pooled juice and wine, so his swollen cock formed a pinnacle, a summit, as if he hoped to complete earth's globe by providing this natural conclusion to it. I planted my mouth there. I might have fallen asleep. He whispered. We kissed. His teeth were small and even, like rows of young corn. I tasted wine and dinner and a musty sugar that seemed to hide in the hollows beneath his tongue. We moved more and more slowly. We fell asleep this way.

In the dead of night the stone walls were still warm because the fire had burned so long and hot. There was no light. I felt the boy beside me, curled around his pillow with my leg drawn between his. I wrapped myself around him. Time and space are so flimsy. This moment cupping my body over his continues, it persists so that we lay now together in Colmars in bed back home in my theatrical city so dark in Paris with Herbert at Boy over dinner under Harry's canopy and slats prone in the courtyard of my school. I laid my arm over his, my chest to his back, and felt him breathing: now, then, now, then, now, then. What kept me in my place, my isolation? The boy shifted, drawing my arms around him tighter, resolving nothing, and the question dissolved into the warm, close air.

"My stomach hurts," the boy whispered, waking me. Still no light. His body burned with fever, so beneath the covers it was very hot. I shifted my head from the pillow but could see nothing.

"Your stomach hurts?"

"Yes, very much."

"I could get a doctor."

"There is no doctor."

"Do you feel nauseous?"

He groaned and said yes. I held my hand on his belly, hoping that would soothe him, but the boy was inconsolable. I made a cool washcloth and looked for more aspirin, but there wasn't any. There were no pills or medicine and the boy wouldn't take solid food, so I gave him water and wine, and he seemed to feel a little better. I kept the washcloth in a bowl by the bed and put out the light again. I talked to distract him from his pain.

"My mother used to make scrambled eggs in the middle of the night, and she'd wake me up and we'd eat them together. I wish we had some eggs."

"I don't like eggs."

"She put cream cheese in them and beat them so they were fluffy. We ate by the window so I could watch the street. It was the middle of the night; there was no one, just cats or sometimes a car that looked lost." I heard no snow against the windows, and where the snow had been it was black. "Do you think it's stopped snowing?" But the boy had fallen back asleep, and soon I did too.

When he woke me the day was bright and sunny and the small room was warm because of it. The boy had made coffee with hot water from the heater and poured bowls of cereal for both of us. "There are letters from Miriam," he said, handing a square blue envelope to me. Letters from Miriam. My heart sank. There were two. Why should she send two? It was a relief to see mine was addressed to *Herbert*. I wondered if the boy had been to the post office and telephoned her.

"Have you gone out?"

"No. The letters came through the door and woke me. I've been up only a little." The boy was pale and his eyes were shadowed; still, he seemed to have gotten better. At least he was cheerful.

"Thank you for making breakfast." The coffee was hideous, tepid and oily, but the milk made it drinkable. "We both got letters?"

"Yes. I have not read mine." He pried at the flap of his envelope.

I took a few spoonfuls of cereal but the milk was warm and thin and I pushed it away. The boy was reading his letter contentedly. I opened mine: "Dear Matthew,

"It is with a kind of vertigo that I address you, since there is no one I know by that name, no man in this world to anchor the name to, and so I feel myself floating just to write it: Matthew. Who is that? My friend, a good friend, Herbert, has been taken away, and I blame you for it. Denis and Hank have been here all morning, and I don't know what to say to you. I'm so angry about Stéphane. I have asked him in his letter to come home at once. It isn't possible for me to come get him from you, but I would do that. You have been selfish and stupid. I did not tell him about your deception; you will do that yourself before he leaves. In any case we will presume he knows when he gets home.

"I can forgive Denis because he has been our friend for so long and he's like this; he has never had good judgment. But you were a guest. You lied your way into our home. We trusted you, we became friends, yet I don't even know who you are. I cannot imagine the arrogance. What right have you to make what you have of our family, to take our son whom you do not even know and use him in this absurd fantasy?

"Your friend Hank thinks it is some adventure made up by you and Herbert, whoever he may be, to get drawings that are apparently the ones you say you're looking for. I'm unable to think of another Herbert, a real Herbert, now that you have erased the one I knew. What do I put in his place? And you, are you the man I knew? Have I only misunderstood your name? That is not so terrible a man to be. I would not be upset by this trip with Stéphane if

I could let myself believe that he was with *you,* with Herbert. But that has become impossible.

"I assume Stéphane is happy. He genuinely liked you. I'm astonished how pigheaded you are to have thought this would lead to anything but disappointment. I don't know how you will explain your lie to Stéphane, but I trust you won't make a burden for him. Just tell him you lied and you're sorry. We'll continue with our lives when he's home, and I'm glad for him to forget you."

The boy had stuffed his letter back in its sleeve and was frowning. He drank the cereal from his bowl and exhaled sharply when I looked at him. "What did your letter say?" I asked.

"She would like me to go to Paris right away. There is a misunderstanding. I am asked to go home."

"I'm sorry. What is the misunderstanding?"

The boy shrugged. "She said the arrangement with you was not understood by her and that I'm to spend the vacation at home. I think it is stupid."

"Mmm." I could not meet his eyes. "I'm sorry," I repeated.

"We will go to Agay. There is no reason to go right now to Paris."

"I don't want you to get in trouble."

"It is fastest to go through Marseille. Who is to say how long we will take, or at what time I read my letter?"

"Yes." I felt myself sinking back again and could not resist it. "It's a miracle the letters even got to Colmars, with that snow and all."

"Who is to say?" The boy flipped his letter from the table, and it helicoptered to the wall. I had already stuffed mine deep in my pants pocket and was glad he didn't ask to see it.

The grocer knew a man who was driving to Nice, and we got a ride in his *2 CV*. The boy slept in the back with boxes of almonds and lavender, while I sat up front and listened to the driver talk. It was all in French. I was tired and distracted. The car was pungent with the acrid nuts and dusky flowers, and the bright sun through the windows warmed them, making the odor stronger. There was no sign of yesterday's snow. We were in Nice in a little more than an hour, and he dropped us at the train station.

The boy looked sick and tired. His color had gotten worse. He put on a show of teenage cool and wore the sunglasses to hide his eyes, but I knew he felt poorly. The train to Agay was plush, and I got us seats in first class so the boy could rest. He fell asleep at once. I went to the dining car and ate a sandwich with some wine. There were decent chocolates and oranges, and I took a few of these to our seats with a bottle of water. The boy was awake. The train slowed and stopped in the shade of a station. Cannes. The oranges smelled terrific, clean as fresh air where the peels sprayed their oils. The boy looked better, refreshed by sleep but still very weak. He put his tape machine away, and I was glad.

"Stéphane." Here I paused, wanting him to look at me. He was watching a comedy on the platform, a man struggling with two burst cases of clothes, which had been strapped together with belts and which the porter was refusing. I looked out there too, then touched his arm. "There's something I need to tell you."

"Mmm." The train lurched and began pulling away from the platform.

"I'm not here to find drawings or do research like I said I was." The boy made no sound, nor did he shift away from me. "I mean I'm doing that, but it's sort of a masquerade. I don't need to do it."

"What." The word was soft and flat.

"I'm not Herbert Widener. Herbert is my friend in America. I'm just pretending to be him."

"What?" Now he drew away slightly and turned toward me. The sun flooded our seats as we cleared the buildings of the old town.

I could see the ocean spread out, deep blue and shimmering toward its curved horizon.

"I'm Matthew. My name is Matthew." The boy shook his head and pushed it back against the seat, saying nothing. "It's important that you know who I am."

I watched his eyes, which were dull and unfocused, and beyond him the sea, which had become busy with great phallic yachts, bright white yachts filling the rocky harbors that sped past our window at an increasing speed.

The boy glanced up at me. "What is 'Matthew'?"

"My name. Do you understand?"

"No." He turned away.

"I only used Herbert's name as a way to get here, but except that, everything we've said and done I really mean. None of it is lies."

He turned his back to me, drawing a pillow up to his chest, and said nothing. I put my arm on him, but he clearly didn't want it.

"You can't do this," I said. "You have to know who I am. None of it was lies. I don't want you to think I lied."

"It doesn't matter," he answered into the air. "Leave me alone to sleep now." After that he said nothing. I sat beside him watching the sea until the train reached Agay and I got off. The boy did not follow. I stood on the platform and watched the train disappear around the headland.

I gave my bags to an old woman who said she worked for the hotel. She had a pushcart littered with dried flowers, and I put my bags on that, then she disappeared down the one narrow road toward town. I went to the wall of the stationmaster's office and sat on a slatted bench in the shade. The hum and clatter of the rails, transmitting the train's prolonged departure, diminished to nothing, so that insects could be heard, together with the waves collapsing on the shore. I ate the last of the chocolate but was still hungry and went into town to find a café. I wandered the small town looking for the hotel of Allan Stein; a woman at the post office gave me directions.

The hotel was now a private home, turned into apartments or condos. In any case it was shuttered and the grounds were in disrepair. I found the terrace where the group had had their dinners, the slope of lawn where Allan had sat beside Sylvia with his great wide watch shown proudly, the sleeve of his summer jacket pulled up. The lawn was overgrown, and the view was obstructed by brown rushes. I ate, and then I walked down the road to the river where the maids had washed clothes. There was no one there. A path wound its way through mimosa and pine along the southern bank and I followed it, searching for any trace of the disappeared boy. The valley it led to was flat and verdant. Horses cantered in a wide green field. Their range was bordered by forested hills and the river. The sun was low enough to lose its strength, and I felt chilly walking through the brush. I was a little drunk already, and the waiter had sold me a second bottle of the mandarin wine I'd been having, a specialty that Allan liked and had written of in his letters.

I lost the trail, then found it again, rounding a great bend in the river. Through the trees a clearing opened up, with a squat, stuffed recliner stuck in the muck of the riverbank. I sat there and drank. The wind blowing on the river made me cold. I wanted the boy back in life with me, just to talk for a while. He'd kept his secrets, even from himself, and I guess he would have had nothing to say to me. It grew dark and stars appeared. Was it safe here? I was tired enough to be overwhelmed by anyone. It wouldn't have mattered. In the clean black night with the refreshing cessation of the wind that convinced me it was summer when actually winter was still transpiring just over the next ridge, I wondered where the boy had gone, dispersed into the air or locked in the ground in a crowded box? I have imagined that whole worlds dwell in the body of a boy and have pried with words to relax these meanings from their hiding place, to coax the boy into the open. He stood still for a moment, caught in the warmth of my regard, and when I reached for him he was gone.

Bibliography

Excerpts from the following works have been quoted in the text:

Baedecker, *Paris et Ses Environs*. Paris: Paul Ollendorff, 1907.

Black, C. B., *The Riviera*, 14th edition. London: Adam and Charles Black, 1905.

DeForest, Katharine, *Paris As It Is*. New York: Doubleday, Page & Co, 1900.

Les Guide Bleus, *France Sud-Est*. Paris: Librairie Hachette, 1929.

Higinbotham, John, *Three Weeks In France*. Chicago: The Reilly and Britton Co., 1913.

James, Henry, *Parisian Sketches*. New York: NYU Press, 1957.

James, Henry, *A Little Tour in France*. London: W. Heinemann, 1901.

Jelencko, Therese, reminiscences as told to Elizabeth Hass, Bancroft Collection, University of California, Berkeley.

Lucas, E. V., *Zigzags In France*. London: Methuen, 1925.

Salinger, Sylvia, *Just a Very Pretty Girl from the Country*, edited by Albert S. Bennett. Carbondale, IL: Southern Illinois University Press, 1987.

Stein, Gertrude, *The Making of Americans*. Normal, IL: Dalkey Archive Press, 1995.

Stein, Gertrude, *The Geographical History of America*. Baltimore, MD: Johns Hopkins University Press, 1995.

Stein, Michael, letters to Gertrude Stein, Beinecke Library, Yale University.

Stein, Sarah, letters to Gertrude Stein, Beinecke Library, Yale University, and Brancroft Collection, University of California, Berkeley.

Stein, Sarah, photo album, Bancroft Collection, University of California, Berkeley.

Tarkovsky, Andrei, *Nostalgia* (film), 1983.